THE RISE OF THE REMARKABLES
BRASSWITCH and BOT

THE RISE OF THE REMARKABLES
BRASSWITCH and BOT

Be the blue train

[signature]

GARETH WARD

WALKER BOOKS
AND SUBSIDIARIES

LONDON • BOSTON • SYDNEY • AUCKLAND

First published in 2020
by Walker Books Australia Pty Ltd
Locked Bag 22, Newtown
NSW 2042 Australia
www.walkerbooks.com.au

A catalogue record for this
book is available from the
National Library of Australia

ISBN: 978 1 760652 21 0

The illustrations for this book were created digitally
Typeset in Stempel Garamond
Printed and bound in Australia at Griffin Press

10 9 8 7 6 5 4 3 2 1

The paper this book is printed on is certified against the
Forest Stewardship Council® Standards. Griffin Press holds
FSC chain of custody certification SGS-COC-005088. FSC
promotes environmentally responsible, socially beneficial
and economically viable management of the world's forests.

For Louise, the privilege is all mine.

1

The crackle-tram lurched and the butterflies already quivering in Wrench's stomach took flight. The summons to Clifford's Tower, the regulators' headquarters, was quite normal, or so her foster-father had said. A random *screening* interview triggered by her upcoming fourteenth birthday. It was a mere formality, he'd assured her, his fingers worrying the wax-sealed envelope, and for anyone else it might have been.

Wrench straightened her brass-rimmed spectacles and glanced across the aisle at a bookish gent with a skew bow tie. Affixed to his bowler hat was the cog and spanner emblem of a university engineering professor and his critical gaze hadn't strayed from Wrench since she'd boarded at Holgate Lane. The row of upmarket terraced

7

houses at the tram stop were the homes of engineers and mechanics, the steel-forged backbone of the Victorian age. She adjusted the cuff on her apprentice's overalls; she was a part of that now, or at least she wanted to be. They didn't allow women to study at the university and perhaps the professor didn't approve of female railway engineers either. She wanted to tell him to park his peepers, but he was gentry, not another steam monkey at the coachworks, and besides, he might be part of her interview board.

Metal screeched on metal and the crackle-tram lurched again. Wrench gripped the handrail atop the seatback. Something was wrong; she could sense it.

"NO BRAKES!" shouted the driver.

With a violent shudder the crackle-tram surged down Mickelgate Hill. The street's shops flew past, their bright awnings nearly scraping the windows. A corset-maker's mannequin suspended as a sign dashed against the roof, sending a thunderous drumming through the speeding tram.

Wrench's heart kicked up a gear. Surely the engineering professor would know what to do?

The driver heaved at the friction brake. "Brace yourselves! She's out of control," he yelled.

An elegant lady seated opposite raised a lace-gloved hand to her forehead and fainted with an exaggerated sigh. The carriage swayed alarmingly. If it jumped the rails it would roll and crush them beneath the heavy iron chassis, just like ... no. She needed to focus. This wasn't like before. She was older now, an apprentice engineer, she could stop this. Wrench slung her tool belt over her shoulder and, grabbing the seat backs for support, she strode down the aisle.

"Young man, sit down. Let the driver deal with it. That's what he's paid for," blustered the engineering professor.

Wrench ignored him and ignored the flushing of her cheeks. With her mess of mousy hair, baggy overalls and chunky hobnail boots she was easily mistaken for a boy.

"No passengers past the yellow line," commanded the driver, still hauling at the brake.

"Nuts and bolts to the chuffing yellow line." Wrench stepped up to the engineer's maintenance hatch and braced herself against the driver's console. She slid a screwdriver from her tool belt and levered the hatch open. It took a tram engineer three months to learn the intricacies of the switches, rheostats and circuit breakers revealed beneath. She glanced through the domed windscreen. In less than thirty seconds they'd collide with the traffic on Ouse Bridge. People would die if she couldn't stop the crackle-tram. She had no choice, whatever the cost to herself.

Wrench reached out with her mind. The power surging through the tram's callan motors was bright in her senses. She took hold of the magnetic fields surrounding the stream of electrons and, easy as breathing, she shaped them to produce a counter force; the motor now acted as a brake, not an accelerator. She flicked a switch on the control board and channelled the electrons back into the batteries.

Electricity crackled beneath the tram, arcing across the carbon brushes. Insulation melted on overheating cables, sending wisps of greasy smoke curling into the carriage. Wrench's face contorted with the effort. The engineering was taking the strain, but it felt like she was stopping all forty tons of crackle-tram with her brain.

Above the granite arches that bridged the turbulent river Ouse, a broken walkomobile blocked the road, one of its steel legs buckled and collapsed. Traffic queued back to the stationary trailer of a Tadcaster Brewery dray that loomed large in their path. Stacked high with beer barrels, the solid steam-powered trailer would provide for an unforgiving collision. Wrench turned up a rheostat on the control panel and pain pierced her skull. Teeth clenched, she forced more power into the batteries.

Its motors screaming, the crackle-tram nudged into the back of the dray. Frothy white plumes of beer fountained into the air. Wrench dropped to her knees, panting. Her body ached, like she'd worked a double shift welding coach wheels. She trembled uncontrollably, a combination of adrenaline, fear and elation. Someone stepped behind her, their boots clacking on the hard wood floor.

"What did you do?" asked the university professor.

Wrench stood, shakily. "I saved us."

"Yes, and we're all jolly grateful, but what exactly did you do?"

Panic squeezed Wrench's chest like a steam vice. They mustn't know her secret. "I rerouted the motor through the bifilar coils, so they act as a regenerative brake." The explanation was at least partly true and may have been enough to bamboozle a layman, but the professor frowned and fiddled with his tie.

"That's not possible. Not without a reductive circuit and only the new B twenty-sevens have those." The professor jogged the control panel door wider and looked inside. "This is truly fascinating. Show me what you did, please. You may have unwittingly discovered something of great scientific importance. Either that or the crackle-tram stopped by magic." He gave a little laugh.

Cold spread through Wrench's veins and she shivered. Why did he have to use the M-word?

A straggly-haired woman lifted an arm and pointed. "She's a witch!"

Wrench stared at the professor. Her fingers picked at her tool belt. "Tell them it's science. They'll believe you. Please."

"I'd convinced myself I was mistaken earlier – I thought you were a boy – but now I've heard you speak I'm certain," said the professor. "You're Finnian Chester's daughter, aren't you?"

Wrench exhaled. Her father had been legend in the world of engineering, designing locomotives like no other, their futuristic beauty matched only by their power. He had been hailed as a visionary of the industrial age, until the accident at least. If the professor knew of her father, surely he'd help. "Yes, I am," she said, a spark of hope rekindling.

"I always thought there was something unnatural about him." The professor backed up the aisle as if Wrench was contagious. "Nobody normal should have such a command of machines."

"She's a Brasswitch," shouted the woman with straggly hair. A collective gasp filled the carriage.

"It was just science. Honestly," protested Wrench. She looked from the suspicious-eyed passengers to the driver. He too shuffled away, refusing to meet her gaze.

"Somebody, fetch the regulators," said the fainting woman, who had made a miraculous recovery.

Wrench clenched her fists and the lights in the crackle-tram flickered. It wasn't fair. She wasn't a Brasswitch. Not once had she used her powers to destroy machinery or cause harm. "I saved you all. There's no need for the regulators."

The driver rapped his knuckles against a window. "They're already here."

Outside, a blue-uniformed constable stood, hands on hips, surveying the chaos. Next to him, their backs ramrod straight, waited two men dressed in the madder-red suits and black bowler hats of the regulators.

Wrench hauled at the crackle-tram door. Latched secure, it didn't budge. Her mind reached out to the locking bar. It would be simple enough to open with a little mental encouragement, but the proximity of the regulators terrified her.

The driver banged on the window again and the regulators' heads turned slowly towards the crackle-tram. Their black tinted goggles gave them a soulless look, which matched their cruel reputation. They strode closer. Wrench's heart thumped like a compression engine and her legs trembled. Stopping the crackle-tram had left her too exhausted to flee.

With the hiss of steam pistons, the door slid open. One of the regulators stepped inside. His pointed black goatee sharpened a cruel, narrow face that crinkled on one side with burn scars glossy as waxed paper.

The driver bowed his head, his cap held in his hands. His voice trembled, weak and afraid. "Sorry about the accident, Sir. The girl did it. She's a Brasswitch."

Wrench raised her eyes to the professor. "Help me, please," she mouthed.

"Whatever happened here, it wasn't science," said the professor. "She's not one of us."

The regulator drew his pistol and pressed the barrel to Wrench's head. "You are under arrest on suspicion of being an aberration."

The cell was sparse. One table and one electric chair. On the table sat a file, neatly bound with brown twine. In the electric chair sat Wrench, neatly bound with brown leather straps. Somewhere behind her a transformer hummed, ready to deliver ten thousand times the voltage required to light the single Edison bulb that hung flickering from the ceiling. The heated filament cast an orange glow on dirty lime-washed walls splattered with blood. It was like a vision from hell. Wrench shivered, imagining that for many it had been.

The cell's heavy iron door swung inwards. The regulator with the scarred face marched into the room. He was taller than she remembered, his pointed beard accentuating his angular face and reedy body. With a theatrical air, he locked the cell door, pocketing the key in his waistcoat. He approached the table and placed his hand flat on the file. "I am Captain Flemington of the Aberration Regulatory Cabal and I will be your interrogator for today." He no longer wore his hat or goggles, but his grey eyes were as cold as the smoke-tinted glass.

Wrench swallowed, her mouth dry. There was something deeply unwholesome about the way he'd said "interrogator", although, to be fair, being strapped in an electric chair in a dungeon below Clifford's Tower hadn't exactly left her with a terrifically positive mindset.

"I've been watching you for some time, Miss Wren Chester-Harris." Flemington paused, stroking the point of his beard, letting his words sink in. Wrench's gaze flicked to the file. It was over an inch thick and stuffed with papers and photographs. What had they seen? What did they know about her?

"In fact, I've had a special interest in you. Ever since the crash of the *Drake*."

Wrench flinched, as if she'd been physically struck. It was eight years ago but the horror of that day was permanently stamped on her brain. The *Drake* had been a revolutionary new express train designed by her father, a miracle of modern engineering. On its final test run it had crashed, killing seven, including her parents.

Flemington smiled, obviously pleased with the hurt he'd caused. "The regulators became involved when they could find no reason for the brakes locking on. I wasn't part of the original investigation, but I have a theory about what happened. Would you like to hear it?"

Wrench was certain that she wouldn't. Whatever the monster in front of her said, he only meant to cause her more pain.

Flemington leant forward. The warped skin of his burn scar glistened beneath the Edison bulb. "Last month I investigated an incident at the coachworks. Torr Morton, a fitter with a wife and children, was crushed when the brakes on a shunter failed."

Why was he talking about Torr? He'd been her shift leader at the coachworks until the accident, and it had been an accident, nothing more.

"Industrial-related fatalities don't normally concern the regulators, but I had a special interest in the case." Flemington's eyes burned with hatred. "YOU!" His face inches from hers, he shouted, "You are an aberration and a killer."

Wrench wanted to lean away, wanted to get away, but the restraints prevented her. All she could do was screw her eyes tight shut and not think about the flecks of spit peppering her skin or what unpleasantness the enraged regulator had in store for her.

She sensed Flemington move back. Then pain stung her cheek.

"Look at me when I'm talking to you."

Wrench opened her eyes. Not because she'd been ordered to, but so she'd be ready if the regulator slapped her again.

Flemington sat back and took a moment to calm himself. He wiped the back of his hand across his mouth and then continued. "You were on Morton's shift. Everyone I interviewed said he was hard on you. Said he didn't like having a girl on his team. The other shift leaders teased him, and he took it out on you, claiming it wasn't safe. He was right. You made the shunter's brakes fail. You murdered him."

Wrench didn't want to remember that day. The terrible shrilling of the shunter's whistle. The panic on the driver's face and Torr's expression of terror when the shunter slammed him into the buffers. She couldn't stop it; she'd been too far away. Torr had seen to that, giving her the task of counting washers rather than letting her get stuck into any real engineering.

Flemington smirked at the hurt in her eyes. Then his face hardened, anger furrowing his brow. He slammed a fist onto the table. "You interfered with the brakes on that day, you interfered with the brakes on the crackle-tram today and you interfered with the brakes on the *Drake*. You killed …" Flemington clenched his teeth, biting back the words. The muscles in his neck tightened. "You killed your parents, Brasswitch."

A tear trickled down Wrench's cheek. She loved her parents and missed them every single day. How could this excuse of a human being suggest she was the cause? She wanted to reach out and stop his heart, squeeze it until it beat no more, but her powers only worked on machines.

Flemington wagged a finger at her. "They said I was wrong. Master Regulator Leech told me the crash of the *Drake* was an accident. I didn't believe him. I kept an eye on you, and today I'm vindicated. You are an aberration. A Brasswitch."

Wrench tried to shake her head. The leather skullcap with its metal electrodes stopped any movement. "Please, Sir. I'm not. I'm innocent." Was she though? She didn't understand her powers, not fully. Could she have used them unwittingly? She'd researched the crash of the *Drake* too. Her father's reputation had been destroyed and she'd wanted to clear his name. Despite her best efforts, she'd never determined how the brakes failed, or been able to explain why she was the only survivor. What if Flemington was right? What if she had killed her parents?

Flemington tutted. "It would be nice if one of you freaks admitted it for a change. Then again, that would stop all the fun." He stepped behind her. The sharp clicks of switches operating cut the air. The transformer's hum became more intense and Wrench sensed the sudden electrical surge through its coils.

"I've triggered a simple clockwork timer," said Flemington. "In a little under two minutes the circuit will complete, and you will be electrocuted. Unless you use your powers to stop the clock." He leant close to her ear. His warm breath stank of garlic sausage. "Tick-tock," he whispered.

Was Flemington telling the truth? She knew that the most dangerous aberrations were executed, their deaths trumpeted in the newspapers' obituaries, but she'd always assumed that was after a fair trial to determine their guilt. Could Flemington really murder her where she sat without recourse? Wrench let her mind explore the cogs, gears and electric cables. Apparently, he could. In ninety seconds, she'd be dead. It was like the witch drownings of old. Tied hand and foot, you'd be thrown into a pond. If you sank and drowned you were innocent, if you floated and lived you were guilty, and would then be burned alive. If she stopped the clock, a simple use of her powers, she'd prove her guilt, and who knew what horrors that would prompt. Maybe it would be better to let the electricity do its work, fry her brain and boil her blood. At least it would be quick.

Flemington sauntered back in front of her and leant against the wall beside the door. "You know how when you walk on a carpet and it builds up static so your hairs stand on end? Then you touch some metal and you get that little prickle of a spark and it makes you jump? It's not going to be anything like that."

Something heavy battered the cell door and it shook.

"Flemmy! Open up. I need the girl," shouted a deep bass voice.

A look of annoyance flickered across Flemington's face. "No one called Flemmy here, and no girl, just a soon-to-be-sizzled Brasswitch."

The voice boomed again. "The manual says we're to call them Technomancers. Brasswitch is an apparently outmoded and inappropriate term in these days of enlightenment." The door shuddered and a dent the size of a dinner plate appeared in the metalwork. "It also says we're not supposed to kill them."

"I believe that's more of a guideline than a rule." Flemington winked at Wrench and whispered, "Thirty seconds."

"I don't have time for this," boomed the voice.

Flemington pulled a pocket watch from his waistcoat and flipped it open. "Actually, *she* doesn't have time–"

With an almighty crash the door swung inwards and slammed Flemington into the wall. The pocket watch fell from his hand. Unconscious, he slid to the floor amidst broken watch glass and scattered cogs.

A massive jet-black mechanoid stooped through the doorway then expanded to its full height. Over seven feet tall with bulbous skorpidium-carbide armour covering its body, it looked like a giant medieval knight.

Wrench strained at her bonds, the leather chafing her wrists. The mechanoid's rounded head turned towards Flemington and the shape of its emerald eyes subtly changed. Somehow Wrench knew it was smiling.

"Good morning," said the mechanoid, then paused, seeming to reconsider. "Obviously it hasn't been a good morning, but I'm optimistic things are about to get a whole lot better. I'm Bot, and I require your assistance, so it would be absolutely top hole if you weren't electrocuted."

Wrench stopped the electric chair's clock.

With frightening ease, Bot ripped away the straps that secured Wrench to the electric chair, the heavy leather parting like tissue paper beneath his chunky fingers.

Wrench ducked out of the skullcap. "Thank you." She rubbed her wrists, feeling awkward. She'd never conversed with a machine before, at least not in the traditional sense.

"You are most welcome." Bot stooped back out of the cell. "Come with me and live, stay here and die. The decision is yours."

The mechanoid stomped down the corridor, not bothering to see if she was following. It was a Hobson's choice he'd offered. When the infamous stable owner Thomas Hobson offered customers a choice of horse, it was the one nearest the door or none at all; the choice offered to Wrench was equally scant. Bot hadn't said what he wanted but it couldn't be worse than staying with Flemington. With a *plink* the Edison lamp overhead burned out. Wrench stepped from the cell. Behind her the transformer glowed red-hot and melted under a massive surge of power, never to electrocute anyone again.

Bot clanked through the stone-lined tunnels deep beneath Clifford's Tower with what Wrench could only describe as a confident swagger. Of course, that was ridiculous; he was a mechanoid, although not like any of the mechanoids she'd encountered before. Automatons were a common sight on the streets of York, fetching and carrying for the wealthier gentry, and she'd even seen some of the more advanced battle-mechs used by the army and regulators. Bot was different. The way he spoke, and the fluidity with which he moved despite his massive size, was almost human. He pounded past a pair of uniformed regulators and they shied away.

A smile curled Wrench's lips; she enjoyed seeing the much-feared enforcers adopting a subservient role for a change. "Where are we going?" she asked.

Bot's voice boomed along the passageway. "The Minster, Brasswitch."

Wrench recoiled. For some reason, coming from Bot the name rankled. "I thought you weren't supposed to call me that?"

"I was just baiting Flemington. Bloody stupid

rulebook. I mean, who the hell's ever heard of a Technomancer? Brasswitch has power. Brasswitch creates fear. Until today, being called Brasswitch would have got you killed. Now, it might save your life."

This was wrong. She wasn't a Brasswitch. They were evil harridans that destroyed machinery, downed zeppelins and sank ships. Or so the superstition of generations believed. The last Brasswitch to be publicly executed was Morag Kennard, a wise woman living in the lee of the Tay Bridge in Scotland. She was blamed for the collapse of the central span on 28th of December 1879, plunging a locomotive and six carriages into the icy waters of the river Tay below. Seventy-five people died as a result of the disaster, seventy-six if you included Kennard, which nobody ever did.

Wrench's father had been called as an expert at the enquiry. He'd claimed the bridge design was flawed, the iron girders being brittle under tension. The engineering company that designed the bridge denied any error and instead involved the regulators. In the end, it worked out better for all concerned to hang a madwoman than to admit a mistake. Well, better for all concerned, except Kennard.

Wrench wasn't evil, or mad; all she'd ever done was help. As she'd grown older she'd become more aware of the technology surrounding her, sensing it like a sleeping dog waiting to be roused. She'd touch a machine and instinctively know how it worked, what it did and if it was *unwell*. She'd used this talent to fix things, to make machines better, never to do harm, but Flemington's accusations niggled her like a squeaking piston. *You interfered with the brakes on the* Drake. *You killed your parents, Brasswitch.* What if she could trigger machines without knowing?

On her eleventh birthday, she'd received a letter confirming her apprenticeship as an engineer at the coachworks. Not everyone was selected and she'd had to battle harder than most to even be considered. She'd been truly happy for the first time since her parents died and at that moment, a nearby gramophone had whirred to life without cause. Other times, when she was irked and moody, Edison bulbs had been known to flare and burn out. The engineer in her said coincidences happened and the events were nothing more than random chance, but the traitorous part of her brain that fed her self-doubt disagreed.

The passage opened into a circular stable, the stone walls and roof reinforced with girders of iron. Large ducted fans drew away the steam and the smoke that spiralled upwards from the rows of waiting walkomobiles. With their domed steel and glass cabins and their shiny brass legs sparkling in the lamplights they looked like giant insects waiting to swarm. A driver dressed in regulator red snapped to attention. "All fuelled and ready, Sir."

Bot led Wrench to a walker, the sides of which were peculiarly angled, giving the carriage the appearance of a squashed dodecahedron. Unlike the other vehicles, which were painted madder-red, the colour of the regulators, the colour of fear, Bot's walker was jet-black, matching his armour. The only embellishment on the machine was the crest of the ARC, the Aberration Regulatory Cabal: a clenched fist dripping blood, with the word *Purity* written beneath.

The Grand Cabal had been formed centuries earlier to rid the population of aberrations, unwholesome tainted people who threatened the natural order of society. Independent of the government and overseen only by the Queen, they met in secret, passing down dictates to be carried out by its operational arm, the Aberration Regulatory Cabal, the regulators.

"Take a seat." Bot pulled open the carriage door and gestured to the bench inside.

Wrench glanced around the bustling garage, looking for a way out. She was surrounded by people who would kill her at the drop of a bowler hat. Escape would have been impossible, even without the armoured mechanoid watching over her.

"No electricity in these chairs. It's the best offer you're going to get," said Bot.

Wrench climbed into the carriage. There was no other choice, for now at least. She settled onto the worn padded leather seat and waited. Bot lowered himself onto the oak bench opposite and rested his shovel-sized hands on his knees. "How much do you know about the Rupture?"

The walker rose on its legs and strode out of the fortified iron gate beneath the tower. Wrench considered the question. "Only what I learned at school," she said. "Three centuries ago a religious order called the Monks of Mayheim tried to open a gateway to heaven; instead they created a connection to another dimension, letting evil into our world. Things came through – horrible, unspeakable things. Some people worshipped them as gods but all they did was destroy. Chaos ensued until an Augustine Knight, Sir Dereleth, drove the beasts back. Shrouded in protective armour, he ventured into the other world, ensuring the creatures' banishment. Months later, he returned mortally wounded but with the knowledge of how to seal the Rupture."

Sunlight filtered through the carriage's smoked-glass window, a refreshing change from the dim claustrophobia of the tower's dungeons. Bot's green eyes shone brighter. "Only some of that is true. The gateways were never closed. It was more like we put nets over them, but occasionally things still punch through. Powerful monstrosities that are responsible for causing aberrations like you."

Wrench scowled. "I'm not an aberration."

"You know that's not true, Brasswitch," said the mechanoid flatly.

Anger flared inside Wrench and the carriage light flickered. It wasn't her fault she was different. She extended her mind, probing Bot's mechanics, searching for some clue about the machine's intent, or for a way to disable him. Blackness surged into her brain and her head snapped back, pinned against the carriage's metal shell by an invisible force.

Bot's eyes flashed red. Quicker than Wrench could blink, he was gripping her head with chunky fingers the size of hammerheads. "Brasswitch, if you ever use your powers on me again I will crush your skull like the most delicate of bird eggs."

The cold metal pressed into her skin, points of pain skewering her head. Blood pounded in her ears, drowning out all other sounds. Fear overwhelmed her, but there was a sliver of something else too. A shard of terror that didn't belong to her, but to the mechanoid.

Bot's eyes faded back to green. "The purpose of the regulators is to hunt down and remove the threat of aberrations." His grip softened and he withdrew his hand. "Fortunately for you, I am one of the few who believe this can be achieved without resorting to murder. In your case at least."

Wrench massaged her skull. "Why don't you want me dead?"

"Right now, I need your skills."

Not the most reassuring of answers. Was she just a tool to him, to be put back in the toolbox or discarded when the job was done? "So, you'll keep me alive because I'm useful?"

"I'm keeping you alive because I believe it's the right thing to do. I am of the opinion aberrations are not bad by default. A viewpoint which has made me unpopular among the majority of my colleagues, so you could show a little more gratitude."

"I shouldn't have to thank you for simply doing what's right."

"And yet, it would be terrifically nice if you did."

"If you wanted nice you should have rescued someone else." Wrench folded her arms and glowered.

"Alas, then I would have squandered a fantastic opportunity to annoy Flemington and the Clifford's Tower Cabal."

Wrench had always considered the regulators as one big scary institution, to be avoided at all costs. However, it was clear that the organisation was divided.

"You're not from Clifford's Tower?"

"Most certainly not. That's Captain Flemington's little empire. They protect the city of York and its surrounds. I have a more wide-reaching remit."

"The regulators at the tower, they were scared of you."

"When the most malevolent aberrations manifest, it's me they send for." Bot leant closer. "They hate me for my beliefs and they fear me because they've heard tell of what I'm capable of."

"What are you capable of?"

"You help me at the Minster and you might just find out." Bot twitched and the armoured plates protecting his workings clanked gently together. "Just so we're clear, that was a bump in the road making me shudder and I am certainly not terrified of what we may find in the casket I want you to open."

Wrench stuck her hands in her overall pockets. "Casket, as in *coffin*? Last resting place of dead people?"

"Sort of. Except what's in the casket isn't a person –" Bot drummed his fingers against a metal plate on his leg, "– or dead."

Wrench's relief at being free from Clifford's Tower was beginning to wane. Flemington had appeared unhinged, and now it seemed Bot had a few cogs loose as well. Perhaps it was in the regulator's job description: *Are you cruel with a tendency towards lunacy? Then join the regulators today.*

She fixed a smile on her face. "You've rescued the wrong person. You wanted the grave robber in the cell next door. If you drop me off here I'll let you return for them."

"I can drop you back to Flemington."

"I'm just an apprentice engineer at the coachworks. I know about steam trains, not coffins. I'm no good to you."

"Oh, but you are. When the Rupture occurred some of the creatures that came through couldn't be destroyed or banished. Those aberrations were incarcerated in special caskets that over time would dissipate their power. These caskets are impossible to unlock – unless you're a Brasswitch."

"You could smash it open. You made easy work of my cell door. I'm sure a coffin would present little problem."

"The caskets were forged three hundred years ago at the time of the Rupture. They drew on the massive flux of power flowing into our world as part of the casting process. With the Rupture now controlled we can't make new ones and we can't afford for this one to be damaged."

Wrench looked out of the window at the bustling streets. Sat astride a monoped, a city gent juddered alongside the carriage. The metal machine shaped like a giant brass boot progressed over the cobbles in a series of small jumps. She could fling the door open, steal it from him, and lose herself in the crowd … no, Bot would stop her in an instant. She relaxed back into the seat. "I don't want to open a coffin if there's going to be something horrible inside."

"That's why I'm here. Dealing with horrible things is somewhat of a speciality of mine. And afterwards, if the Minster, and indeed the city of York, isn't destroyed in a frenzy of metal-tentacled mayhem, you're free to go," said Bot. "Technically at least."

"What do you mean technically?"

Bot rolled his shoulders. "Should you choose to leave, I won't stop you."

The carriage hissed to a halt.

"But?" said Wrench.

"But Flemington is a vindictive little git and will

undoubtedly make it his business to hunt you down and kill you."

Wrench adjusted her glasses. Outside, flanked by two wrought-iron gas lamps, a flight of wide stone steps led to the Minster's doors. In times of old, churches were seen as a place of sanctuary, but not now. Not for the likes of her. "So, if I want to live, I'm stuck with you?"

Metal plates around Bot's mouth slid into different positions so he appeared to be grinning. "Yes. But look on the bright side."

"What bright side?"

Bot punched her on the shoulder with a surprising lightness. "I'm terrific fun."

"Yeah, I can tell. All that stuff about crushing my skull. You're a real hoot."

4

To call the Minster a church would be like calling Big Ben a timepiece. The biggest, most impressive building in the city of York, the Minster dominated the skyline. Constructed from thousands of tons of carved stone, the western facade was decorated with a breathtakingly complex stained-glass window the size of a locomotive turntable. The south-west tower, with its brass gargoyles and aluminium-bronze spires, offered tribute to the one true god. The blackened melted stump of the north-west tower, with its purple haze of swirling energy and roiling clouds, was a stark reminder of the power of the old gods. Worshipped in a frenzy of madness, the nightmares that squelched through the Rupture brought chaos to the country. They thrived on destruction, drawing power from devastation, opening new rifts to their dimension. They sought to obliterate the world and without the bravery and sacrifice of Sir Dereleth, they would have succeeded.

Wrench climbed the steps to the western doors. The hairs on her arms stood on end, as if she was in the presence of a strong static field. But this wasn't electricity. This was power of an entirely different nature, and one she felt viscerally drawn to. She gestured to the desecrated tower. "So, the portal up there isn't actually sealed and at any time something horrible could just pop through?"

Bot pushed the Minster's heavy iron-bound doors open as if they were nothing and stepped inside. "Not at any time. Certain celestial events seem to bring the worlds closer, making the Rupture more vulnerable."

Wrench had never been a fan of churches – the faithful hounded aberrations with more malice than the regulators. Anyone judged to be different was cast from the congregation, or worse. The justice of the good book meted out with pious zeal. She clenched her fists and stepped through the door.

The interior of the Minster was as impressive as the outside with high vaulted ceilings, ornately carved arches and magnificent stained-glass windows. Wrench hurried after Bot, marvelling at the engineering prowess required to build such a place. The construction would have been a major undertaking even today, using steam cranes, hydraulic lifts and all the modern technology of the industrial revolution. How people had managed it five hundred years ago was beyond belief.

Bot stomped down the southern side of the nave. The clanking of his mechanics garnered him unchristian looks from the faithful praying in the pews. Wrench adopted an awkward skipping run to keep pace. "Where are we going?"

"St George's chapel. Or to be more precise, an undercrypt, which thanks to Master Regulator Leech and a large sledgehammer, is now accessed via St George's chapel."

Legend heralded that a thousand years ago St George had slain a dragon. Since the occurrence of the Rupture many now claimed evil had come into the world once before and St George had driven it back, just like Sir Dereleth had done. Wrench had always been sceptical, preferring science to stories. Bot's revelations about the Rupture made her wonder if the superstitions of old held more credence than she'd believed. If the fact of the matter was that the Rupture had never been sealed, what other truths had been kept secret? Her foster-father had complained only recently about the regulators when the railway lines to the port of Whitby were closed for two weeks. Allegedly the sailors on a foreign ship were afflicted with a virulent disease and so the area had to be quarantined. Now she wondered if that really had been the case.

At the far end of the chapel a rectangular altar bedecked in blood-red cloths and dedicated to St George the dragon slayer rested on a dais. To the left of the altar a pile of rubble lay next to a ragged doorway smashed into the church wall. Through the doorway a flight of steps led down to the under-crypt. A balding reverend knelt at the top of the stairs reciting a Latin incantation. An expression of loathing crossed his face when he glanced at Wrench. He knew she was an aberration, the hate in his eyes telling her plainly as day.

The smell of smoke filled the under-crypt, but not from the flickering candles; it had a pungent tang that Wrench couldn't place. They walked between thick stone columns that supported the arched ceiling and Wrench sensed a change in Bot's demeanour; he was more alert, his movements controlled and measured. The back of her neck prickled. He was hiding something from her, she was sure of it. Why bother? How could it be worse than a coffin containing a monstrosity from another world?

Surrounded by twisted railings, a baroque phosphor-bronze casket rested on a marble plinth. Chains and locks inscribed with strange symbols secured the casket closed. The sooty silhouettes of a man and a child tarnished the white plaster wall behind.

"Time to earn your keep, Brasswitch," said Bot.

Wrench placed her hands on the coffin. "Inside there might be a murderous monster from another dimension that wants to rip us to pieces before destroying all humanity."

"If we're lucky."

"And if we're unlucky?"

Bot's hands clenched into fists. "It'll be empty."

It didn't make sense; she wasn't getting the whole story. "I'm still a bit thin on why you need to open it."

"One of my officers, Master Regulator Leech, uncovered reports of an aberration from the original Rupture that hadn't been destroyed. Historic documents suggested it had been captured and contained for centuries in a casket of phosphor-bronze."

"And Leech thinks this is that casket?"

"Indeed."

"So why doesn't Leech open the coffin?"

Bot clapped his hands together, the metallic clang echoing around the under-crypt. "Enough stalling with the questions, Brasswitch. Get it done."

Wrench examined the phosphor-bronze, a metal known for its strength and resistance to corrosion. Perhaps that was why the craftsmen had chosen it, knowing the casket would be required to maintain its integrity for centuries. She ran her fingers over the locks. The metal felt abnormally cold, and the locks had no keyholes. There was no way to open them, or at least no way unless you were a Brasswitch. She pushed her mind into a lock's mechanism and aligned the pins. A mental nudge rotated the barrel and the lock sprung open. Wrench shuddered. She'd removed the first defence without problem. Would the others prove so easy? And if so, what unimaginable horror would she release? Her focus shifted from the mechanism to herself. The palms of her hands tingled, and her heart thudded faster, but all things considered, she felt remarkably calm. Perhaps that was the thing with unimaginable horrors: you couldn't imagine them, unlike the crash of the *Drake*, which even in her nightmares was so very real. She pushed the thought away, distracting herself with the remaining restraints.

With six of the locks now sprung open, Wrench's palms prickled uncomfortably. There was something different about the last lock. She wriggled her fingers, trying to force the unpleasant feeling away.

Bot moved closer. "The moment you're done, run to the carriage and bolt yourself in."

"And I'll be safe there?"

Gears grated inside the mechanoid, making the mechanical equivalent of a laugh. "Don't be stupid. This is an eldritch being from another dimension. The only way to be safe would be to get across the sea to France. They hate the sea."

The final lock had an added safeguard, but it was already deactivated, not needed. The discomfort in her fingers lessened. "No point in hiding in the carriage then."

"It would save you from a horrifying sight."

"The eldritch being from another dimension?"

"No. Me whimpering like a girl."

Wrench put her hands on her hips and turned to face the mechanoid. "I am a girl, and I never whimper."

"You're a Brasswitch – that's different."

"And you're a skorpidium-carbide armoured mechanoid, so toughen up."

Bot eased closer to Wrench. "That's an oxymoron."

"No. You're a moron. There's nothing in the casket."

"How do you know?"

"There's something odd about the last lock. It's got a counterbalance that won't allow it to open if there's a weight in the casket."

"Are you sure?"

"See for yourself." Wrench pushed the lid free. The sarcophagus was empty except for a thin layer of what looked like ash covering the hazel wood interior.

Bot's shoulders slumped. "Tarnation!"

Wrench prodded the ash in the coffin with the shackle of a padlock. "Maybe Leech was wrong."

"I think not. I was hoping I was mistaken, but Leech beat us here and released it. He knew it would be weakened from centuries of containment and he thought he could handle it."

"So, we find Leech and we find the unimaginable horror."

Bot motioned to the soot-stained silhouette on the wall. "Leech must have miscalculated. It was still too powerful. A mistake he didn't live to regret."

"That's not possible." Wrench raised one of the padlocks. "He couldn't have opened it without a Brasswitch."

"He had one. How does it feel to be the only

surviving Brasswitch in the country?"

Wrench stared at the second silhouette on the wall. It was not that of an evil harridan, some hideous monster to be despised, but a girl not much younger than her.

"Dangerous," she said.

5

An intricate brass relief covered the door that led to the ruined north-west tower. The detailed frieze, depicting an armour-clad Sir Dereleth forcing a betentacled behemoth back through the Rupture, did little to camouflage the immense strength of the heavy steel door beneath. The things that came through the Rupture were said to have taken many forms, some no bigger than a man, others purportedly the size of a battleship. Wrench had always struggled to believe a creature that size could exist. Even the dinosaur skeletons in the Yorkshire Museum would be judged small by comparison. It seemed impossible that Sir Dereleth could have battled such a beast, as impossible as St George slaying a dragon.

Bot raised his arm and made a fist like a battering ram.

"You want me to open that?" offered Wrench, concerned the mechanoid would adopt a similar approach to the one he'd used on the cell door.

A three-pronged key extended from Bot's knuckles. "I've got this."

Bot inserted the key in the lock and twisted his fist. A series of loud clunks echoed from deep within the door. Wrench didn't need to use her powers to tell that the lock's mechanism was both complex and robust. Accompanied by the staccato clatter of a ratchet, the door slid aside to reveal a spiral of thick stone steps, leading upwards.

Somewhere overhead lay the ravaged remains of the tower and above that was the Rupture, not permanently sealed, as Wrench had been taught, but a thinly netted hole to another dimension. A shiver slithered up her spine. She should be terrified but the strange energy seeping down the staircase exhilarated her.

"We've got some climbing to do," said Bot. "Can you keep up or shall I carry you?"

Wrench bristled, anger burning away any exhaustion. She was nearly fourteen, and she most certainly wasn't going to be carried like a child. "I worked ten-hour shifts at the coachworks; I can manage."

The stairway spiralled around and around. Wrench trudged relentlessly upwards. The clank of Bot's feet on the worn stone steps echoed from above and the faint smell of oil and steam hung in the air. Why couldn't they install an Otis elevator or an Armstrong hydraulic lift?

Probably the same reason why every fifty steps there was another of the heavy steel doors. For anyone without a key or a hulking metal mechanoid they would present an almost insurmountable obstacle.

She passed through the fifth such door, the muscles in her legs burning like the finest Barnsley coal. At the coachworks, she'd had to prove she was a match for the boys, never once complaining, and now she pushed through the pain with the same dogged determination.

A violet haze filtered into the stairwell. It played in dappled patterns on the walls like sunlight reflected from water. Except up here, hundreds of feet above the ground, there was no water. It was the flicker of raw thaumaturgy, the name given to the energy leaking through the Rupture. The public were told it was safely contained at the top of the tower, nothing more than a spectacular light show. Was that another lie?

The substance of the walls had changed too; no longer sandy-coloured limestone blocks, they were glassy and smooth with candlewax-like drips. It was as if the tower had been melted in a great furnace.

The clank of Bot's footsteps stopped. Wrench rounded one more bend and she emerged into daylight, or what would have been daylight if it weren't for the roiling storm cloud surrounding them. The Rupture swirled and pulsed, casting a surreal hue across the smelted stone.

A grid of titanium bars arced over the ruined tower top, encaging it in a protective dome. Bot waited at the cage's centre, alongside a tarnished gold ball the height of two men. A steel pole skewered the ball's centre, disappearing into the angry clouds far overhead. Seven brass and platinum discs rotated around the ball. Something that wasn't quite electricity arced between the discs and crackled along thick copper cables that trailed from the base of the machine and over the tower's edge.

"This is the odic capacitor," said Bot. "It absorbs surges of power from the Rupture, stopping it gaining enough energy for anything to break through. Since we added it to the earth coils a decade ago, breaches of the Rupture have more than halved."

The capacitor had a feeling of familiarity to it. A distant memory nagged at Wrench. A blazing fire, the smell of pipe smoke and lying on a soft carpet playing with her favourite toy, a puzzle ball. Overhead, the Rupture thrummed and sparks crackled across the capacitor's discs.

Wrench extended her mind into the machine. Beneath the globe's shell Faraday shunts, Edison coils and all manner of other components fizzed with power. Yet they weren't as she knew them. Subtle differences repurposed the technology to change the way it functioned. No. It wasn't possible. It didn't make sense – this wasn't science. Wrench pushed harder, trying to sense the flow of electrons passing through the wires, but there were no electrons, only –

Pain lanced her skull. The copper cables that snaked from the base of the machine squirmed towards her and encircled her arms and legs. One grabbed her head, snapping her neck back, forcing her to stare directly into the heart of the turbulent cloud. A face appeared, massive and morose.

Wrench fought back tears. It was her father. "Help us," he said. Behind him, a second face emerged from the haze, her mother. "Wrench. Help us, please."

"You killed us. Left us here in limbo. Free us now," said her father.

Tears rolled down her mother's cheeks. "You crashed the *Drake*. You must free us, Brasswitch."

"Brasswitch," said her father, his voice distorted. He reached out to her, a greedy smile on his face. His fingers elongating into metallic tentacles.

"Brasswitch!" Bot's hand seized her head and forced her gaze from the cloud. Wrench clawed at her neck, but there was nothing there. No copper cable strangling her. The thick wires lay dormant, unmoved, trailing from the machine. What had happened? It had been so real. Her mother and father talking to her after all these years. She rubbed a hand across her eyes, fighting back tears. She hadn't killed her parents. It had been a terrible accident, nothing more. It wasn't her fault.

"It doesn't pay to stare into the Rupture," said Bot. He removed his hand from her head. "Not if you don't want to end up a gibbering lunatic."

"I saw my parents," said Wrench, ashamed of the tremble in her voice.

"Whatever you saw, it wasn't your parents. Reality is thin here; the old gods can sense your power, but they can't break through, not without help. That's why I needed to check the thing from the casket hadn't tried to destroy the odic capacitor."

Wrench stepped away from the cables and made a mental calculation of the strength of the titanium cage surrounding them. "I hope it's well guarded."

"It is." Bot waved in the direction of the adjacent undamaged tower. "Snipers keep it under constant vigil. The stairs are the only way up. And I've taken a few secret precautions of my own."

"But you still had to check?"

Bot ran his fingers over a blob of melted stone. "You need to understand the world you're a part of now. The thing from the casket is an NIA, a Non-Indigenous Aberration from beyond the Rupture. Not as powerful as an Old God, a lesser-servitor maybe, but still stronger than a charging bull, deadlier than a striking snake and with the ability to access powers we barely understand. It will be weakened by its incarceration, but it's only a matter of time before it recoups the rest of its strength." Bot twisted his arm and checked the chronograph inset in his wrist. "Time we don't have. Chattox, my previous Brasswitch, was brilliant, resourceful, and tough beyond her years. She was well trained too, yet the NIA turned her into a sooty smudge. We can't afford for it to get any more powerful."

Wrench removed her glasses and polished them with a grubby handkerchief from her pocket. She had always wanted to be a part of something, to belong. When she'd become an apprentice at the coachworks she'd thought at last she'd fit in. She couldn't have been more wrong. Now she was being offered another chance to belong; however, she wasn't sure it was a chance she wanted. So far, the regulators had brought her nothing but pain. Flemington with his accusations that she'd crashed the *Drake* and then Bot with the visions of her dead parents. If she joined them, what additional suffering would she endure?

"So, what do you plan to do about the NIA?" she asked.

"I'm going to find it and then I'm going to ask it politely to return to the casket."

"Really?"

Bot laughed. "Of course not. I'm going to kill it with extreme prejudice."

6

The carriage ran down Queen Street, its steel feet sending sparks flying from the cobbles. Out of the window a fortified stone wall stood atop a steep grass bank, the medieval defences still providing a robust barrier around the old city. Further down the hill the grandiose glass canopy of York railway station glinted in the sunlight. Steam and smoke billowed from dragon-shaped roof vents that kept the platforms free of smog.

"I thought we were returning to your headquarters?" said Wrench.

"I'm not part of the Clifford's Tower Cabal. I head up Cabal Thirteen."

Wrench rolled her eyes. "Oh, let me guess. You're called Cabal Thirteen because all the bad people get sent to you and it's a really unlucky posting."

"Actually, we recruit only the best regulators because our work is so dangerous. Whether that's unlucky or not depends on your viewpoint."

"So why are you called Thirteen?"

"Because thirteen is the platform number our train's stationed on."

Wrench put a hand on Bot's arm; he didn't seem to notice. "You have a train?"

"York is the centre of the Rupture, but the rest of the country still suffers its effects. Being able to move our cabal using the rail network has proved invaluable."

A train of their own. Railways fascinated Wrench. As far back as she could remember she'd felt drawn to the majesty of steam locomotives, and the crash of the *Drake* had only served to strengthen the allure. If she got to know the engineer, she might get a chance to help on the footplate. "What class of train is it?"

"Oh, the usual: big wheels, three chimneys, pointy bit at the front," said Bot, casually waving a hand.

"You don't know, do you?"

"It's just a train."

Wrench removed her hand and sat back. "The railways are the lifeblood of the country."

"People are the lifeblood of the country and my job is to keep them alive. I can't get bogged down in the details."

With a hiss and a clatter the carriage drew to a halt at

the front of the station and settled onto its haunches.

Bot squeezed through the door and dropped onto the road, the crash of his feet on the hard flagstones frightening the horses of a more traditional carriage nearby. He offered his hand to Wrench. She ignored it and jumped down the steps. "Tell me about Cabal Thirteen."

Bot strolled into the station. "We deal with the most dangerous aberrations and all NIAs – the things that break through the Rupture from other dimensions."

They crossed an iron lattice footbridge spanning the station's many platforms. Below, locomotives and rolling stock of all colours, shapes and sizes filled the tracks. A Caledonian blue express thundered along the mainline, dirty smoke billowing from its graceful curved chimneys.

"The twelve fifty-three to Edinburgh," said Wrench.

Bot glanced sideways at her.

Wrench pointed at the locomotive. "It's a four-six-four Stephenson rotary piston with over-boiler."

"You know this because you're a Brasswitch?"

"I know this because I'm an apprentice mechanic at the LNER engineering works. Or at least I was until this morning."

"You're still an apprentice." Bot drummed his fingers on the footbridge's metal rail. "Just not to the London North-Eastern Railway."

"I'm an apprentice Brasswitch?"

"You were born a Brasswitch. You're an apprentice regulator."

Wrench stopped. The regulators were the enemy, or if not the enemy, the bogeyman. The people mothers would frighten their children with. Eat your turnips or the regulators will come for you. Holding more power than parliament, people feared the regulators like they used to fear the inquisition. The regulators could change your life in an instant, or end it.

"What do you mean I'm a regulator?"

"You're an aberration, so you either work for Cabal Thirteen, in which case I can protect you, or you take your chances with Flemington. I thought you understood that?"

"I didn't know I'd be a regulator."

"We're not all bad people. Heck, we're not even all people."

"But you do bad things."

Bot moved beside her and stared over the rail at the disappearing twelve fifty-three powering into the distance. "We do terrible things. The public don't know the half of it. However, the consequences of not doing them would be catastrophic."

Wrench's grip on the rail tightened. Everyone had heard horror stories of the regulators, and if what Bot was saying was true, the reality was worse than the rumours. In the under-crypt, she'd sensed the mechanoid's fear, not for himself but for what would happen if he failed. She'd seen the Rupture and the odic capacitor and had been introduced to the world as the regulators saw it, a world where the fortunes of the country, and possibly the world, could be destroyed in the blink of an eye.

Could their iron-fisted reign of terror be justified? Was it necessary? She'd learned in school that the sea prevented the creatures that came through the Rupture from spreading beyond the English isles, but the history books also told what a close-run race it had been. In 1620 a ship called the *Mayheim Flower* had set out for the new world with three NIAs aboard. Only the might of the Royal Navy, and their resolve to sink the *Mayheim Flower* despite the loss of innocent lives had stopped the spread. It was from the Navy's Regulatory Branch that the initial regulators had been recruited, men who would punish and kill without question to put a halt to the threat of aberrations.

"Come on. You'll like our train," said Bot.

"The train that you don't ..." Something Bot had said earlier caught up with Wrench. "What do you mean, you're not all people?"

Bot drew to a halt alongside the train "stabled" in the siding of platform thirteen. The carriages were double decked, two tall rows of smoked-glass windows set into the angled armoured sides. He pressed a panel on the carriage's door and with a whoosh of steam it slid open. "Here, I'll introduce you to the team."

The carriage was set out like a lecture theatre, admittedly a long narrow one. Bot pulled a vocal annunciator tube from the wall. "Code Dead, cabal

51

briefing now." He let go of the conical mouthpiece and the VA tube retracted. After a short pause his words repeated through a rosette of flared trumpets attached to the ceiling. He dragged a chair to the front of the carriage and turned it around to face the rows of seats. "Please, sit."

Wrench lowered herself into the chair. Her stomach churned. At least this chair wasn't electric. She was a regulator, or it seemed she was going to be. One of the people she'd spent her whole life avoiding. Could she do that? Join the enemy? Cause others to cower in fear and worse? It felt wrong, but she had no choice, not for the moment at least. She glanced out of the smoked-glass window. York station was the hub of the railway network from where trains traversed the length and breadth of the country. She could escape to one of the big cities. London, Edinburgh, Birmingham, Manchester and many more were all but a ticket away. Lost among the crowds of such a teeming metropolis, not even the regulators could find her. She'd be alone, but since the death of her parents she'd always felt alone.

After the accident, Horace Grimthorpe, her father's chief engineer, had taken her in and looked after her. He'd got her the apprenticeship at the engineering works and his wife, Elsie, had mothered her as best she could, but she wasn't Wrench's mother and it was never going to be the same. Despite all their kindness, nothing could fill the emptiness deep inside of her.

Wrench straightened her shoulders, determined to hide the unease that twisted her stomach. The rows of chairs began to fill with a mixture of red-suited regulators, and more traditionally attired personnel. Unlike apprentice meetings at the engineering works, where the air would be thick with banter, nobody talked. Even Bot stood motionless, ignoring the arrival of the staff. Wrench wondered if the sombre quiet was something to do with the strange message he'd delivered over the vocal annunciator: *Code Dead.*

A delicate tip-tapping of high-heels on metal grew louder from further down the train and then a sylphlike lady, dressed in a silk cheongsam and teal sequined turban drifted into the carriage. Her skin appeared to be of the darkest black until she walked beneath the carriage's lamps where it glistened with a sheen of midnight blue. "I'm the last," said the lady, her melodic tones soothing the knot in Wrench's stomach.

The lady flowed onto a seat and with a whirr of gears Bot straightened.

"Master Regulator Leech and apprentice Chattox have left Cabal Thirteen," said Bot. "We will hold a retirement party in due course, but we have more pressing needs. Leech was tracking a possible Non-Indigenous Aberration, which I now believe to be in the wild. Get your desks clear because this is our priority. I will allocate tasks after the meeting but first I would like to introduce our new Brasswitch."

Wrench waited, expecting Bot to say more, but he simply motioned towards her with his chunky arm. The silence lengthened. Wrench stood. She'd spent three years at the engineering works battling to be accepted just because she was a girl. If she was to start a new apprenticeship here, she was going to set her stall out from the start. In a voice made strong by anger she said, "I have a name actually." She waited a moment; Bot didn't respond to the prompt. "My name is Wren, although everyone calls me Wrench. Well, everyone apart from him," she said, pointing towards the mechanoid.

The sylphlike lady stood. "Delighted to have you on the team. I'm Octavia." From beneath her turban slithered a dark glossy tentacle. It waved at Wrench.

7

Bot left Wrench in Octavia's charge while he organised the hunt for the NIA and assigned tasks to the regulators. Octavia radiated a calm confidence that dulled Wrench's unease. They walked in companionable silence along a wood-panelled corridor running down one side of the carriage's upper deck. Wrench had never met anyone like Octavia before and her mind was full of questions but something about the woman's soothing presence quelled her urge to ask them.

Octavia stopped at a polished cedar door and pushed it open. "This will be your cabin."

The room was small but well appointed. Opposite the door, beneath a large tinted window stood a chunky desk. A high, brass-framed bed ran the length of the cabin, okcase and chest of drawers fitted snugly below.

"This is the bathroom," said Octavia, pushing an adjoining door. "And this is your wardrobe and weapons cabinet."

Wrench wrapped her knuckles against the steel plating of the wardrobe. "Why do I need a weapons cabinet?"

"You probably don't, but for most of the regulators the only thing that stands between them and a horrible death are their BBGs."

"BBGs?"

"Bloody Big Guns." Octavia checked her reflection in a mirror screwed to the wall and preened an eyebrow. "It will take a while, but you'll get used to the TLAs in time."

"TLAs?"

"Three Letter Abbreviations. The regulators sprinkle them about like salt at a summoning."

The wardrobe was cavernous and empty. Back at her bedroom in the Grimthorpes' house Wrench had one frock for Sunday best and three sets of overalls. The size of the steel cabinet was somewhat excessive for her needs.

Octavia closed the wardrobe door. "Among my many talents, I'm Thirteen's outfitter. I'll get you measured and run up some garments fit for a queen."

"I'm not a queen," said Wrench, bristling.

"No. You're not." Octavia took Wrench's hand and gave it a squeeze. "You're far more important."

✿

Octavia's cabin was considerably larger than Wrench's and decorated with a flamboyant confidence. An industrial steam-powered sewing machine was bolted to a large workbench on which were draped swathes of fabric. There was no sign of a bed and Wrench guessed one of the three doors that led from the room provided access to Octavia's private quarters.

Her arms held outstretched, Wrench waited awkwardly. Tentacles emerged from concealed slits in Octavia's cheongsam and she began taking measurements.

"You're obviously ... different," said Wrench.

"You mean I'm an aberration."

"No. I hate that word. Why can't different be good? Look at you. You're magnificent."

Octavia's tentacles gave a delighted ripple. "I sensed I was going to like you."

A warmness filled Wrench's chest. For the first time since this terrible day had begun she felt comfortable, even welcome. She wanted to know more about Octavia. She wanted to be friends.

"I can't imagine Bot recruited you for your tailoring talents. So what is it that you do in the cabal?"

"You mean bringing some much-needed sartorial style and a sense of panache isn't enough?" A tentacle uncurled from Octavia's head and formed a circle in front of her face. She stared at Wrench through the impromptu eyepiece. "Much as I appreciate the practicality of shapeless overalls, I think tartan dungarees and a double-buttoned blouse would do wonders for your appearance."

"Clothes aren't important. It's what's up here that counts." Wrench tapped a finger against her temple.

Octavia's elegant eyes widened. "Dressing correctly is oh so important."

"Not to me." Much to her foster-mother's dismay, Wrench had never been concerned about appearance. What mattered to Wrench was mechanics. The way a worm drive changed torque, that was something to get excited about, not having matching gloves and hat.

"You're not doing it for you. You're doing it for the job. There will be times when you have to bluff, times when people are looking for sanity in the madness, times when you have to convince an angry mob to follow you rather than lynch you, and at those times looking the part and feeling the part goes a long way towards playing the part."

Wrench shrugged.

A tentacle curled into a question mark over Octavia's head. "If a Stephenson RP class locomotive was painted dull grey instead of Caledonian blue and the shiny brass fittings were replaced with iron, would it still go as fast?"

"Obviously."

"And if you put the grey train next to the blue train which one would the passengers choose?"

Wrench didn't answer. She wanted to disagree, but

Octavia was right. Deep down, Wrench knew she'd always been the grey train.

Octavia rested a tentacle on Wrench's shoulder. "My mother was pregnant with twins when she was attacked by a NIA that had punched through one of the secondary Rupture sites. I survived but not without my 'peculiarities'. My sister's aberrations were too great and she died. Some would say she was the lucky one. I've had to try harder than most to be the blue train. You will be a gleaming golden express locomotive, my dear Brasswitch."

Wrench took a step back. She'd warmed to Octavia – she hadn't expected to be called a Brasswitch.

"Don't be ashamed of what you are," said Octavia. "You asked me what I do here. Well, I'm a sensitive. I feel aberrations. I could walk down any street in York and fill a prison-wagon before I'd taken more than twenty steps. Most don't even know they're tainted; they're not victims of an attack like my mother, so why should they think they're anything other than normal? The prevalence of these minor aberrations is a mystery; perhaps as Gregor Mendel suggests they've inherited them from their parents, who inherited them from their parents and so on, all the way back to the time of the original Rupture. What we do know is they'll never be able to do anything special. You, on the other hand, have been given a gift, and a powerful one at that."

Wrench didn't consider it a gift. She'd always had a fascination with machines, which her talents encouraged, but at the age of ten her world had changed. A boy at school had told their teacher about a strange dream he'd had and the next day, when the bell rang, the regulators were waiting. The boy had tried to run, and without hesitation the regulators had shot him down. After that Wrench knew she had to keep her talent secret. It wasn't a gift; it was a noose.

"You know what I can do?" asked Wrench.

"I can only sense the power, not how it manifests." Octavia uncurled a couple of tentacles towards Wrench's head. "May I touch your face?"

"Will it hurt?"

"I promise not to sting."

Wrench bit her lip and nodded. She fought the urge to pull away, expecting the tentacles to be slimy. Soft like velvet, they caressed her face, leaving only a pleasant warmth behind. A pang of guilt swept over her that she'd made such a prejudiced assumption.

"It's fine – everyone always expects the worst," said Octavia. She closed her eyes and her forehead furrowed. "I haven't sensed power like this in a long time and there's something else. Strange."

"What's strange?"

The warmth left Wrench's face. Octavia's tentacles recoiled and her eyes snapped open. "People, my dear. People are strange. I can see why Bot likes you."

"He doesn't like me. He threatened to crush my head and he won't even use my name."

"Cabal Thirteen staff tend to 'retire' early. Bot was close to Pippa." Octavia swallowed. "Sorry, Regulator Chattox. She was more than his Brasswitch, she was his friend. He doesn't use your name, like he never used Pippa's, because it makes the potential loss easier. Under all that armour he really is quite sensitive."

"Brasswitch!" boomed Bot's voice outside in the corridor. "Come hither. It's time to say goodbye to life as you know it. Then we have things to kill."

Wrench raised her eyebrows at Octavia. "Sensitive, huh?"

8

Wrench looked around the small box room that had been her home for the last eight years. She wouldn't miss the floral wallpaper or the horsehair mattress, which no matter how she lay had always been uncomfortable. No, what she would miss were the things that made it hers, the things that marked out her history. The gash in the dresser where a mechanical broom she'd been building had malfunctioned. The brass gas lamp she'd modified with a re-burner to produce more light. The scratches on the window ledge she'd used to track the path of the moon. Those were hers, and she couldn't take them with her.

"Might as well pack everything," she said to the walkomobile driver who waited with a trunk on the narrow landing.

"Very good, Brasswitch," she said.

Wrench squeezed past her and headed to the polished wood stairs. Pictures of locomotives lined the wall on the stairway down, all creations of her father. The *Elmsworth Flyer*, the *Sheffield Stallion*, and last of all the *Drake*. Elsie Grimthorpe had wanted to take it down, but Wrench had insisted it stayed. After all, it was a part of her father's legacy.

For the last time, she walked along the hallway that smelled of carbolic soap. She purposefully avoided the black tiles in the chequered floor, although no longer quite able to convince herself they would activate traps of ingenious horror, a game she had played as a child. Her eyes picked out the repaired rip in the wallpaper behind the hatstand, hers and Horace Grimthorpe's little secret, the result of another mechanical misdemeanour. The oak front door opened with a familiar judder and a squeak. Without looking back, she stepped outside.

Tears rolled down Elsie Grimthorpe's cheeks. She hugged Wrench to her chest with an embrace like a steam clamp. Warmth radiated from Elsie's considerable presence, as did the stale reek of sweat. A nauseous claustrophobia gripped Wrench; it was like being smothered by an unsavoury sofa.

"We really must be going now," said Octavia. Bot had sent the seamstress to chaperone Wrench, wanting to avoid any emotional goodbyes. For her part Wrench felt little sadness. Elsie had been kind to her, perhaps too kind, trying to be something she never could. Trying to be Wrench's mother.

"Excuse me, luv," shouted the driver of the walkomobile. She stood trapped in the compact terraced house's doorway. In her arms rested a single small trunk containing the sum total of Wrench's possessions.

Elsie reluctantly released Wrench and stepped into the street.

The driver stowed the luggage and slammed the cargo compartment shut. With a wounded wail, Elsie grasped Wrench again.

Octavia placed a hand on the distraught woman's temple. "Shush. Shush. Everything's good. Be happy now."

A stillness overcame Elsie. Her tears stopped then a smile brightened her face.

"Come," said Octavia to Wrench. "Time to go."

Elsie waved at the departing walkomobile, her demeanour now one of happy optimism. Rows of identical railway cottages that made up Rosary Terrace flashed past the windows. Wrench sat back in her seat and eyed Octavia suspiciously. "What did you do?"

"I made her happy."

"How?" Throughout Wrench's childhood Mrs Grimthorpe had been many things, but as a rule, happy wasn't one of them.

"Deep down we all want to be happy. It's just a case of finding that one special thing that will let it happen," said Octavia, folding her hands in her lap.

"And what did you find?"

"She wants a puppy. I told her she could have one."

Mr Grimthorpe hated dogs. In fact, he hated all animals, but dogs most of all. He'd once told Wrench that as a boy a feral stray had taken a chunk out of his calf. Wrench gripped the edge of the seat. "She can't have a puppy. Mr Grimthorpe won't allow it."

Octavia winked. "Fortunately, I believe we're seeing Mr Grimthorpe next."

✿

Mr Grimthorpe's office stood on a raised gantry overlooking the coachworks. Down below, giant steam cranes manoeuvred heavy axles, boilers and chassis into place. Bright sparks from welders illuminated the gangs of fitters who laboured, turning metal into majesty.

"And I have no choice in the matter?" said Grimthorpe. He folded his arms across his chest. A gesture of annoyance Wrench knew well.

"You do have a choice, and I'm sure that you'll make the correct one," said Octavia in honeyed tones. "This really is what's best for Wrench. You do want what's best for her, don't you?"

"May I have a moment alone with Wrench, please?" requested Grimthorpe.

"Absolutely. I'll be just outside." Octavia pulled the door closed behind her.

Grimthorpe unfolded his arms and took Wrench's hand. "Is this what you want? To go with the regulators? You know what they do to people like …"

"People like me," said Wrench. "How long have you known?"

"I didn't know. Not for sure. I've suspected for a long time," said Grimthorpe, toying with the cuffs on his overalls. "That's why I kept you away from the interviews after Torr's accident."

"I wondered why they didn't question me."

"I thought I'd gotten away with it. However, it seems they already had their suspicions and didn't want to tip their hand."

"What gave me away?" asked Wrench.

"Nothing for certain. The crash of the *Drake* was wrong. It shouldn't have happened and you shouldn't have survived."

"The regulators think I caused the accident." A lump built in Wrench's throat and she swallowed. "What do you think?" she asked, her voice trembling.

"I'm an engineer. I deal in formulas and numbers, quantifiable calculations. This is far in excess of my understanding. What I do know is that you would never have intentionally hurt your parents."

Wrench looked down at her feet. "Could I have done it by accident?"

"I don't know. Maybe. Perhaps you'll find your answers with the regulators."

"You think I should go with them?"

"Only you can decide that." Grimthorpe ran a hand over his wiry hair. "The regulators terrify me, they truly do, but I'll fight them hammer and nail to protect you."

"Thank you. I know you would." Wrench flung her arms around the engineer. "I need to find the truth about the accident, about me. I need to go with them."

Grimthorpe gripped her shoulders. "Whatever you discover, know that you were made this way for a reason. A layperson may look at a steam train and not understand the need for a chimney shroud, but the engineer designed it so for a purpose."

His words were little comfort. If she'd been made like everyone else perhaps her parents would still be alive. She could have led a normal life. One without fear of discovery. One without fear of the regulators. One where she felt like she belonged.

There was a knock on the door and Octavia entered. "Are you ready?"

Wrench gave Grimthorpe's arm a squeeze. "I'm ready."

"Please let me escort you to your carriage," said Grimthorpe.

"Really, there's no need." Wrench's bottom lip trembled. Despite her best intentions she was now in danger of being the one wailing, desperately seeking more hugs, and she didn't want to depart like that.

Octavia raised a hand to Horace's head. "You can stay in your office and let Wrench go now, happy in the knowledge that you and Elsie will experience much joy from the puppy you are going to bring home tonight."

9

Wrench led Octavia through the hangar-like building that made up the coachworks. The sounds of industry surrounded them, the hiss of steam and metal clanking on metal. Fountains of sparks illuminated the air and the tang of scorched iron filled Wrench's nose. A steam trolley pulling wagons of boiler pipes puffed across their path. White clouds vented from its brakes and it stopped, blocking the way.

Behind her, a voice full of malice rose above the cacophony of the coachworks. "Someone said you'd finally turned up for shift."

Aaron Coltard: bully, chauvinist and the bane of her apprenticeship. Wrench turned to face him. Her hands clenched into fists. Behind Coltard, backing him up, stood the Clamp twins, Ray Daley and a gaggle of other apprentices. They scowled at Wrench, trying to look mean, trying to impress.

"You know the punishment for being late." Coltard smacked his fist into his palm.

Wrench squared up to the bully. He was a good six inches taller than her and more heavily built, but throughout her apprenticeship she'd never backed down and she wasn't going to start now. "I wasn't late. I've left," said Wrench.

Coltard frowned. "No one's told me that."

"Why would they? You're not as important as you think."

"We all got punished, double shift because you didn't turn up. They wouldn't have done that if you'd left."

Behind Coltard voices raised in murmurs of discontent. Being put on a double was the worst punishment you could get. You weren't paid for the second shift and it left you exhausted for the rest of the week.

"They probably put you on double-up because I do twice the work of the lot of you. With me gone you'll have to put in the extra hours to catch up."

"Let her have it. She needs to pay," shouted Ray Daley.

"Yeah. Pay her back," yelled another of the mob.

Coltard slammed his grease-stained fist into his palm again. "You're lying. You're scared of getting a battering."

Wrench lowered her head and flexed her arms.

Things were about to get ugly. "It's not me who's scared. I didn't have to bring a gang along for support."

Octavia stepped alongside Wrench. "She is with me and you will leave her alone."

Bewitched by Octavia's presence, Coltard faltered.

From the mob someone shouted, "Let them both have it."

A lump of coal sailed past Coltard and struck Wrench on the shoulder. A spike of pain shot through the muscle. She clasped the injury but refused to back away.

Octavia grabbed Wrench's arm. "Come on. We're leaving."

Ray Daley joined Coltard. "Oy! We ain't finished with her."

A second piece of coal flew wide of its mark and knocked Octavia's turban to the floor. The mob quietened, silenced by the angry flailing tentacles atop Octavia's head.

Wrench scooped up the fallen turban and backed away from the mob. She pulled Octavia with her. The sensitive was woozy and dazed; from her temple ran a trickle of blood.

"Holy mother of God protect us," said Coltard, shocked back to sentience.

Ray Daley seized a shovel and brandished it. "She's an aberration. She'll kill us all."

"Not if we do for her first," said the Clamp twins in unison, and grabbed iron bars.

Wrench shook Octavia's arm. "Use your mind thing."

71

"Only works on one person and I have to be touching them," said Octavia, her words a little slurred. "You need to be the blue train."

Wrench had spent her life sticking up for herself. She wasn't one to run from a bully; win or lose she'd fight her corner. However, this was an angry mob, fuelled by hate and prejudice. A mob had a mind of its own and one that wouldn't listen to reason. A mob responded to fear and power. She took a deep breath. "Be the blue train," she whispered to herself and stepped forwards.

"I work for Cabal Thirteen, for the regulators, and you will not impede us," she shouted, her voice far stronger than she felt.

The mob faltered. Wrench drew herself taller. She could do this; she could be the blue train.

"You ain't no regulator," yelled Daley. "You're a freak who killed your own parents."

"I ... I didn't. That wasn't me."

"You did so. That real regulator said. Came looking for you and told us. Only one reason he's interested in you." Daley pointed at Octavia. "You're an aberration just like her."

The mob surged, anger in their eyes. Wrench stepped in front of Octavia. Coltard lowered a shoulder, and slammed Wrench in the ribs. She dropped to one knee, winded. The Clamp twins swung their iron bars. Wrench raised her arms over her head, knowing the gesture was futile. Metal slammed into metal, the sound ringing loud in her ears. A shadow loomed and the metal bars were yanked from the Clamp twins' hands.

"Cease and desist or cease to exist," shouted Bot, a mechanical growl adding menace to his words. Without effort, he bent the iron bars in half. The mob quietened. The Clamp twins scuttled backwards, seeking anonymity in the crowd.

Bot tossed the folded metal aside and held out a hand to Wrench. "Are you all right, Brasswitch?"

Wrench took his hand and pulled herself up. The metal was surprisingly warm against her skin, almost human.

"I'm fine," said Wrench. "How's Octavia?"

"Nothing a good strong cup of tea won't fix," answered Bot.

From behind the mechanoid, Octavia offered Wrench a wan smile, her willowy frame trembling like an autumn leaf in the wind.

"Come on, let's go," said Bot.

"No." Wrench pulled free. She gestured to the loitering mob. "One of them hit Octavia with a lump of coal. She needs an apology."

Bot faced the gaggle of apprentices and retrieved the coal from the floor. He held it out on the flat of his palm. "One of you struck my regulator with this." Bot's fingers curled around the coal and crushed it, motes of black dust escaped through his fingers. "You were brave enough to throw it. Are you brave enough to apologise?"

Nobody stepped forward. All eyes cast downward, the floor suddenly of particular interest.

Bot turned his fist sideways. Coal dust trickled to the floor. "You have until my hand is empty. Confess now or every one of you will suffer the consequences."

A murmuring ran through the group and a skinny apprentice was jostled to the front. A sickening jolt lurched Wrench's stomach. Freddy Jessop was his name. She hadn't exactly been friends with him, but they'd often sat and had their lunch together. They'd both been outcasts in their own way, she because she was a girl and him because he was malnourished and weak.

Freddy tried to push back into the crowd but a host of strong hands ejected him from the group. He stumbled and fell to his knees.

Bot took two giant strides to tower over him. "You attacked my regulators."

"Don't hurt me, please. I'm sorry." Freddy cowered, tears streamed down his cheeks.

"Sorry isn't good enough." Bot raised a fist like a wrecking ball and slammed it down.

"No!" shouted Wrench.

Bot's fist shuddered to a halt, inches above the quivering apprentice. He unfurled his fingers, showering coaldust onto Freddy's head.

Wrench rushed to the apprentice and pulled him to his feet. "Get along with you, Freddy Jessop," she said, pushing him away. "And think about this the next time you're going to bully someone. That goes for all of you."

The group hesitated. Bot emitted a rumbling growl and they scurried away.

"Thank you," said Octavia, curling a tentacle around Wrench's shoulders.

Wrench wasn't sure whether she was thanking her for getting an apology or for stopping Bot from smashing Freddy. She guessed it didn't much matter either way. She lifted her face to Bot and glared up at his angular metal features. "You were going to kill him."

"Was I?"

Wrench kicked her boot in the dust. "Yes, you were. How did you put it … you would have crushed his skull like the most delicate of bird eggs."

"I thought you wanted justice."

"That wouldn't have been justice; it would have been murder."

"Not legally speaking. Attacking a regulator is an offence punishable by death."

"He only threw a lump of coal."

"They were going to kill you."

Wrench folded her arms. "It still doesn't make it right."

"Perhaps I was going to stop anyway." Bot clapped his hands together, freeing them of coaldust.

"Were you?"

"I guess we'll never know," said Bot sulkily.

10

Wrench sat adjacent to Octavia in Thirteen's sickbay. The floor was made of polished brass and the walls and ceiling were plated with copper. Both materials had recently been discovered to kill bacteria. Too expensive to be used in hospitals, price did not appear to be an issue for Thirteen. Rowed opposite were three beds, also brass, their sheets folded with surgical precision. Further along the carriage private rooms were reserved for the treating of more serious cases.

The bruise on Wrench's shoulder was sore, but she'd had far worse. It wasn't something she'd normally trouble a doctor about; however, Octavia was still shaken and Wrench wanted to keep her company.

"Reckon you're going to get a good-sized egg," said Wrench.

"Egg?" queried Octavia.

Wrench tapped her temple. "You know, bump. Egg on your head."

"Oh, that's terrible," said Octavia. "None of my hats will fit."

After their near miss with the mob, Wrench couldn't believe Octavia was still worried about her appearance. "We're lucky to be alive. Reckon your hats not fitting doesn't matter."

Octavia wriggled the tentacles on her head. "With an aberration like mine, hats always matter."

Wrench supposed she was right. At least with her own aberration there were no physical signs. "Sorry I couldn't stop them. I guess I'm not the blue train."

"I think we can cut you some slack. It is only your first day. It took Pippa several months to come to terms with being a Brasswitch, to truly believe in herself, although, perhaps it was her belief that got her killed. Leech should never have taken her; she was only ten, for goodness' sake." Octavia's expression hardened. "She should have said no. That's the problem with Bot, hang around him for long enough and you end up thinking you're bulletproof."

"What was she like, Pippa?"

A sad-eyed smile formed on Octavia's face. "She was the sweetest little thing to look at, golden ringlets, big blue eyes, you'd think butter wouldn't melt, but get on the wrong side of her and she could pack a tantrum worse than Bot. He adored her, she had no family and I sometimes think he saw himself as her father. He always got the best out of her. She was wonderful. A true inspiration. You know, one of those people who could brighten a room just by their presence."

Wrench did know, and she knew she'd never been that person. Never would be. If that's what they wanted from her, it wasn't going to end well.

A regulator dressed in red with a white cross on her tunic bustled into the sickbay and handed Wrench a sealed envelope. "Orders from Bot. He says I'm to clear you fit for duty. You've got a mission."

Wrench had twenty minutes to unpack her possessions from the Grimthorpes' before she was expected to meet Bot in the briefing carriage. She hung her dress and overalls in the wardrobe and placed her best shoes and two sets of work boots in the foot locker. From the centre of a soft woollen shawl, she removed the only item she really cared about, a framed photo of her with her parents. It was taken on a station platform alongside the *Drake* a matter of minutes before the fateful accident. She had no other photographs of her family, and it brought her joy and sorrow in equal measures.

She placed the photo on her desk and stared out of the carriage windows across the platforms. Over half of the trains that passed through the station had been designed by her father. Could he really have got it so wrong with the *Drake*? She rubbed a tear from her eye and removed her last few possessions from the trunk. On her bed, she placed her dressing-gown. It had been a long day and all she wanted to do was climb under the covers and sleep. But the orders from Bot made it clear her day was not done and they still had work to do. He had tracked her and Octavia to the coachworks because he'd discovered a potential lead in Master Regulator Leech's desk diary and he wanted Wrench to accompany him. Or as he put it *I might need a Brasswitch to throw a spanner in the works and you'll have to do.* She didn't know where they were going or what they were doing but she suspected it was likely to prove as eventful as the rest of her day.

⚙

The walkomobile cantered through the arch beneath Mickelgate Bar. Built in medieval times and further fortified with towers and a portcullis, the stone structure looked more like a castle in miniature than the gate out of the city centre. The sharp clatter of the walkomobile's steel shoes changed to a dull thud, the cobblestone of Mickelgate left behind, replaced with the wooden block paving of Blossom Street. Three-storeyed Georgian townhouses lined both sides of the wide thoroughfare, their bright red brick and fine stonework porticos marking them as the homes of the wealthier residents of York.

Raindrops big as marbles slammed into the roof and

splattered against the armoured glass windows. Bot had elected to drive the carriage, leaving Wrench sat opposite a near-skeletal boy who looked like he might puke at any moment. Bot had called him Plum. Whether that was his name, an insult, or a reference to the mauve three-piece suit and fez that he wore, Wrench couldn't be sure. The boy stared out of the window from behind dark glasses, his fingers twitching into all manner of strange positions. A bolt of lightning forked across the sky and the coach's electric Edison lamp flickered. The boy's fingers splayed involuntarily, the muscles in his hands locked rigid.

"The electricity. You can feel it?" asked Wrench.

"Master says I'm not supposed to talk about it," stammered Plum.

"He should have sat with us instead of driving then, shouldn't he?"

Plum shook his head. "Not Bot. Master Tranter."

"Is he the man you were with at the Code Dead meeting? The one who looks like a surprised rat?"

Plum snorted a laugh then guiltily clasped a hand over his mouth. "No. That was Bartholomew. Master Tranter – well, Master Tranter doesn't get out much," he said from between his fingers. "Is it true you're a Brasswitch?"

"That's what they tell me."

Plum lowered his hands. "You can sense the carriage's mechanics right now?"

"I guess so. It's sort of there all the time, like when

you see something out of the corner of your eye. I have to concentrate to bring it into focus."

"And what about the other stuff. The magic and that?"

Wrench leant closer. "What do you mean magic?"

Plum looked directly at her and removed his glasses. His eyes were the deepest purple. He made a sign with his fingers and gestured towards the carriage's window. Outside, trees and tall hedgerows flashed past, the city left behind as they headed into the countryside. However, Wrench's focus was firmly on the raindrops that stopped running down the glass and began streaming to a central point, forming an amorphous blob of water. The blob wobbled up the window to a narrow gap where the glass met the frame. Droplets squeezed through the slit, but instead of emerging as a blob they took the form of a tiny humanoid arm. A second arm appeared, and the water gave the impression of heaving its body through the gap until a watery man was standing on the glass. The little man marched to the middle of the window where he bent his legs, brought his arms together and dived into the carriage. He somersaulted downwards and his body froze into a humanoid icicle. With a crack, he shattered across the floor.

Wrench's mouth hung open. She forced it closed and frowned. "How did you do that?"

Plum smiled, and his whole face brightened. "I'm a thaumagician."

"A what?"

"A thaumagician. They call the power that leaks through the Rupture thaumaturgy because if you know how to harness it, you can do magic."

"Magic's not real." Wrench pushed herself back in her seat. How could it be? She believed in machines, the laws of physics, the science of engineering.

"Can you explain what I did in any other way?" Plum paused, his eyebrows raising.

She couldn't. Like employing aberrations, and the odic capacitor, magic was another secret the regulators kept from the public.

"Master Tranter says I'm the best he's seen. Says in another ten years I'll be better than him." The smile faded from the boy's face. "Not that anyone in Cabal Thirteen lasts that long."

"Is it hard, doing magic?"

"Not hard. Sort of knacky, a bit like riding a monoped. It seems impossible at first, then something clicks and you can't understand what the problem was before. Only a few aberrations can do magic – the gifted, as they call them. Being a Brasswitch you should be a natural."

"Can you teach me?"

Plum sniffed. "Dunno. Maybe. I taught Pippa, much good it did her. She never should have gone with Leech. She wasn't supposed to leave the train without Bot." Wrench remembered the sooty smudge on the under-crypt wall and shivered. She'd not even been in the regulators for a day and had already opened a casket that could have contained an NIA, been mesmerised by an Old God through the Rupture and suffered an attack by an angry mob. If this was the life of Cabal Thirteen, no wonder Plum thought he'd never last another ten years. At the moment, making it to the end of the week seemed like an outside chance.

"So, do we need spell books and wands and magic ingredients?" said Wrench.

Plum frowned. "There are spell books. Although, written incantations are mostly used for rituals and we don't do them, rituals are dark magic. All you really need is a good imagination and a heck of a lot of patience."

Wrench wasn't sure that she had either, but she was determined to give it a go.

"Why do I need imagination? I want to do real magic, not just pretend."

"Think of a bright green juicy apple and imagine taking a bite."

Wrench closed her eyes and thought of biting into a Ribston Pippin, her teeth cutting through the fruit's smooth skin and the taste of the juicy flesh sweet on her tongue.

"Your mouth's watering, right?" said Plum.

"That's not magic. Anyone can do that."

"Your body just made water; it controlled it. That's the start."

Plum made a complicated sign with his fingers.

"Hold your hand like this. It's the sigil for water."

"Sigil?"

"It's how we thaumagicians refer to magical signs."

Wrench ignored the arrogance in Plum's tone, too eager to perform magic of her own. She copied the shape of his contorted fingers and said, "Ready."

"Now think of biting into a lemon, the sour taste in your mouth."

Saliva pooled in Wrench's mouth. She stared at her fingers waiting for something "magical" to occur. Eventually, she swallowed. "Nothing happened," she said.

Plum smiled. "Even for a Brasswitch magic isn't that easy. You're just learning the feeling. Master Tranter calls it anchoring. You need to keep practising the sigil and think of things that make your mouth water."

"Great. If I practise hard I'll be able to do the magic of dribbling."

"You have to be able to cause your mouth to water by just making the sign, then the feeling's properly anchored and you're ready to start controlling water outside your body."

With the toes of her boot Wrench prodded a piece of ice on the floor, possibly the remains of the tiny figure's head. "And how long until I can do what you did?"

"Water is the easiest element to control. It only took me a year to have a handle on it."

"A year!"

"You'll probably have the basics in six months. Master Tranter says, if it was easy it wouldn't be magic."

"Yeah, well, Master Tranter sounds like a chuffing great—"

An explosion rocked the carriage. It slewed sideways and crashed lopsided to its knees. Hurled from her seat, Wrench slammed against the door. Outside the staccato rat-a-tat-tat of gunfire rent the air. The rattle of lead pinging from the carriage's metal plates drowned out the drumming rain. A burst of bullets smashed into the door's lock and with the click of turning cogs it sprang open. Wrench tumbled sideways into the mud. Greenery lined both sides of the narrow country road, although a section of the hedgerow was blackened and burned, a result of the explosion that had crippled their walker. Ahead, an armoured walkomobile squatted, blocking the puddle-strewn country lane. Atop its roof a stream of brass cases ejected from a maxim cannon that sent a hail of lead slamming into the driver's dome.

Starbursts blossomed over the armoured glass hemisphere and it deformed, sagging under the onslaught of bullets. In an explosion of sparkling shards Bot leapt through the weakened glass. He thumped into the muddy road and with surprising agility rolled sideways, dodging the lethal stream of projectiles that followed his course.

A pair of armoured boots squelched into the mud beside Wrench. Above her towered a brown-clad soldier, his leather and ceramic armour making him look more mechanical than human. The goggles on his respirator helmet cast a red glow. The soldier raised his machine musket and aimed at her head. He pulled the trigger. Wrench pushed her mind into the mechanism and the firing pin shuddered to a halt a fraction of an inch shy of the bullet's percussion cap. The soldier dragged the bolt back, trying to clear the stoppage. Wrench's focus moved from the gun's clockwork to the man's goggles. They shone intensely bright and burst into flames. The soldier staggered backwards clutching at his face. Behind him a similarly dressed comrade took aim with a sabre-rifle.

Cracks propagated through the mud surrounding Wrench, the road becoming suddenly parched. From the desiccated ground a wall of water reared up in front of her.

The second soldier's finger tightened on the sabre-rifle's trigger and the weapon fired.

Cold enveloped Wrench and the wall of water transformed into ice that shattered under the bullet's blow.

"Get back in the carriage," shouted Plum, his purple eyes wide with fear.

The soldier sprinted closer and lunged, the sharpened point of his sabre-rifle heading straight for Wrench's heart.

Bot grabbed the blade, stopping it instantly. With a ferocious growl, he ripped the rifle free and flung it into the surrounding fields. His palm slammed into the soldier's chest plate. The ceramic armour fractured, and the soldier flew backwards into a hedgerow.

Puffs of dust exploded in the dried mud around Wrench, the maxim gun barking with renewed vigour.

Bot leapt into the path of the bullets and they

ricocheted from his armour. "Brasswitch, stop that cannon!" he shouted.

Wrench peered from behind the mechanoid's legs. Her eyes narrowed and her face tightened with concentration. She pushed her mind into the machine gun and fused the carrier bolt to the breach. The weapon jammed.

"Excellent. Get back in the carriage while I finish this," said Bot. His metal-jointed knees bent as he prepared to charge.

"Wait!" yelled Wrench. "I can do it." She clenched her teeth and forced her mind into the walkomobile's firebox, turning up the heat while locking the boiler's safety valves closed. Wisps of steam vented from the armoured gun slits and then the vehicle's doors flew open. The crew scrambled out in a state of panic, surrounded by scalding white clouds. Wrench concentrated on the boiler, superheating it. The walkomobile shuddered, then with a boom it exploded, sending the maxim gun cartwheeling through the air.

Bot nodded his approval. "Nice."

Wrench grabbed the carriage step and pulled herself to her feet. Her legs felt like jelly and she thought she might puke. Bot rested a hand on her shoulder. "You did well, Brasswitch, but next time stay in the carriage with Plum."

"You think there's going to be a next time?"

Bot's head tilted. "There's always a next time."

✿

The mournful twang of melting clockwork punctuated the crackle of the burning armoured car. Wrench probed the workings of their own carriage, tweaking valves and rerouting steam pressure in an attempt to get them mobile again. Silhouetted by the flames, the chunky form of Bot scouted the ambush site. Plum had been instructed to keep watch, although how he could do that cowering in the carriage Wrench wasn't sure.

Returning to Wrench's side, Bot said, "The perimeter's clear. They all seem to have scarpered."

Wrench heaved at a metal sheet that the explosion had pushed against one of the walkomobile's legs. "Who were they? And why did they attack us?"

"The who is easy. They're the Future Watch. The paramilitary wing of the Epochryphal Brotherhood. Why is straightforward too: we were on our way to raid the Brotherhood's Priory. The question you should be asking is how?" Bot leant down and with one hand pulled the crumpled metal clear of the leg.

"How?"

"Indeed. How did they know we were coming?"

Wrench ran a hand over the walkomobile's dented armour. When she'd first seen the carriage at Clifford's Tower she'd thought it was ridiculously over engineered. Now she owed her life to the angular plates covering the vehicle. "Somebody at the regulators must have told them."

"Unlikely. The Brotherhood have been in our sights for some time. We've had suspicions that they're sheltering aberrations, possibly even using them."

"Using them for what?"

"We don't know. I hope to discover more when we get to the priory. Will the walkomobile make it that far?"

"It's not pretty, but it'll get the job done." Wrench patted the carriage's sides. "A bit like you."

Bot's green eyes widened. "That's all the thanks I get for saving your life?"

"I told you before, if you wanted nice you rescued the wrong girl."

Plum poked his head out of the window, his face pale. "Surely we're not still going. They'll be expecting us now."

"No. They were expecting us. Now they'll think they've bought themselves some time, so we have the element of surprise."

"Because only someone suicidally stupid would carry on with their original plan," said Plum.

"Exactly." Bot clapped his hands together. "He who dares, wins."

"Or dies horribly," mumbled Plum and slumped back into the carriage.

11

"I should stay and guard the carriage," said Plum, cowering behind Bot.

The mechanoid squatted next to a high, ivy-covered wall that surrounded the priory. Gears ground beneath his chest plate, making a rumbling chuckle. "Oh, Plummy, you do make me laugh. We need you, and not just for your sense of humour in times of mortal peril."

"I wasn't joking," complained Plum.

"Nor was I," said Bot. "This is dangerous; keep those magic fingers at the ready."

Wrench peered through a wrought-iron gate barring their way. The priory dated from before the Rupture and the crenellated rooftops gave it a medieval air. Four long, dark windows, not much wider than arrow slits, stood sentry over a metal studded door set deep in the thick stone walls. An array of broader windows divided by masonry pillars bestrewed the remainder of the priory in a seemingly random pattern. Low gardens and a considerable distance of open lawn lay between them and the L-shaped building. The rain had stopped but heavy cloud hung thick in the sky, covering the moon.

"Coast's clear. Let's go," said Wrench. With the tiniest of mental nudges the gate's lock clicked open.

They stole across the sodden grass, the squelch of Bot's footsteps uncomfortably loud, his chunky feet leaving deep divots in the turf. Ahead, a bulbous shadow with what looked like giant horns detached itself from a bush and prowled towards them. Wrench froze, her heart thumping. "What is it?"

"Trouble," said Plum.

The shadow began to pant, gulping down giant breaths of air and the black outline of its body expanded.

"It's a Scotch dog. You need to stop it, now," said Bot, but it was already too late. The shape emitted a low droning sound then the distinctive skirl of bagpipes filled the air.

"Run," shouted Bot and sprinted for the priory.

Electricity crackled, and giant spot lamps burst to life around the house. The Scotch dog consisted of a set of bagpipes with four clockwork legs. What would normally act as the mouthpiece wagged like a tail, sucking in air. The chanter formed a head-like structure, mechanical valves opening and snapping closed to elicit the tune, while three different-length drones ranged along the top of the bag like spines. Excited by the light, the Scotch dog pranced over the grass, its tartan bag body puffing in and out, fuelling the rendition of 'Flower of Scotland' that droned from its pipes.

Wrench dashed past the beast. Her mind dug into the machine's innards and she froze the master cog on the air bellows. With a mournful wail the droning died.

The metal studded door in the priory house burst open and out charged a brown-habited monk. He held a giant cross in one hand and a giant crossbow in the other.

The monk slammed the sharpened end of the cross into the turf and rested the crossbow on top. He dropped to one knee and took aim.

Wrench reached out with her mind, but the weapon's mechanism was somehow fuzzy, almost resistant to her thoughts.

Bot detached a bronze star from his collar and held it out in front of him. "Regulators. Lower your weapon," he commanded, his voice booming.

The bow twanged then a crack rent the air, the steel-tipped bolt ricocheting from Bot's skorpidium-carbide armour. "That hurt," he said and hurled the brass star. "Admittedly only my feelings, but it hurt nonetheless." The monk collapsed to the floor, clutching his neck where the brass star had embedded.

"So much for the element of surprise," grumbled Plum.

The door the monk had used led into a large, warm kitchen. Heat radiated from a chunky, cast-iron Yorkshire range set into a wide chimney flue. Coals glowed beneath the stove's firebox, which had been well stoked to keep it smouldering through the night. A pile of unwashed vegetables graced a counter below the window, somebody's chores for the day to come. On a solid and well-worn table that squatted in the centre of the kitchen rested a stack of crockery. Sprigs of herbs hung from the gnarled oak beams, and the scent of rosemary flavoured the air.

Bot picked a meat cleaver from a hook on the wall and weighed it in his hand. "Brasswitch, discover what they're up to.'

"How am I supposed to do that?"

"There'll be a significant machine involved; feel for it."

Wrench cast her mind about. A strange energy thrummed through the air, like a sound you couldn't hear. Not electromagnetic and not thaumaturgy, the pulses were powerful yet alien. She walked to one of the kitchen's three doors, letting her feelings guide her. "It's that way and underground," she said.

Moving with the same caution he'd shown in the under-crypt, Bot joined Wrench at the door. "Master Regulator Leech's desk diary is harder to decipher than a doctor's prescription note. The one thing I could make out was a line connecting the casket and the Epochryphal Brotherhood." Bot grabbed the doorhandle.

"The Brotherhood were excommunicated by the church for their tolerant views towards aberrations and if they're involved with the NIA we can only assume the worst. This could be dangerous, stick behind me."

Plum rolled his eyes. "It wasn't like I was thinking of taking the lead."

Raising the cleaver, Bot pulled the door open. The corridor beyond had rustic whitewashed plaster walls covered in clocks, watches and hourglasses. However, its most noticeable feature was the brass automaton armed with a four-foot long Draeger tank rifle.

Bot slammed the door closed and pushed Wrench and Plum against the wall. "Change of plan," he said. The cleaver clattered to the floor and he embraced them in a metallic hug, his bulk acting as a shield. A massive explosion rocked the kitchen and the door disappeared in a shower of splinters.

An armour plate on Bot's leg slid open and he withdrew a hefty-looking hand cannon. "Time for the big guns."

"His is bigger," said Plum.

"Always with the glass half empty Plummy boy," said Bot and stepped into what remained of the doorway.

Wrench clasped her hands over her ears. Jets of flame spurted from the hand cannon, sending a deluge of titanium-tipped carnage along the corridor.

Bot lowered the smoking weapon and strode through the doorway. A tangled mess of brass lay scattered across the floor. In its midst rested the angular Draeger, a dismembered metal hand still clutching the stock.

"Looks mean, shoots mean, reloads slower than a sleeping sloth," said Bot, picking up the gun and returning the hand cannon to the holster in his leg.

"It was a mechanoid. I could have just stopped him," said Wrench.

Bot tested the weight of the Draeger. "Where's the fun in that?"

"The fun bit is not dying," said Plum.

Apparently satisfied he could manage the weapon one handed, Bot pulled the stock into his shoulder. "So where now, Brasswitch?"

Wrench nodded to a low arched door the automaton had been guarding. "We want to go that way."

Plum frowned. "I think 'want to go' is not the sentiment of the entire group."

Bot clapped Plum on the back with his free hand, knocking him forward. "Don't be such a sourpuss. You know Master Tranter wants you to gain practical field experience."

"That's easy for Master Tranter to say; he's not left the train in years. The most dangerous thing he has to worry about is whether his bath is too hot."

A flight of stone stairs spiralled down from the door. Wrench followed Bot, whose overly large feet made negotiating the narrow steps awkward. A loud electrical hum rose up from below. The hairs on Wrench's arms stood on end and her skin prickled with static electricity … or with what she hoped was static electricity.

"I don't like what I'm feeling," said Wrench. "It doesn't seem natural."

"Can you tell how far away it is?" said Bot.

"No. I can't even tell what it is. Some sort of machine sucking masses of electricity. It's not like anything I've ever encountered before."

The stairs opened into a cellar crammed with two giant humming transformers. A tower of ceramic discs acted as insulation to three silver globes mounted atop each machine. Continuous sparks crackled between the globes. Thick cables snaked across the floor and trailed through an arch at one end of the room. From beyond the arch flickered a harsh blue light.

Wrench peeked into the adjoining room. Laid into the floor, a copper pentagram stretched to the extremities of the cellar. At each point, a thick tinted glass tube rose to the ceiling, inside of which writhed a robed monk. Like some sort of horrific zoetrope, the faces of the monks flicked through expressions of agony in a not-quite-linear fashion. Copper wire spiralled from the tops of the tubes, to something resembling a diver's helmet worn by a rubber-suited monk who sat serenely at the pentagram's centre.

"Time to kill their power," said Bot and cocked the Draeger tank rifle.

Wrench spun around. "Nooooo!" she shouted, clasping her hands to her ears, but it was too late.

Bot pulled the trigger. A deafening boom filled the cellar and one of the transformers exploded in a shower of sparks.

Inside the pentagram thick blue bolts of electricity arced from the tubes to the diving-suited monk. His body spasmed, his expression now anything but serene.

A scowl darkened Wrench's face. "You idiot! That wasn't supplying the power. It was draining it."

The monks in the glass tubes screamed, surrounded by lightning. On the floor, the pentagram glowed red-hot.

Wrench understood the machine more clearly now, and it was angry. She couldn't pinpoint the source of the power but she sensed the surge in energy, no longer being dissipated by the transformers. She ran for the stairs. The crackle of electricity grew louder, vivid white flashes leaching all colour from her surroundings. Ahead, Plum's feet disappeared up the spiral steps while from behind echoed the metallic clunk click of the Draeger being cocked. "In for a penny," said Bot.

Her feet hammering the stone, Wrench lunged up the stairs. The retort of the Draeger again filled the cellar, followed by muffled screams. She barrelled into the corridor where Plum waited, his hands held over his head. Standing in front of the wrecked kitchen door, a monk pointed a clockwork-crossbow at Plum.

Wrench pushed her mind into the weapon, which this time offered no resistance. She locked the release catch in place and grabbed Plum's sleeve. "We need to run."

The monk levelled the bow. "You're going nowhere."

Plum's fingers twisted in complex patterns and fire flew from his hands. The monk staggered backwards, his robes ablaze.

"Running away is one of my specialities," said Plum and he sprinted along the corridor. Wrench raced after him, through the kitchen and back outside. She hurdled the smouldering monk, who rolled moaning on the wet grass and rushed past the stationary Scotch dog to the boundary wall. Her legs aching, she drew to a halt. Panting, she sucked in air, her chest heaving like bellows.

Plum's skinny frame shook. He bent double and coughed, then spat on the ground. "Where's Bot?"

"He's–"

Pain gripped Wrench's head and she sank to her knees. The machine in the cellar had gone critical, sending out debilitating waves of energy. Plum towered above her, an expression of panic on his face. Through eyes squinted in agony she followed the direction of his gaze.

The kitchen door burst open and Bot came surging through. He raced onto the lawn and with one massive hand scooped up the smouldering monk. The ground shook and the priory exploded in a crackling mass of electrical discharge. A shock wave swept from the burning remains and Bot stumbled. Momentum carried him onwards, his feet dug into the soft turf and he regained his balance. Behind him the priory roof collapsed, sucked inwards by a vacuum's void.

Bot reached the wall and dropped the monk on the ground. Brushing dust and ash from his arms he said, "I think that was pretty successful, don't you?"

Heat and the smell of ozone surrounded Wrench. Her ears filled with the discordant sound of thousands of voices. Bright colours swirled across her vision. From somewhere far off she heard a mechanical voice yelling "Brasswitch" but it was lost among the chaos. The cool wet grass was a relief as it came up to meet her, slamming into her face.

12

The crackle-tram trundled down Mickelgate and slowed to a sedate halt behind a Tadcaster Brewery dray. Wrench gazed through the window at an irate-looking regulator with a large burn on his face. She tensed, and not just because he was staring straight at her. There was something frighteningly familiar about him; she felt like she should know him. The scene shimmered and she was in a vaulted crypt unlocking an ornate phosphor-bronze casket. Metallic tentacles, thick as ship's hawsers, writhed from beneath the lid and grabbed her around the throat. Her windpipe constricted; she struggled to breathe and everything went black. A gaslight flared; she was in a dungeon corridor, steel cell doors lined the walls. Ahead, a door pockmarked with bullet holes lay ajar. She peered through the gap. Plum was tightly chained to the wall, shackled by his hands and ankles. A brazier glowed red-hot before him, iron brands heating in the coals. Livid scars in the shapes of strange sigils smouldered on his skin. His eyes met hers, pleading, no longer purple but a soulless grey. She fell into their smoky depths and was on the footplate of the *Drake* with her parents. The countryside rushed by, the wind tearing at her clothes. Her father laughed, clutching her mother's hand as he encouraged the driver to go faster. A knot of fear burned in Wrench's chest. The brakes on the engine locked on and the air filled with the scream of metal on metal. The scream transformed into that of a young lady. She sat on a rug spread out in an empty carriage, before her a magnificent picnic. Her handsome beau clung in terror to a seat. The carriages jumped from the rails, twisting like a leaping salmon. The young lady catapulted towards the glass. Ahead of her a bowl of strawberries smashed against the window in a splatter of red mush. Flames engulfed the railway carriage and then Wrench was atop a black scorched tower, hundreds of feet above the ground. In her hands, she held the odic capacitor, no longer massive but the size of a football, nothing more than a toy. A monstrous beast flailed at Bot with huge tungsten tentacles, their sharpened points scoured deep gouges in his armour. With bladed hands Bot slashed and parried but the beast advanced, ensnaring the mechanoid, pinning his arms. More tentacles wrapped around Bot. His armour deformed, constricted and crushed. The crack of breaking metal echoed across the tower and the glow in Bot's eyes dimmed. "Brasswitch!" he cried.

"Brasswitch! Brasswitch, wake up – we've got work to do."

Wrench's eyes snapped open. Bot leant over her, his large angular head uncomfortably close.

"See, I told you she'd live," said Bot with an air of triumph.

"It wasn't about her living. It was whether she was going to be a dribbling idiot for the rest of her days," said Octavia.

Wrench pushed herself upright. She was on a narrow bed in the sickbay. "What the chuff happened?"

Bot clicked his fingers together. "Look, no dribble. I win."

"Keep calm," said Octavia, taking Wrench's hand and passing her glasses. "You've had a bit of a moment."

"And by *moment* she means you were hit by a vast temporal shock wave that could have turned your brain into tapioca when the machine in the priory malfunctioned and exploded," said Bot.

Wrench scowled. "It didn't malfunction. You destroyed an integral part of the feedback system."

"Causing it to malfunction," said Bot. "The important thing is we're all alive, and not tapioca-ish, and the mission was a success."

"You found the NIA?"

"No, but we've ruled the monks out of our enquiries. In fact, we've ruled them out of existence."

Images of Bot running from the priory and grabbing a monk from the grass filled Wrench's mind. She couldn't be sure if it was a memory or an alternative past she'd seen in her visions.

"I thought you rescued one."

"More arrested than rescued. Unfortunately, he didn't survive his burns. He did confess that the monks were trying to make a machine that could see into the future. He claimed the brains of the monks in the glass tubes were affected by the massive electrical fields, opening their third eye and allowing them insights of possible events to come."

Octavia withdrew and poured two cups of tea from a pot resting on a cabinet. "He wasn't able to tell us anything about the NIA, though."

"So, you're no further forward." Wrench swung her legs from the bed and accepted the bone-china teacup offered by Octavia.

"Actually, we are." Bot lowered his voice to a whisper. "What I'm about to tell you doesn't leave this room, and that goes for you too, Octavia."

"Cross my tentacles and hope to die."

Bot turned towards Wrench. "Brasswitch?"

"You mean this is more secret than the fact that the Rupture isn't closed, the odic capacitor keeps us safe and we have an NIA on the loose?"

"Yes," said Bot.

"Hookey-Walker!" Wrench adjusted her glasses. "My lips are locked tighter than a Tesla-welded rivet."

"The monk said shortly before we arrived yesterday they were visited by another regulator. He wanted them to use the machine to look into the future for a specific person."

"Who?" Wrench took a sip of tea, enjoying the warm tang of tannins that soothed her whole body.

"You, Brasswitch. That's how they knew we were coming."

The cup in Wrench's hand trembled, sloshing tea into the saucer. "Why are the regulators interested in me? I thought I was part of the cabal now?"

"You are," said Bot. "Although, perhaps not everybody sees it that way."

"Who was it?" asked Octavia, taking the cup from Wrench before she spilled any more tea.

"The monk didn't hear a name, although he described the regulator as having a very bad burn on his face."

"Flemington!" said Wrench.

Octavia's tentacles quivered. "We need to discover what he's up to."

"He wants to kill me, that's what he's up to." Wrench scowled, remembering the electric chair.

"Maybe." Bot drummed his fingers against his leg. "He's a misguided zealot, for sure, but there's something else going on. I'll make some discreet enquiries. You'll be safe enough at Thirteen for now."

Octavia's tentacles wiggled. "She needs training. Pippa wasn't ready and neither is Wrench. We can't lose another Brasswitch."

Bot patted the bed. "Get some rest and tomorrow Plum can start teaching you magic."

"Plum?" Octavia folded her arms, and several of her tentacles. "Master Tranter should teach her."

"Tranter's got one of his migraines," snapped Bot. "Plum's good enough to cover the basics."

"The basics weren't good enough for Pippa."

Gears whined. Bot squared up to Octavia, towering over her. "You think I don't know that?"

Octavia lifted her chin. Uncowed, she met his gaze. "So don't repeat your mistake."

"It wasn't my mistake." Bot clunked to the door. "She wasn't supposed to leave the train." He stomped from the sickbay, his thudding footsteps receding down the corridor.

One of Octavia's tentacles encircled Wrench's hand, spreading a comforting warmth through her fingers. "He'll come around."

"You don't trust Plum?" asked Wrench.

"Plum's good, but he's no Master."

"He saved my life when we were attacked by the Future Watch."

"Oh, he's got the skills …"

There was something Octavia was holding back. Some detail she was hesitant to share. Wrench needed to tease it out gently, like removing a smudgel pin from its casing. "Did Pippa and Plum get along?"

"As much as anyone gets along with Plum. He's different, had a harder time than any of us."

"How so?"

"That's for Plum to tell, not me."

"And you think that affects his ability to teach me magic?"

"Not his ability." Octavia looked down at her feet. "Pippa told me she thought Plum was holding back in his lessons."

"Holding back, how?"

"She felt she'd mastered water and wanted to move on, but Plum insisted she keep at it. She asked me not to tell Bot, so I didn't. Only now I feel as guilty as him about her death."

"We should let Bot know, then he might insist I train with Master Tranter."

"It wouldn't make a jot of difference. He's made up his mind. You'll have to work with Plum. For now, at least."

Wrench's hand twitched and seemingly from nowhere the thought of juicy, bitter lemons popped into her mind. She swallowed, her mouth watering. "Great. I survive the temporal shock but Plum's going to have me dribbling like an idiot anyway."

13

Wrench concentrated on the glass of water resting on her desk, trying to feel the magic, trying to sense the change in the state of the molecules. Plum slouched against her steel wardrobe. He hitched up a sleeve on his lilac suit and made a gesture with his hand. The water emitted a faint crackling sound, then in an instant it was solid ice.

"Did you feel it that time?" said Plum, fixing her with his magenta eyes.

Wrench shook her head. It was three days since the incident at the priory and Wrench was fed up with thinking of mouth-watering fruit. She could now dribble at will, and was certain that her finger positioning of the sigil for water was perfect, but she still failed to have any noticeable effect on the contents of the glass.

Plum unfroze the water. "Your turn," he said.

Wrench repeated the sign and reached out with her mind to the water, slowing the molecules, taking their energy, willing them to bond together, to freeze. The surface of the water began to shake, concentric circles expanding from the centre. She focused harder, she could do magic, this time it would work and she would wipe the bored look from Plum's face. Her jaw clenched, and she screwed up her eyes in concentration, then the surface became calm and the moment was lost.

"I did it. Did you see? I did it," she said excitedly. She hadn't frozen the water but she'd had some effect, made the surface move. That had to be a start.

Plum pulled a fob watch from his jacket pocket. "No, you didn't."

Wrench put her hands on her hips. "I bally well did. Maybe you should have been paying more attention rather than gazing out of the window. I made the surface ripple and everything."

"That wasn't magic," said Plum.

"Oh, what was it then?" challenged Wrench.

Plum flicked the fob watch open. "The military express. It comes hurtling through once a week on the next platform and always shakes the train."

Wrench slumped onto a chair. "It's not fair."

"Welcome to the cursed life of an aberration," said Plum and sighed.

"Octavia calls it a gift."

"Yeah, well, even with an aberration like hers she can hide it. I spent the first nine years of my life with bandages swaddling my head, pretending I was blind. My ma only let me take them off when I was safe inside. All I saw of the world was the view from my bedroom window and that was nowt but the dirty wall of a mill."

"Being able to do magic though, that must have made up for some of it?"

"Not really. Until Master Tranter taught me control, I just made weird stuff happen. And now it's not like I can use it for anything fun. The only time I get to do magic is when some horrible thing is intent on eviscerating me. It's not exactly a right royal barrel of monkeys working for the regulators."

"How long did it take Master Tranter to teach you?"

"After about three months I had a basic control of water, then another nine months to become expert. The first form is always the hardest," said Plum. "Once you've mastered your first spell you have a feel for it. Don't be hard on yourself – you've only been at it three days."

"I need to learn magic now." She needed to be able to protect herself, to protect Plum. The image of the thaumagician chained in the cell, his eyes pleading for help, surfaced again. She pushed down the guilt-fuelled urge to confess. The other visions hadn't been right. The tram had hit the brewery dray and there were no passengers on the *Drake* when it had crashed. They probably weren't even visions at all but more like dreams where her brain was scrambling images, trying to make sense of them. And it wasn't as if Plum needed the warning to be careful, or any additional encouragement to be paranoid. She thumped her fist on the desk and the water's surface rippled again. "I have to be able to protect myself. I could be dead in three months."

Plum showed her genuine interest for the first time that morning. "That's the spirit. You're coming around to my way of thinking." He shuffled closer to her and held out his arm. "Take my hand."

Wrench grasped his fingers. The cold, clammy skin was how she'd imagined Octavia's tentacles might feel, almost slimy, like holding a dead fish. She bit the end of her tongue, using the pain to keep the revulsion from showing on her face.

"Feel the magic," said Plum. Once more he froze the water and the coldness of his fingers intensified. A chilling ache spread from her hand through her bones to her brain. She shivered involuntarily and squeezed tighter. "Again," she said.

Plum melted the water and the ache intensified. Her arm trembled, the tightness in her muscles somewhere between pleasure and pain. She let go of Plum's hand and focused on the glass. "My turn."

Her fingers contorted into the symbol for water and saliva pooled in her mouth. She remembered the sensation in her arm, recreating the feeling, the ache, the power. Magic was real. Like gravity or electricity, it obeyed physical laws; its effect could be reliably repeated, like a scientific experiment. She imagined the water in the glass becoming colder, bleeding heat into the air, and she convinced herself the tiniest of ice crystals were forming at the water's meniscus.

A knock at the door broke her concentration. Octavia breezed into the room. Behind her she dragged a large steamer trunk, which she deposited in front of Wrench's wardrobe. "Bot doesn't really care about clothes," said Octavia. "Probably because he doesn't wear any, but it's important for us, so I've made you some things."

Wrench didn't care about clothes either; however, she liked Octavia and didn't want to offend her. She forced a smile. "Great. What have you got?" she said, faking interest.

The tentacles on Octavia's head quivered. "Limited extrasensory perception for a start, so there's no point in pretending. Although, I do appreciate the effort, and who knows, once you've stripped off those overalls we may discover there's a young lady underneath."

"ESP? You can read minds?" Wrench swallowed. All the time she'd spent with Octavia, what had she been thinking about? Nothing bad, she hoped.

"I try not to. It's ghastly what most people think." Octavia opened the trunk and fixed her gaze on Plum, whose cheeks glowed red. "I can also tell that Plum is feeling awkward and uncomfortable and so perhaps he should leave now."

"Keep up with the practice," mumbled Plum and scurried out of the door.

Octavia winked at Wrench. "Although I didn't need ESP to tell that, which is fortunate as he seems to be becoming somewhat resistant."

She removed a set of plaid dungarees from the trunk and held them up. "Not entirely regulator red, but oh so much more stylish."

Wrench took them from Octavia and flattened them against her body. Despite her initial reservations she had to agree. They did look fantastic.

Octavia slid a shiny black shirt from a hanger inside the trunk. The sleeves and torso were patterned with chunky ribbed braiding. "This little number is both elegant and practical. Made of double woven silk from the kevlaris moth, it will deflect a sword blow or stop a bullet."

Wrench rubbed the material between her finger and thumb. The delicate fabric seemed fragile as a butterfly's wing. She gave the sleeve a tug and the cloth pulled taut, the immense strength of each individual fibre becoming clear in her mind.

"Your dungarees are lined with kevlaris too, as is your hat," said Octavia, tossing a rather splendid black bowler to Wrench. On the front of the bowler, attached to the hatband was a brass star bearing the regulators' crest.

"You really expect me to wear all this?" said Wrench.

"I heard about your near-death experience during the ambush of the Future Watch. You're lucky to be alive, and I for one would like to keep you that way."

Wrench shrugged out of her overalls and slipped the shirt over her broad shoulders. "I'm fairly keen on it myself."

"That's why I thought a little extra care in your defence wouldn't go amiss. Especially as Bot tends to forget that everyone else isn't bulletproof."

"He does seem to favour the 'wade in guns blazing' approach," said Wrench.

Octavia's tentacles squirmed. "Bot's certainly offensive."

"Yes. That too."

"No. I meant he believes the best form of defence is to attack."

Wrench flushed. "Sorry. I thought you were referring to his rudeness."

"I can see how you'd be easily confused. It's really just another form of armour. He was particularly close to Pippa, and I can tell he's hurting at her loss."

"Your ESP works on Bot?"

"No. He's got magical protection, so I get nothing."

Wrench remembered the force that had pinned her to the carriage when she'd tried to reach inside him. Presumably that was the magical protection repelling her.

Octavia seemed to sense her thoughts. "Pippa managed to find a way through. I think that's why they were so close. He'd spend hours sparring with her on the range."

An odd sense of jealousy built in Wrench's chest. She'd only known Bot for less than a week, but she somehow felt threatened by the other Brasswitch's memory. Did Bot view her as an impostor, a substandard replacement, a temporary part bolted on to the engine, so the train could limp home? She bit down on her tongue again, feeling cold inside.

Octavia encircled Wrench's hand with a tentacle. "Oh, there's nothing substandard about you, girl. It was a year before Bot took Pippa to the Artificer. You're going this evening."

"Who's the Artificer?"

"I wouldn't want to ruin the surprise." Octavia caressed the plaid dungarees. "Even with Bot the Shambles are dangerous, so please wear your new clothes."

"Thanks, I will."

Octavia pushed the door open to leave, then turned back towards Wrench. "Why've you got a glass of ice next to your bed?"

Wrench looked at the glass of water she'd been practising on with Plum. It was frozen solid.

14

With Plum nowhere to be found and having no other commitments until her evening visit to the Artificer, Wrench found herself at a loose end. She'd spent an unproductive hour failing to freeze a fresh glass of water, achieving nothing more than to give herself a splitting headache. Now in a stinking mood to match her stinking head, she kicked about the lower decks of the train.

She paused at the iron gate forged with complex sigils that secured the stairs leading to the "the magic department". It was one of the few areas of the train she'd not been encouraged to visit, Plum always seeking her out for their lessons. Her desire to investigate what lay at the top of the stairs was tempered by the inadequacy she felt at her failure to perform magic. Could it be that everyone was mistaken in their belief that she was a Brasswitch? Yes, she had an affinity for machines, but did that of its own right truly make her so special?

Carrying on further down the train, she continued walking until she came to what she now realised had been the object of her meanderings all along. She had reached the final carriage, beyond which lay only the locomotive and tender, and what a locomotive it was. The Robinson four-six-three with dual turbo-underboilers was a beast of a machine. Her father had referred to it as an iron stallion and she knew it had heavily influenced his design of the *Drake*.

With a flick of her mind she unlocked the door that led to the tender and snuck inside. Her back pressed against the water tank, she squeezed through the dimly lit passage then eased open the door to the footplate and peeked out. In front of one of the Robinson's dual fireboxes stooped a stockily built engineer dressed in regulator red overalls and cap. Slinging a shovel of coal chunks the size of house bricks into the firehole, the muscles on the engineer's bare arms pulled taught, warping the elaborate tattoos that covered them into strange patterns. Other than the ink, the engineer's skin was surprisingly unblemished, bearing none of the burn scars and blisters Wrench normally associated with working on a great locomotive's footplate.

"I wondered when I'd be seeing you." The engineer turned and beamed a white-toothed smile that lit up a face radiating elegance beneath the smears of oil and coaldust.

"I'm Darcey Jones," she continued, holding out a hand. "And you must be Wrench, or do you prefer Brasswitch?"

Wrench stepped onto the footplate and took the offered hand. The skin was rough and calloused, not unlike her own. "Definitely Wrench."

Firm and friendly, Darcey pumped Wrench's arm up and down like she was pumping water into the locomotive's boilers. "Good to meet you, Wrench."

"I hope you don't mind. I wanted to see the Robinson up close."

Darcey beamed again. "Of course you did. I'd expect nothing less. I'm firing up the second boiler. You can give me a hand if you want?"

Now it was Wrench's turn to smile. Rolling up her sleeves, she said, "What do you need?"

Darcey handed Wrench the shovel. "You can stoke the firebox, for starters."

Delighted to be doing some hard, physical labour for a change, Wrench slammed the shovel into the coal spilling from the tender's chute. Lifting the laden shovel, she threw the contents into the firehole. Only then did she realise something was wrong. "The firebox, it's not lit," she said, surprised.

"Things work a little differently on this footplate," said Darcey, winking at Wrench. "Just like you and Octavia, I was recruited by Bot." She knelt down and took a sizeable breath, filling her lungs to bursting. Placing her mouth by the firehole, she exhaled. A roar filled the cabin, orange flames shooting from Darcey's mouth into the firebox.

A wave of heat washed over Wrench, the coals in the firebox now burning brightly. She tightened her grip on the shovel, trying to hide her surprise.

Darcey stood. "To be honest, I think Bot had wanted to use me as a weapon. Only I'd never hurt another aberration, or indeed a person, so he put me to work on the footplate."

Wrench shovelled another load of coal into the firebox. "Does Bot rescue many aberrations?"

"I'm not sure he rescues any of us. If an aberration is useful he may recruit them, which comes with its own chains attached, otherwise they end up in prison, or if deemed too dangerous, executed."

"Executed?" In the carriage Bot had said he didn't believe in murdering aberrations. Was that a lie?

"Bot's not like the rest of us. He's seen more of the horror caused by the Rupture than anyone. I'm not sure I believe the rumours, but some even say he's faced down the old gods."

How was that even possible? The old gods had been beaten back by Sir Dereleth hundreds of years ago at the time of the original Rupture. Unless that wasn't true, like the fact that the Rupture wasn't closed. Was this another secret, the real dangers of NIAs and the old gods being kept hidden from the public?

"Do you trust him?" asked Wrench.

"I was twelve when he saved me. I'd been bedridden and coughing up blood for a week. They thought I had tuberculosis, then I coughed up a jet of flame and set fire to the poorhouse. The nurses left me inside to die and called the regulators." Darcey stared into the firebox, the flames reflecting from the glossy sheen of tears that welled in her eyes.

Wrench placed a hand on Darcey's tattooed arm. The skin was hot beneath her fingers, like a freshly baked loaf. "But you didn't die."

"I was fortunate that it was Thirteen that arrived first. Bot stormed into the burning building and rescued me. Although undamaged by the fire, I was struggling to breathe. He brought me back here and with Octavia's help I learned to control my aberration." Darcey grabbed the locomotive's regulator lever. "I love my job here; I have a good life. I owe that all to Bot. He can be a bit like a tempest at times – he's like a whirlwind – and sometimes it's best to just go with the storm and see where it takes you."

"It's taking me to see the Artificer," said Wrench.

Darcey smiled again, her face pulled taut, accentuating high cheekbones dusted with soot. "Then you're in for a most wonderful surprise."

15

The Shambles were the meanest, roughest, most villainous maze of streets and snickelways in the city of York. It was a place where for their own safety the muggers went around in pairs and the constables just plain went around, avoiding it entirely. The buildings were old, even by York's standards. Twisted and bowed, they leant across the cobbled streets so their eaves nearly touched.

"Never come down here without me, Brasswitch," said Bot.

"Why on earth would I want to?" Wrench tugged at her collar. Despite fitting perfectly, the new outfit Octavia had tailored felt peculiarly uncomfortable. Her clothes no longer helped her blend into the background; instead they screamed "look at me".

"You're a Brasswitch; the Artificer is going to have a natural appeal to you. It's the way of things."

"I've met craftsmen before, and engineers. What's so special about this one?"

"Everything." Bot ducked into what passed as the main street of the Shambles. He'd taken no more than twenty steps when a couple of shadows detached themselves from a doorway, blocking his path.

"Got to pay the toll," said one of the shadows, his voice filled with menace.

Bot's mechanics emitted a growl. "My young associate here is wearing brand-new clothes. I would be in most bad disgrace with her tailor were they to get blood on them."

"Best you pay the toll then. Cheaper than new threads," said the shadow.

"You miss my point. More specifically your blood. I'm giving you an opportunity to beat it." Bot's hands clenched into fists the size of footballs. "Before I beat it for you."

The second of the shadows produced a large truncheon, one end of which was ringed with copper coils. He powered on the Tesla club and the flickering light of arcing electricity filled the alley. Blue sparks crackled along the stack of coils, the harsh glare emphasising the shadow's rat-like features.

"That's the problem with you mechanoids. You don't know your place," said Rat-face, brandishing the club.

The pulse of electricity filled Wrench's senses. The surge of the capacitors inside the club rapidly charging and discharging thrummed in her mind. It was a simple task to stop the flow of electrons, keeping them stored in the metal plates, letting the charge build.

The sparks of electricity dwindled to nothing. Rat-face frowned at the weapon. He shook it but to no avail, then whacked it against the palm of his hand, as if hoping to jog a loose connection.

Wrench released her control and the electrons burst free, into the head of the club, into Rat-face's hand. A white flash of electricity filled the alley. Rat-face flew backwards and slammed into the street wall.

His colleague fled into the dark. "See ya, Rex," he shouted, his voice drowned out by the slap of his feet on the cobbles.

Slumped in the gutter, Rat-face groaned. "I'll let you both have a free pass this time."

Bot stamped on the Tesla club, crushing it beneath his considerable weight, then marched past the prostrate robber. "I could have handled that, Brasswitch."

"Would either of them have walked away if you'd handled it?"

"Not so much walked away, no. More carried away in several buckets."

"My way's better then," said Wrench.

Bot shrugged with a mechanical whirr. "Only for them."

The Artificer's workshop was along a snickelway so narrow that Bot had to turn half sideways to walk down it. Damp brick walls towered overhead, a network of cast-iron drainpipes climbing them like an industrial ivy. There was no sign or nameplate marking the shop, just a low, tar-tarnished door, but Wrench knew it was the place. From inside she could sense machinery of such awe that it glowed gold in her mind.

Bot pushed the door open and, squatting awkwardly, manoeuvred inside. Wrench followed the mechanoid into the low-beamed room. Glass-fronted cabinets lined the walls. Secured behind the lead-crossed panes gleamed devices so fantastical that even with her abilities Wrench was at a loss as to their purpose. A workbench occupied the centre of the room, scattered with tools nearly as marvellous as the gadgets they created. At the workbench sat a man tinkering with the clockwork engine of what looked like a tin tortoise. He had rosy red cheeks, a bulbous nose and a long white beard that tapered to a point over his rounded stomach. The thought *gnome* immediately sprung into Wrench's mind and she blushed guiltily, hoping the man didn't have ESP like Octavia.

"Brasswitch, this is Mr Todkin."

"Another Brasswitch?" said Todkin in a high-pitched, melodic voice. He pulled a platinum gizmo the size of a pocket watch from beneath his leather jerkin and flicked it open. Viewing Wrench through a crystal in the device's lid, he said, "And this one has real power. I can see it in her aura."

"Auras? I thought I was supposed to be the witch?" said Wrench.

Todkin snapped the device closed. From a chest of miniature drawers he took a compass and placed it on the bench next to a thick copper wire. "Observe." He connected the wire across a battery and the compass needle twitched then spun.

Wrench could sense the magnetic field created by the flow of electricity pushing the needle. "That's science, as explained by Maxwell's treatise on electricity and magnetism," said Wrench.

"Galvani tells us of animal electricity. Is it so hard to believe we don't emit a similar field?"

Wrench cocked her head to one side. "Volta disagrees with Galvani, but point taken."

Todkin clapped his hands together in delight. "Magic. Science. They're just words. Young Plum will try and tell you different but in the end it's what we do with it that counts."

"What I want you to do with it," said Bot, "is to give my Brasswitch a way to defend herself."

"And by *defend herself* you mean cause heinous injury to someone else," said Todkin.

"Defend. Heinous injury. It's just words. It's keeping her alive that counts."

"Touché!" said Todkin. "Is there a specific threat?"

"We're not certain. A possible NIA turned my last Brasswitch into a sooty smudge." The corners of Bot's mechanical mouth turned down. "We think there's a human element involved too."

Todkin looked crestfallen, and his lower lip trembled. "Pippa is gone?"

"She retired a few days ago."

"I'm so sorry. I know you–"

Bot slapped a hand onto the workbench, making the tools jump. "We're not here to talk about the past. Can you help or not?"

Todkin sniffed, wiping his eyes. "I always do." He donned a pair of ocular analysers and squinted at Wrench. Flicking levers on the side of the brass arms, he aligned lenses of differing shapes and materials over the eyepieces. A dazzling red light at the top of the frames glowed to life. Rotated by miniature gears, the light played across Wrench. "Hmm, you have a natural feel for electricity, yes?"

Wrench nodded.

"Good. I think the 'Bracers of Zeus' would be most effective." He depressed a button on the side of the glasses and the lenses flipped upwards. "They didn't really belong to Zeus, but it sounds a whole lot more fun than 'the wrist-mounted Wimshurst air discharge device'."

Todkin threw open the doors of a glass-fronted cabinet and took out a pair of tan leather armguards. On each were fitted two counter-rotating ceramic discs decorated with copper plates that connected to a pair of spherical brass electrodes. "I built these as an experiment, only I've needed a Brasswitch to test them. It's basically a modified Wimshurst machine where your body acts as a Leyden Jar to store the charge."

Wrench frowned. They'd used massive Wimshurst machines to generate electricity for arc-welding at the engineering works. It had been the job of the apprentices to hand-crank the giant discs, a thankless and back-breaking chore. She inspected the bracers, which appeared to have no means for turning the discs. "So how do they work?"

"Well, the counter-rotating discs build up opposing charges—"

"No. I understand the science of a Wimshurst machine. I mean what powers the discs?"

"You do, my dear. You are a Brasswitch." Todkin passed the bracers to Wrench. "Here, put them on and give it a spin."

Wrench strapped on the bracers, tightening the brass buckles so the leather snugly gripped her muscled forearms. Her mind merged with the machine and the discs turned. She pushed them faster until they vibrated, and the discs emitted a low hum. The air became dry and she sensed the electrical charge building.

"Bring your wrists together," said Todkin, a look of excited anticipation on his face.

Wrench moved her forearms inwards and a crackling flash of electricity jumped between the spherical brass electrodes. Instinctively, she pushed the bolt away from her. It shot across the room, seeming to grow in magnitude, and thumped into a wooden chest. Electricity arced over the metal hinges and the chest shattered in a shower of splinters, scattering tools across the workshop.

"Chuffing heck," said Wrench, panting. She pulled her arms apart and the discs slowed. The remnants of the chest toppled forward, molten metal dripping from between the charred boards.

Todkin clapped his hands together delightedly. "Fan-bally-tastic," he said, his singsong voice even higher than normal.

"Sorry about your tools," said Wrench. "It just sort of happened."

"No matter. No matter." Todkin turned to Bot. "Suitably heinous?"

Bot's eyes changed shape, so he appeared to be frowning. "So long as she can aim it. I don't want to end up like that tool chest."

Todkin stroked his beard. "I'm sure she'll be fine with a little practice."

"She needs to be a damn sight better than fine. She needs to be able to hit a snipe at fifty yards if she's firing them anywhere near me."

Wrench smiled and patted Bot on his thick bulbous arm. "Have a little faith. It's not like I'm going to be reckless. In fact, I'll show all the restraint that you did at the monks' priory."

16

Electricity leapt along the length of the weapons range illuminating the windowless walls. Double rows of interlocked sandbags lined the train carriage to head height, above which protruded steel-plated reinforcement. The crackling bolt struck one of two wooden targets. The figure-shaped board split in two and burst into flames.

"Chuff it." Wrench stamped her foot.

Plum made a gesture with his hands and water condensed in the air over the target, extinguishing the fire. "What's wrong? That was a direct hit."

"I was aiming for the other one." The discs on her bracers stopped spinning and the spark pulsing between the two electrodes died.

Wrench dropped onto a low sandbag wall, designed

as a firing point for more traditional weapons. The indoor range was about sixty feet long, the length of the carriage, and housed two shooting lanes with a gangway between them. She picked at the sandbag's faded hessian and tried to slow her racing heart.

Controlling the electricity wasn't like controlling machines; it was wilder and reflected its excitable nature back on her. She'd been overconfident when she'd told Bot to have faith. Unlike Plum, who had Master Tranter to train him, she had no one. Without any guidance, she was making it up as she went along. Over the years, as her powers had developed, that approach hadn't been a problem. She'd been careful to ensure no one was watching when she'd tried her skills on machines. There had been no consequence of failure or pressure to succeed. With the regulators, it was different. Bot wanted to see that she could use the bracers properly before she took them on missions. More importantly, she wanted to be able to use them properly. Her life might depend on it.

Plum dropped onto the sandbags and looked up at her. His irises were a pale violet colour. Over the days they'd been practising he'd explained that the purple faded from them as he used magic, like some sort of indicator of charge. She pushed the premonition of them, tortured, grey and pleading, from her mind.

"Taking a break. Good idea. Putting out all those fires is draining me," said Plum.

Wrench suspected that wasn't the reason. She'd only

hit the target a handful of times and she was certain that Plum could manipulate water with the most limited of effort. Octavia had told her that Plum was entering a new phase of training and Master Tranter was pushing him hard in the manipulation of air. She wondered how many years it would be before she could progress to the other elements. Despite her best efforts she'd failed to freeze the water again. In fact, as far as she could tell she'd failed to have any effect on it at all.

Plum's fingers twitched. "Octavia said you had visions of the future after the machine exploded at the priory. What did you see?"

The memory of her dreams still haunted her. She'd hoped Plum wouldn't raise the subject, not knowing what she should tell him. A picture of the boy beside her, chained in a cell, his body burned and branded filled her mind. The skin on her arms rose into goose bumps and her throat went dry. She pushed away the image. "It was hard to be sure. There was so much going on, I couldn't make much of it out."

"Did you see me? In the future, I mean?"

"No. It was mostly Bot," lied Wrench.

Plum nodded, making a deep in thought hmming sound. Wrench wondered if she should have simply told him the truth. Would her falsehood make Plum believe he'd soon be dead and not part of the future? Or worse still, would her lies lead to the thaumagician being captured and undergoing the very events she'd seen? It was so hard to know what to do, but she simply couldn't bear to relay the account of her vision to Plum.

The vocal annunciator in the ceiling buzzed and then Bot's voice blared from the trumpets in the ceiling. "Plum and Brasswitch, to the DC. QRF to REDCON-1. This is an ACS. Message ends."

Plum clenched his fists, and his face drained of colour. He pushed himself from the sandbags, his legs trembling.

"Well, that was clear as engine oil," said Wrench, standing. She still didn't understand most of the acronyms used by the regulators.

"Come on." Plum hurried towards a steel-plated door protected by a wall of sandbags. "The QRF is the Quick Reaction Force. ACS is an Aberration Containment Situation. Something must have gone badly wrong on a regulator mission and we're the cavalry."

The carriage jolted, and the train began to move away from the siding that acted as its home in the station. Wrench grabbed onto the sandbag wall, steadying herself. The DC was the drop carriage. Darcey had given Wrench a special tour of the carriage because of its unique mechanical design. About half the length of the other carriages and only single storey, it could disconnect from its chassis when the train neared their destination and walk the rest of the way.

"Do you think they've found the NIA from the Minster?" asked Wrench.

Plum swallowed, the bulbous Adam's apple in his scrawny neck quivering. "I really hope not."

The only two carriages after the weapons range were the QRF's quarters and then the drop carriage. Wrench followed Plum through a heavily armoured door into the equally well-protected drop carriage. A team of six rugged-looking regulators dressed in chunky red battle armour occupied most of a bench that ran alongside one side of the carriage. On their knees rested a variety of bizarre, oversized guns. Beyond them a pilot strapped himself into a complex articulated chair. Distorted by the thick glass cockpit surrounding the pilot, the city of York was rapidly disappearing into the distance.

Plum stood awkwardly in the carriage's corner, as far away from the surly-faced regulators as possible.

"Aren't we going to sit down?" said Wrench, gesturing to the bench.

Plum fiddled nervously with the tassel on his fez. "There's not enough room and they don't play nicely with others, especially not aberrations."

"I hate that word," said Wrench. "Different shouldn't necessarily mean wrong. We're not aberrations, we're … remarkable."

"It doesn't matter what you call yourself. They're still not going to want to sit with you."

"Then they're going to have to learn. I've had enough of being treated as a second-class citizen. I am the blue train." Wrench ignored Plum's look of confusion and strode over to a regulator who had three gold chevrons on his shoulder armour and appeared to be in charge. "Budge over please, Sergeant. Plum and I need to sit down."

The sergeant raised his head, hostility in his dark eyes. "This is the QRF bench."

"We're part of the Quick Reaction Force and we need to sit down."

"You're not QRF; you're ab– "

The magazine dropped from the sergeant's massive steam rifle, cutting his sentence short, then the weapon's trigger mechanism disassembled itself, shooting a hefty recoil spring across the carriage.

"I really hope you were going to say *you're not QRF; you're absolutely too remarkable for that*." Wrench made a sweeping movement with her arm and the Bloody Big Guns belonging to the remaining QRF disassembled themselves. "Because it would be terribly unfortunate for your weapons to fail in battle."

His fingers balling into an armour-gloved fist, the sergeant raised a hand. Wrench's heart skipped. Unflinching, she stood her ground, daring him to strike her. Bot clanked into the carriage. The sergeant leapt to attention. The QRF followed suit, scattering more rogue weapon parts onto the floor.

"Sergeant, get those weapons squared away. Now's not the time for field stripping," commanded Bot.

"Yes, Sir."

The QRF scrabbled on the floor, retrieving fallen

weapon components. Bot winked at Wrench. "Brasswitch. Take a seat."

Wrench dropped onto the bench and beckoned to Plum. He slid next to her, ensuring she was between him and the QRF. "You don't want to make enemies of these people," whispered Plum.

"I'm not. I'm making friends." Wrench tapped the sergeant on his armoured shoulder pad. He turned to her, on his face a look of contempt.

"I'm no expert with weapons but the fourth bullet in your magazine is significantly different to the others. I can't tell what effect that will have but I'd seriously consider removing it."

The sergeant stared at her, scrutinising her face, then slid the magazine from the weapon. He pushed the first three rounds free with his thumb and examined the round that now rested at the top. The brass case appeared tarnished and the percussion cap on the cylinder's base was warped. He prised the round free and pocketed it.

"You're welcome," said Wrench as the sergeant reloaded the top three rounds and clicked the magazine back into place.

The train slowed and Wrench sensed something happening in the mechanics of the carriage. Heavy cogs turned, unfurling six massive legs. The carriage shuddered to a halt, the musty rubber smell of overheating brakes filling the air. Steam hissed from pistons and the legs fully extended, lifting the carriage clear of the chassis-cradle.

The pilot feathered the drive-sticks and, with a lumbering gait, the drop carriage walked away from the train.

Bot stationed himself across the aisle from the QRF and rapped his fingers against his head. "Eyes and ears on me." After a brief pause to ensure he had everyone's attention he continued. "Mission information is sparse. A regulator arrest squad attended St Andrew's Church in Bishopthorpe this morning to apprehend an aberration. They were met with resistance and casualties have been reported."

The QRF sergeant raised his hand. Bot nodded at him and he spoke. "Civilian or regulator casualties?"

"Both," answered Bot.

There was a murmuring among the QRF then another member of the team, who had something that looked like a giant rocket strapped to his back, asked, "Who's heading the arrest team?"

Bot's head didn't move but Wrench was sure that he glanced at her before answering. "Captain Flemington."

"Was he the casualty?" asked the same member of the QRF, an almost hopeful tone in his voice.

"No. Regulator Thurston was." Bot cut short the further murmurings of the QRF. "Thurston was a good woman and a capable regulator so we know this isn't going to be a cakewalk. When we touch down the QRF will reinforce the internal perimeter while I liaise with Captain Flemington. Brasswitch, Plum, you will assist me. Any questions?"

"Do we want the aberration alive?" asked the QRF sergeant.

"That is not a priority."

"Do we want Flemington alive?" piped up another of the QRF who had a gun the size of a small artillery cannon resting across his knees.

"Hudson, lock it down," snapped the sergeant.

Steam hissed from Bot's joints and his metal torso grew by several inches. "Captain Flemington may have botched the original operation, but we need to be professional. It's going to be dangerous and I don't want any more regulators retired today. Is that clear?"

"Yes, Sir," barked the QRF in unison.

"We have been through many tough situations together and you guys are the best. I love you guys." Bot paused, letting his words sink in. "But I can replace any one of you with a single telegram to the Grand Cabal." He rested his right hand on Plum's head and his left on Wrench's. "These two are special. They are unique. I cannot replace them. There are dark times ahead and I feel it in my pistons that they will be of the utmost significance in the days to come. Whatever happens out there, you will protect them with your lives."

Bot withdrew his hands and, making a fist, slammed it against his chest. "Ready for anything," he shouted.

The QRF repeated the gesture. "Yield to none," they chorused.

17

The carriage jolted. "Ninety seconds to touchdown," shouted the pilot.

Wrench gripped the edge of the seat, her bracers of Zeus pulling tight against her forearms. When the time came, would she be able to use them? It was all well and good blasting lightning at wooden targets but to use them against an actual living person? She wasn't sure that she could. She guessed most of the regulators didn't see remarkables as people and perhaps that made it easier for them to justify their actions. And if the person in the church had killed one of their colleagues they were unlikely to show much compassion. But having witnessed Flemington's cruelty firsthand, who was to say the regulator hadn't deserved whatever happened? Who was to say the person in the church wasn't a victim rather than a villain?

With a bump, the carriage came to a halt straddling a hedgerow that surrounded the St Andrew's Church graveyard. It settled on its haunches, snapping branches and crushing bushes, the natural barrier no match for the drop carriage's mechanical might. Steam pistons lowered a ramp and double doors in the carriage side slid open. Clanking noisily, their armoured suits venting steam, the QRF stormed down the ramp and onto the fresh mown grass that separated the graves. Neatly tended headstones extended in rows towards the church. The QRF picked their way between them, using the granite monuments as cover.

"Stick with me, Brasswitch." Bot strode after his squad, scanning the graveyard for danger.

Obviously, she was going to stick with him. Flemington had tried to kill her, and just the thought of seeing him again made her nauseous. While she was with Bot she'd be safe, from Flemington at least. She tried to bury the thought of what might happen if the mechanoid didn't survive the encounter. There was little doubt that given the order the QRF would turn on her in an instant, and with the best will in the world she could hardly count on Plum to have her back. If she wanted to live she had to make sure Bot survived the mission too.

On any other day, the large stone church with its terracotta tiled roof and rectangular belfry tower would have looked picturesque. However, today dirty black smoke vented from a broken stained-glass window through which hung the badly charred body of a regulator.

Flemington crouched behind a broad, lichen-covered tomb, from where he surveyed the porch leading to the church door. Next to him a regulator sighted down a chunky steam rifle, wisps of smoke rising from her singed uniform.

Wrench jogged adjacent to Bot, keeping pace with his long strides. Behind them trailed Plum. In her heart Wrench wished she could swap places with the young thaumagician, so the big mechanoid was between her and Flemington. It was clear that wasn't going to happen, and she'd be damned if she was going to give the regulator the satisfaction of seeing her cowering. She pushed her chest out and raised her chin. She was the angry, red train.

Bot drew to a halt beside the tomb, not bothering to use it for cover. "Once again it seems you quite literally need me to pull your ass out of the fire, Flemmy."

Flemington eyed Wrench with a look of malicious disdain before addressing Bot. "I wouldn't be so smug if I was you. It's your mistake I'm rectifying. Leech cleared the aberration who has now killed several civilians and a regulator." He pulled an official-looking notebook from his chest pocket and flicked it open. "I quote from his report: *Carwyn Ddraig is no more a threat to society than I am.*"

Bot growled. "The Grand Cabal forbade you from meddling with my officers' cases after the Whitby debacle. It took us two weeks to clear up that mess."

"I think you'll find I have treated Cabal Thirteen with all the respect they deserve," sneered Flemington. "Leech is dead, and so it's no longer his case. By the looks of things, he and your little brasswitchette were flambéed by the same aberration he cleared."

Wrench winced at Flemington's deliberate goading. Bot appeared to let it go, for now at least.

"If you don't have enough of your own work to do I'm sure the Grand Cabal can find some additional tasks in line with your abilities," said Bot. "I'm thinking nothing too taxing, sweeping up, cleaning the toilets, that sort of thing."

"I have more than enough work cleaning up your messes. That's the problem with recruiting aberration filth," said Flemington, gesturing to Wrench and Plum. "Someone has to make sure Thirteen aren't turning a blind eye to their friends."

There was a roar from inside the church and a window exploded, a jet of blue flame melting the glass. Flemington ducked behind the tomb. "That will be my squad of mechs resolving the situation, so it appears the overrated heroics of Thirteen aren't required after all."

Wrench guided her mind towards the robot regulators inside the church. Machines weren't supposed to have feelings, but she experienced what in a human might have been described as fear. The church's windows glowed bright, illuminated by long tongues of flame. The light faded, and she sensed the robot regulators changing from glorious machines into fused lumps of metal. "Your mechs are dead," she said, not really sure if a machine could die, but that's how it felt to her.

"When I want your opinion, I'll torture it out of you, aberration," said Flemington.

The Wimshurst discs on Wrench's bracers spun and sparks crackled from her fingers. "It's not me who's going to be electrocuted this time." Wrench brought her arms together and a spark crackled between the electrodes. Bot jogged her shoulder and the charged bolt that arced from the bracers sizzled past Flemington and shattered a gravestone.

"You nudged me!" complained Wrench.

"I can't let you kill Flemington," said Bot, with a hint of regret.

"I may have been going to miss anyway."

"Were you?"

Wrench clapped her hands together and a flurry of sparks discharged into the ground. "I guess we'll never know," she said in a sulky voice. The discs slowed, and just for a moment a peculiar sensation overcame her. The mechanics of her bracers were distant and distorted and her brain felt fuggy. It was like at the Epochryphal Brotherhood when the monk's crossbow had been out of focus to her, only this time the feeling was stronger, more direct.

Flemington stood and stepped in front of Bot. "I told you my mechs are taking care of it. Your interference isn't required."

"Out of my way. Thirteen's in control now." Bot towered over the regulator.

"Well, I'm coming with you. Someone responsible has to make sure you don't let the aberration go free again." Flemington drew his pistol.

"Over your dead body. I can't be watching my back for you as well as the target."

"I'm the commanding officer on the scene. You can't stop me."

"I don't have to. Plum, come here."

The thaumagician, who had been standing well back from the confrontation, scurried over.

"If Captain Flemington tries to follow us into the church, do something nasty to him with magic," said Bot.

"You want me to hurt him?" queried Plum, wringing his hands.

"Nothing fatal. Maybe just wither an appendage."

Flemington's eyes narrowed. "You wouldn't dare."

"Plum, I command you to answer truthfully," said Bot. "In the Bradford Mill incident did the officer in charge disobey my direct command?"

"Yes, Sir."

"And what happened to that officer's left arm?"

"It was turned to dust."

"If required I expect you to do the same today as you did then. Is that clear?"

"Absolutely, Sir," said Plum, adopting a magical pose.

Bot brushed Flemington aside and strode towards the church. Once again Wrench jogged to keep up with him. "Did Plum really turn a regulator's arm to dust?" she said when they were out of earshot.

"Plum? Don't be daft. The regulator took a team in against my orders and the aberration desiccated his arm."

"But you said Plum did it?"

"No. I implied Plum did it."

"So, what did Plum actually do that day?"

"Made the tea, I think."

Bot slowed, his gait taking on the wary prowl Wrench had observed in the Minster's under-crypt. A modest porch jutted from the church's wall. Inside, the studded oak door stood ajar. Smoke drifted through the gap, sooty swirls curling into the porch. Bot banged his fist against the woodwork and shouted. "We're unarmed and want to talk. I'm from Cabal Thirteen of the regulators and I would like to resolve this without anyone else getting hurt." He lowered his head to Wrench and whispered, "Especially us."

There was no reply from inside.

Wrench pushed her mind towards the remains of the robot regulators, hoping some functionality remained. Again, she experienced the odd sensation, stronger this time, like a viscous barrier to her thoughts, the mechanoids shielded from her.

"Keep close," said Bot. "We've got to win him over. Hearts and minds, that's the way, hearts and minds." He pushed the door further open and said, "We're coming in now. I'd consider it a great gesture of goodwill if you didn't try and set fire to us."

They stepped through the doorway.

18

Smoke drifted from smouldering pews. The pulpit lay shattered, a mess of splintered wood, and the scorched font leaked water through a crack in the stonework. The regulator mechs stood inert, their bodies melted and twisted. Penned in the choir stalls, a handful of villagers cowered. Ahead of them paced a thickset remarkable with a dragon-like face. Iridescent scales freckled the skin around his blackened nostrils, from which rose twin streams of smoke. He looked too young to be the cause of so much destruction, barely out of his teens.

Wrench sidled behind Bot. She didn't know if her new clothes were flameproof, and seeing what remained of the melted mechs she didn't want to have to find out. What Darcey could do to a lump of coal was formidable and, judging by the dragon-like remarkable's appearance and the carnage all around, he was even more powerful. Wrench forced her mind through the strange oily fug that impeded her senses, searching for any machine that could offer them an advantage. She found only the lifeless mechs, the clockwork church-bell ringers, and the steam organ.

"Carwyn. May I call you Carwyn?" said Bot, holding his palms out to his sides in a gesture of openness. "Can we please let these poor villagers go? They've done you no harm. Your quarrel is not with them."

"That shows what you know. Nothing." A jet of flame shot from Carwyn's mouth into the air. "The good reverend preached that I was an abomination. I was a demon sent to taint us all. The villagers shunned me. When my mother took ill no one raised a finger to help. They were too scared in case the regulators found out."

Bot shuffled further into the church. "I understand it can't have been easy, but this isn't the solution. I'm sure this isn't what your mother wants now."

"My mother died. They wouldn't even bury her in the churchyard. Instead of helping, the parish council informed on me to the regulators."

"Great work, hearts and minds," whispered Wrench. "I think you're really winning him over."

"That isn't the fault of these good people gathered here. Can you at least let them go?"

"These are the parish council. All except Reverend

Peatry who is currently indisposed," said Carwyn, gesturing to a sooty silhouette on the wall that looked uncannily like the ones from the Minster.

Ever so slowly, so as not to draw attention, Wrench began to spin the discs on her bracers. It didn't take the genius of a clockwork-brain mechanic to tell the conversation wasn't going as planned, and she wanted to be ready if things heated up.

"I'd like to help you, truly I would, but you've got to help me, Carwyn."

"That's what the other regulator said."

Bot's eyes narrowed. "What other regulator?"

"We could do a deal, he said. I did what he asked, and he tricked me." Flame shot from Carwyn's mouth. A streak of white heat aimed directly at Bot.

With a speed not in keeping with his size, Bot shoved Wrench sideways, while throwing his massive bulk in the opposite direction.

Wrench thudded on to a collection of cross-stitched kneelers. Heat from the blast scorched her back. The ancient wood pew shielding her burst into flame. Keeping low on her belly, she scrabbled to the end of the flaming wood. She peeked out. Carwyn inhaled rapidly in a series of short breaths. If he was anything like Darcey it would take him a moment before he could breathe fire again. Hoping her assumption was correct she darted across the aisle to join Bot, who had taken refuge behind one of the wide stone columns supporting the roof.

His lungs now full, Carwyn launched a torrent of flame at the pillar, pinning them in position.

"I'm giving you this one last chance to surrender before anyone else gets hurt," shouted Bot. "And by anyone else I mean you."

White-hot flame seared across the flagstones beside their feet.

"Come out and I'll make your deaths quick," roared Carwyn.

"I bet you're really glad you left the thaumagician who can conjure water babysitting Flemington," said Wrench.

"You were supposed to be learning magic."

"I am. When you catch fire, I can think of lemons and spit on your molten remains."

"You've changed," said Bot.

Wrench pressed her back flat against the pillar. A gout of flame shot past, inches from her chest. "Repetitive near-death experiences will do that to a girl."

"Don't get me wrong. I like the new you. Much more how a Brasswitch should be."

"Living in perpetual fear of dying horribly?"

"Welcome to the team," said Bot.

The column cracked under the onslaught of fire. A huge chunk of stone flaked away and crashed to the floor.

"So much for a peaceful resolution. I'm going to have to drop Carwyn before he drops the roof on us." The plates in Bot's leg slid open and he withdrew the hand cannon. "I'm only going to get one shot at this; I need you to provide a distraction."

"You want me to run out there and draw his fire?" said Wrench incredulously.

"If you want." Bot nodded to the spinning wheels on her bracers. "Or you could just do something really cool with electrickery, Brasswitch."

"On the third stroke of the bell," said Wrench. She forced her mind through the fug to the church organ and it began to play. Given the gravity of their situation something dramatic by Bach or Mozart would have been appropriate, but unfortunately the only tune Wrench knew was "Ring a Ring o' Roses", which she'd been forced to learn at school on the recorder. Her mind fumbled through the notes while flicking off the pivot brake on the clockwork ringer in the bell tower. Gears whirred, and three deep chimes rang out. Wrench brought her arms together, leaned from behind the pillar and directed a bolt of electricity towards Carwyn. The streak of lightning landed wide, hitting a large brass crucifix above the altar and earthed in a shower of sparks.

The boom from Bot's hand cannon echoed around the church.

Carwyn exhaled but instead of a jet of flame he coughed blood. His head tilted down, a surprised look on his face as he saw the smoking hole in his chest. He mumbled something unintelligible, red bubbles frothed from his lips then he dropped to the floor.

"… we all fall down," said Bot, as the nursery rhyme finished playing on the organ.

A tearing sound emanated from Carwyn's corpse. His stomach ballooned, inflating like a blimp. Then with a rumbustious squelch he exploded.

A splatter of warm goo covered Wrench. She removed her glasses and wiped the back of her hand across her face. Radiating out from where Carwyn had fallen was a starburst of blood and entrails. In the choir stalls the parish councillors sat in a state of shock, fleshy red gunk dripping down their horrified faces.

"Well, that was a tad unexpected," said Bot, flicking a wobbling tubular mass, which may have once been intestines, from the barrel of his hand cannon.

"Really! Because I'm kind of getting the impression that you and total devastation go hand in hand."

"Harsh," said Bot.

"But fair," said Wrench.

Bot shrugged. "I tried to end it peacefully. I wanted to end it peacefully. I wanted him alive, so he could tell me about the NIA."

"I thought he was the NIA? The sooty silhouettes at the Minster are the same," said Wrench, gesturing towards the carbonised smudge that had once been Reverend Peatry.

"I'm picking he murdered Leech and Chattox, but he's no NIA."

"How can you be sure?"

"Because we're still alive, and the church is still standing."

With a thud, a section of the stone pillar crumbled to the floor.

"We nearly died, and the church is only just standing," said Wrench.

Bot brushed flakes of singed stone from his armour. "It's hard to understand the power of a Non-Indigenous Aberration until you encounter one. Their worshippers call them gods. For all I know they might be gods. Think of biblical devastation with a surfeit of smiting thrown in for good measure and you might begin to get the picture."

"So how do we find the NIA if you've just killed our only lead?"

"Carwyn may have told us more than he realised. I have some suspicions, but this isn't the place to air them."

"Suspicions of what?"

Bot stared towards the church door. "Not what. Who."

19

"Flemington?" said Wrench. She looked from Bot, to Plum and Octavia to see if they were as dubious as her. Plum slouched in one of the briefing carriage's chairs, his head swaying with the motion of the train as it returned to York station. He was barely able to keep awake, his lids drooping over his grey eyes. Octavia's tentacles undulated, a sign Wrench had come to associate with deep contemplation.

"I thought you'd welcome an opportunity to do him down," said Bot.

"Obviously he's not on my Christmas card list." The discs on her bracers spun, emitting a shower of sparks. "I just don't think he'd release a NIA. He detests remarkables."

"He does indeed. Or at least pretends to. Maybe he's just a little bit too zealous, trying to make sure no one would suspect," said Bot.

The tentacles on Octavia's head ceased their rhythmic movements and curled tightly to her skull. "I try not to go near the man, however, Wrench is right. I've never sensed anything other than complete revulsion from him."

"We're talking about a Non-Indigenous Aberration, a lesser God. In his eyes, other aberrations are, well, aberrations of the perfect being," said Bot. "It would stand to reason that he'd want to destroy them."

Wrench dragged herself from her chair. The post-adrenaline slump and the gentle rocking of the train was making her feel drowsy and she didn't want to nod off like Plum. She paced the width of the carriage. "If Carwyn was involved with Flemington why would he call us to the church? That's just asking for trouble."

"He didn't; Regulator Thurston did. She sent an emergency response pigeon and then was conveniently incinerated for her efforts. Carwyn said he did a deal with a regulator and that regulator tricked him. Suppose Flemington got Carwyn to take out Leech and Chattox at the Minster, then tried to silence Carwyn at the church."

The carriage clattered over some points. Octavia reached out a tentacle to the dozing Plum, keeping him from sliding off his chair. "Isn't it more likely Flemington had simply gone to the church to detain Carwyn?" she said. "He would have promised anything to try and defuse the situation and then got all heavy handed when he thought he had the chance."

Bot's skorpidium-carbide eyelids half covered his eyes, making it seem like he was scowling. "Why was Flemington investigating Carwyn in the first place?"

"Because, however much it pains me to admit it, Flemington was right," said Octavia. "Leech made a mistake in clearing Carwyn. I'm beginning to wonder if Leech hadn't lost it some time ago. He deliberately avoided me for that past few months. In hindsight, I think he was worried I'd sense something was wrong."

Bot looked to Wrench. "You were at the church. Did Flemington's behaviour strike you as odd?"

Wrench wasn't sure she had the most objective of viewpoints. She'd only met Flemington once before and on that occasion, he'd been trying to kill her. She cast her mind back to the conversation outside the church; something had been out of kilter. Flemington had cowered behind the tomb intent on stopping them going into the church, and when his protestations had failed he'd tried to insist on going with them. "He did seem to rather change his tune." She gestured to Plum, who mumbled in his sleep. "If you hadn't threatened him with our terrifying thaumagician he would have been in the church with us."

"Exactly," said Bot.

"Exactly what?" Octavia rested her head on a tentacle, her brow furrowed.

Bot threw his arms wide open in frustration, the clank of his armoured plates filling the carriage. "He didn't want us talking to Carwyn, did he?"

Octavia raised her chin. "You didn't talk to Carwyn. You blew a bally great hole in his chest."

"True." Bot's arms dropped to his sides. "Contrary to popular belief it wasn't my preferred outcome. Flemington sent his mechs in as a kill squad. I at least tried to negotiate."

The memory of the strange sensation surrounding the mechs haunted Wrench. What she'd experienced was wrong, but she couldn't explain why. It was like looking at one of those black-and-white pictures where one moment you'd be staring at a vase and then your focus changed, and it would be two people talking. Yet, no matter how hard she concentrated on the feeling, she could only see the vase. The others were more used to dealing with the abnormal; maybe it would hold some sort of meaning to them.

"There was something else in the church," said Wrench. "When I tried to sense Flemington's mechs there was a force blocking me, resisting my powers. I can't really describe it. Maybe a bit like my mind was swimming through treacle. I know that sounds weird."

"Weird is what we do," said Bot. "Why didn't you mention it at the time?"

"I was somewhat distracted by trying not to be incinerated."

"Fair one."

Octavia pressed her hands against her temples. "Could you tell where it was coming from? Was Carwyn the cause?"

The feeling had surrounded her, like a cloud; she couldn't pinpoint the source. Had it stopped when Carwyn was shot? Possibly, but she'd encountered no resistance when she'd played the organ or operated the church's clockwork bells. Surely if Carwyn could sense her powers he would have blocked her there too. Or at least been less surprised by their activation. "No. I don't think it was Carwyn."

"So, we're back to suspecting Flemington as the guilty party," said Bot with a triumphant air.

The train's brakes screeched as it pulled back into platform thirteen at York station. Plum rocked forward, his head lolling to one side. Once again Octavia steadied him. "Supposing Flemington is up to no good, what do you intend to do about it?"

"We need to investigate him, take his life apart, find out what he's hiding," said Bot.

"This has 'terrible idea' written all over it," said Octavia. "Not that it matters, the Grand Cabal will never allow you to investigate Flemington."

"The Grand Cabal aren't going to know. We'll keep it a secret," said Bot.

Octavia's tentacles quivered. "Right, because stealth and guile are such a key part of your modus operandi."

"Admittedly I'm not known for my tact and subtlety, but that's why I'm not going to do it. I'm giving the task to Plum and Wrench."

It took three days, the burning of several markers accrued over many years of saving regulators from horrible endings and Octavia's remarkable skills to unofficially pull Flemington's personnel file from the Clifford's Tower Cabal. Like most of York's regulators, the captain was barracked at Clifford's Tower; however, a footnote in the file mentioned he also rented rooms above Humbug and Mints confectionery shop on Low Peter Gate. This was to be the target of Wrench and Plum's investigation.

Barely wider than the pinched lanes of the Shambles, a shadowed gloom hung over Lower Peter Gate. The merchants did all within their means to brighten their shopfronts: oil lamps flickered outside Malone's Chandlers, bubbling rainbow-coloured elixirs graced the window of Gilmour's Chemists and a mechanical rug sweeper marched up and down brushing the pavement in front of Beale's Brush and Mat Warehouse.

Wrench crossed the cobbled street and took shelter beneath Humbug and Mints' candy-striped awning. A pervasive mizzle dribbled from the sky and her sodden clothes clung uncomfortably. She noted with a certain amount of ire that Plum had surreptitiously used his powers to stay dry, a courtesy he had not extended to her. Maybe he thought it would act as motivation to encourage her to try harder in her magic practice. He was wrong. All it had achieved was to make her angry.

She peered through the lattice of small glass panes that made up the shop's window and her mouth watered. Sturdy rectangular jars of chocolates, toffees and coloured bonbons lined the shelves. A stunning red locomotive engine made entirely from liquorice formed an edible centrepiece that took pride of place in the window.

"What do you reckon?" said Plum, fiddling with the cuff of his bone-dry damson-coloured suit. On the journey over Wrench had ribbed him about his choice of dress, which he mistakenly considered inconspicuous. Possibly another reason why he'd let her get soaked.

"I reckon we should buy some bonfire toffee. Just to maintain our cover, of course." Wrench pushed the door open and a bell tinkled. Inside, the sweet scent of sugary delights filled the air.

"Welcome! I'm Horatio Humbug," said a man in a

frilled white apron and straw boater. His right eye was covered by an eye patch which looked suspiciously like it was made from liquorice. From his pocket he took a crumpled white paper bag and offered it to Wrench. "Pineapple lozenge?"

"What's a pineapple?" asked Wrench.

"They're giant lemons that grow in the Americas," said Horatio.

"I'm not sure they are." Plum thrust his hands into his jacket's pockets.

Wrench retrieved a yellow-coloured sweet from the bag and popped it into her mouth. Her cheeks drew in and her eyes watered. Against all logic the lozenge conspired to be sweet and bitter at the same time. "It certainly tastes like lemon," she said, chasing the lozenge round her mouth with her tongue.

Plum shook his head. "The fact that the sweet tastes like lemon doesn't mean that's what pineapples are."

"Why would they be pineapple lozenges if they didn't taste of pineapple? That would be stupid. You might as well just call them lemon lozenges," said Wrench. Tart sherbet from inside the sweet leaked across her tongue and her face scrunched up. She shuddered, her skin tingling, feeling like the bitterness had spread throughout her body.

Plum frowned. "That's precisely—"

"Would you look at that?" interrupted Horatio, pointing at the window. "It's snowing. In July."

Outside, the mizzle had turned into powdery ice flakes that drifted to the cobbles.

Wrench squealed, Plum's boot landing on her foot.

"It can't be snow," said the thaumagician, making a symbol with his hand behind his back. "It's probably just ashes blowing down the street."

The door's bell tinkled again as Horatio hurried outside to look.

An icy chill filled the shop. "What are you doing?" hissed Plum.

"What do you mean, *what am I doing*? You stamped on my foot."

"Because you were making it snow."

"Don't be ridiculous, how could I …" Plum was right. The pineapple lozenge had made her mouth water, then the sherbet had made her wince and that was when it had started snowing.

Horatio stepped back inside and removed his boater. He ran his fingers through his hair, confused. "Sorry about that. I could have sworn it was snowing. How odd."

"Not in July," said Plum.

"No, not in July," repeated Horatio to himself. "That would be miraculous."

Plum rubbed his hands together. "Sooo, can we have a quarter of bonfire toffee?"

"And a bag of pineapple lozenges, please," added Wrench.

The musty smell of damp decay hung in the snicket that led to the rear of the shop. Midway along the narrow passage, where the light was gloomiest, Plum stopped and pulled off his dark glasses. His eyes glowered purple. "Give me the pineapple lozenges," he said, holding out his hand.

Wrench hesitated. Her fingers rustled the crisp paper bag nestling in her pocket. She'd done magic. She didn't know how, and she certainly hadn't intended it to snow, but even so the sweets had triggered the magic in her. It wasn't enough; she wanted to do it again. She needed to feel the tingling like her whole body was surging with power. Plum was trying to take that away from her, trying to thwart her. Maybe Pippa had been right, Plum didn't want the Brasswitches to learn magic. "No. They're mine."

"Look, I get it; I honestly do. Magic is like opium – once is never enough. The feeling, the power, you become addicted to it." Plum scratched at his arms. "The thing is, you have to learn to control it otherwise it controls you."

"I will learn. I was just surprised."

"Which is my point. If you accidentally do magic–" The colour drained from Plum's cheeks and he clutched his arms across his chest. "Well, bad things can happen."

He was right, and she knew it. They were supposed

to blend in, be sneaky, and she'd made it snow. Even so, she damn well wasn't taking orders from Plum. "They're mine. You can't have them," she said, squaring her shoulders.

Plum hesitated, obviously wondering whether to push the issue. He was no match for her physically, Wrench's apprenticeship at the coachworks having built her strong and broad, but she suspected he could annihilate her with a flick of his fingers.

"I promise I won't eat any more until we're back on the train where you can help me practise safely."

"Good enough." Plum replaced his glasses and carried on down the passage.

A tatty wooden door with peeling paint blocked the back stairs. Wrench reached out to the door's lock with her mind and encouraged it open. Despite her disdain for Flemington, a feeling of guilt stole over her. Bot may have directed them to break in, but their burglary wasn't officially sanctioned by the Grand Cabal. Only the four of them knew of the mission. If they were caught would Bot deny all knowledge to save his precious Thirteen? She pushed the thought from her mind and eased the door open.

A set of rickety stairs led to the flat above the shop. A sudden weariness gripped Wrench as she began to climb. Her legs became leaden, heavy chunks of fatigue that required concentrated effort to haul them step by step up the stairs. She panted, her breathing laboured and ragged, the painful process of dragging air into her lungs an almost unbearable strain. Stumbling onto the small landing at the top of the stairs, a light-headed euphoria engulfed her. She bent over, resting her hands on her knees, willing herself to recover.

"Take a minute," said Plum. "It's the magic catching up with you."

Wrench wheezed and coughed. "You what?"

"Magic takes energy. That energy comes from the cells of your body. That's why all good thaumagicians are so skinny."

"I've seen you do magic, and you don't get like this."

"Over time your body adapts and learns to deal with it. You've just done the equivalent of a magical marathon without any training."

Her body ached worse than it had done at the end of her first day at the coachworks. The team leaders had pushed them hard, wanting to sort out any malingerers. She'd been determined to make a good showing and by the end of the shift she was exhausted. She'd wondered how she'd ever manage another day, but she had. Her body adjusted, and she'd soon become fit and muscled. Perhaps magic was the same. "Can you build up magical stamina?"

"To an extent, but there are still limits. If you're clever, or evil, you can get energy from elsewhere: a sacrifice or magic stored in a totem that acts like a magical battery."

Wrench fought through her exhaustion and heaved herself upright. The landing was barely large enough for them both to stand. Ahead, a grimy window looked out over the street and to her right a steel-plated door barred the way to Flemington's rooms. "Looks like he's got something to hide," she said, her breath still coming in pants.

"Maybe. Or he's just being cautious. You've seen some of the things we deal with. I think I'd sleep better knowing there's hardened steel between me and any remarkables."

"We are remarkables," said Wrench.

"Yes, but we're the good ones. We don't harm people."

Not on purpose. But she'd accidentally made it snow. Could she accidentally have activated the brakes on the *Drake* without knowing? She'd been only five years old at the time, and as best as she could remember she wasn't aware of having any powers. However, the memory of that day mithered her. She remembered the fear she'd felt when the *Drake*'s steam turbo kicked in and the way the train had careered around the bends, tilting at frightening angles. Her father crouching down, wiping away her tears, explaining he'd designed it like that to counter the centripetal force, yet all she could do was screw her eyes tight shut and say *Daddy, please make it stop.*

"When you're ready," said Plum, rapping his knuckles on the steel.

Recoiling from her thoughts, Wrench probed the door's mechanism. It was far more substantial than the back door's simple mortice lock, like a puzzle waiting to be solved. She coerced the gears, tumblers and pins into cooperating and with a click the door opened a crack.

"Right, let's see what the captain's hiding," said Plum, his fingers worrying at his shades.

Wrench ignored him, her mind still in the lock's enigma. There were wheels and cogs, pistons and pinions that weren't required, or at least weren't required for opening the door.

His body trembling with the effort, Plum pushed at the heavy steel plate. The door swung slowly inwards.

Wrench's brow creased. The connecting rods and cables led to a second mechanism. One with multiple laths and stirrups. Strings and flight grooves. Bolts and triggers.

"Get down," she shouted and slammed into Plum.

With a solid-sounding twang, three crossbows released their bolts.

21

Wrench sprawled across Plum, pinning his skeletal frame to the floor. A trio of crossbow bolts whooshed overhead and thudded into the wall, showering them in splinters and brick dust.

"Ow. That hurts," said Plum, squirming beneath Wrench.

"It hurts a damn sight less than those bolts would have."

Plum rubbed his elbow through the sleeve of his jacket. "That's going to leave some bruising for sure. You're heavy, you know."

"Sorry–"

"That's all right. Just get off me."

Wrench pushed herself upright. "No. I meant sorry,

I must have heard incorrectly, because I was expecting some sort of thanks for saving your life, not pathetic whingeing and ungentlemanly comments about my weight." She offered her hand to Plum and hoicked him to his feet. He was surprisingly light.

"Thanks," said Plum. His eyes fixed on the damage done to the wall by the bolts. "And thanks for saving me from a horrible death."

"Any time," said Wrench. Except it wouldn't be any time. The image of Plum being tortured in the cell played across her mind. She hadn't saved him from a horrible death, merely postponed it.

She killed the image and brushed brick dust from her dungarees. The fabric appeared untarnished by her dive to the floor. Just how strong were her reinforced clothes? Strong enough to stop a crossbow bolt? Hopefully she'd never have to find out.

With renewed caution, she stepped through the doorway. The room's floor was covered with a hideous patterned rug on one corner of which sat a well-worn armchair. Horsehair stuffing leaked from its sides where the leather was clawed and ripped. Curled up on the chair, eyeing them with a mild curiosity, lay a cat. Or at least what Wrench assumed was a cat. It had ears like a bat, eyes like an owl, each of which was a different colour, webbed feet and no fur.

"Now that's an aberration," said Wrench.

"I kind of like it." Plum scratched the creature behind

its ears and was rewarded with a robust purr.

Shelving crammed with a higgledy-piggledy array of books and journals filled the wall opposite the door. Star-shaped explosions of paper jutted from ragged holes in the centre of three faux encyclopedias, behind which Wrench sensed the now redundant crossbows. She let her mind wander around the remains of the room feeling all manner of machines, but nothing threatening.

"I'll check here, you can do the bedroom," said Wrench, gesturing to a plain oak door in the right-hand wall. Flemington gave her the creeps and the last thing she wanted to do was rifle through his underwear drawer.

It felt wrong to be handling Flemington's possessions, digging into his personal life. They were only looking for evidence that implicated him as being involved with Carwyn, but it wasn't that simple. Until you started reading the paperwork you didn't know whether it was the vital clue you were looking for or, as in this case, a letter of lovesick platitudes, returned from a quite clearly disinterested debutante.

"Is there anything worse than badly written love poems?" yelled Wrench to Plum in the next room.

"Torture," shouted Plum in reply.

"Yes, it is." Wrench returned the letter to a sheaf of similar forlorn ramblings.

"No. I meant I've never been overly fond of torture. I'd take sentimental slush all day long over pillories and red-hot pokers."

Despite his jocular tone there was an edge to Plum's words. He couldn't possibly know of her dream; he would have said something if he did. So that left the unpleasant thought that he'd been a victim of torture. What had happened to him before he'd been recruited to Cabal Thirteen? Had Bot rescued him from Flemington's clutches too? Plum was no fan of the captain but that was hardly an exclusive club. He'd not shown any fear or hatred when they'd joined Flemington outside the church, or at least no more fear than his baseline level of mild terror.

Wrench had always been able to keep her peculiarities secret, but Plum, with his violet eyes, was going to stand out. Even now, when he was part of the regulators, he wore his large dark glasses everywhere. *If you accidentally do magic, bad things can happen*; that's what he'd said earlier. She hadn't picked up on it at the time, but perhaps that wasn't just a warning, perhaps he was talking from experience.

"Lordy-Lawks! This you need to see," shouted Plum.

Wrench stuffed the sheaf of papers back onto the shelf and hurried into the adjoining room. It contained a narrow bed pushed up against one wall and a simple Elmwood wardrobe into which Plum gazed.

The half-open door obscured the cabinet's interior. Wrench moved further into the room, eager to see what had Plum so transfixed. When working at the coachworks she had prided herself on her unflappability but as the wardrobe's contents came into view her hand went to her mouth, stifling a gasp. It contained not clothes but a montage of photographs, letters, documents and drawings, pinned to the wood. Connecting various items were lengths of knotted string, labelled with neatly written index cards. And in the midst of it all, a spider's web of strings emanating from its centre, was a large photograph of Wrench, the one they'd taken when she joined the coachworks.

"Looks like you've got a secret admirer," said Plum.

With trembling fingers Wrench traced a string back from a photograph of the mangled remains of the *Drake*. She grasped the label tied halfway along the string, holding it so she could see the words: *Is the Brasswitch to blame for the crash?*

She staggered backwards into the bedframe. Her legs gave out and she slumped onto the mattress. "It wasn't my fault. I was just a child," she mumbled, cradling her head in her hands.

Plum joined her, sitting on the bed. "Are you all right?"

"No. I'm bally well not." Wrench lifted her head. "A sadistic psychopath has been prying into my life."

"I know. It's just wrong snooping into people's private possessions. Who would do such a thing?"

Wrench's fingers tightened on the edge of the mattress. "We're not snooping. We're investigating."

171

"Yeah, well, Flemington's been investigating you and that doesn't bode well. Bot carries clout with the Grand Cabal but there's only so much he can shield you from."

"What do you mean shield me? I've done nothing wrong."

"We're aberrations. We were born a crime." Plum gestured towards the wardrobe. "Although this goes way beyond that. Even for Flemington it's obsessive. He must reckon you're pretty special."

"Is there anything on Carwyn or the NIA?"

Plum scanned his gaze over the documents. "No. It's all about you."

Why was Flemington so obsessed with her? There had to be a reason. It was more than just the fact that she was a remarkable, it had something to do with the accident that had killed her parents. She needed time to study the documents. She checked her fob watch – time that they didn't have.

"Bot is going to want to see this. We'd better take it all," she said.

Plums fingers twitched nervously into a succession of shapes. "We're not supposed to leave any sign we've been here."

"Well, that went out of the window when those crossbow bolts put whacking great holes in the wall."

"That could have been ordinary housebreakers. If we take all the stuff about you, Flemington's going to suspect it was Thirteen."

Wrench began unpinning the documents. "He'll never know. I've got a plan," she said.

"Why are you smiling?" asked Plum nervously. "I'm not going to like this, am I?"

"You don't have to like it. You just have to do a tiny bit of magic."

22

Bot stormed into the briefing carriage where Plum and Wrench waited. "How does setting fire to Flemington's rooms fit in with the modus operandi of stealth and guile?" he bawled.

Wrench glared at the mechanoid. The moment she'd seen the contents of the wardrobe she'd known she was taking the documents; there had been no other option. When she'd been strapped in the electric chair Flemington had shown that the regulators had a file on her. However, what she'd retrieved from the wardrobe went well beyond the call of duty and was straying very much into the behaviour of a lunatic.

Besides, who was Bot to lecture her? He'd blown up the Epochryphal Brotherhood's manor house without a second thought. He'd nearly blown them up too in the process. At least she'd thought her plan through. Like the best machines, it possessed a simple elegance.

"No one saw us go into his rooms, so that was stealth," said Wrench.

"And the guile?" asked Bot.

"Plum left sooty shapes on the wall like the ones in the Minster and the church. Flemington will think it's a remarkable like Carwyn seeking revenge. And while he's busy chasing his tail we can find out what he's up to," said Wrench.

Bot loomed over Plum, who concentrated on the cat curled in his lap. The strange-looking beast purred contentedly.

"What is that thing and why is it on my train?" said Bot.

"She's not a thing." Plum toyed with a silver name tag on the madder-red collar the cat wore. "She's called Lady Lovelace and I rescued her from the fire."

"The fire which I thought you were merely ineffectual in stopping but are apparently complicit in starting."

Plum scratched Lady Lovelace behind the ears. "I didn't have any choice. Wrench made me do it," he mumbled.

"You were the senior regulator on the scene. I trusted you to keep her out of trouble," said Bot accusingly.

"Stop being such a big brass baby." Wrench slapped Bot's arm. "You sent us in there to gather information and that's what we did." Plum swallowed loudly beside her, his body trembling. Wrench clenched her teeth and squared her shoulders towards Bot. She didn't care that the robot could crush her with a single blow; she wasn't scared of him. Being in charge didn't give him the right to bully them. Plum might not stand up to Bot, but she refused to submit. He was only a machine, and she controlled machines, not the other way around.

Bot raised a hand and Plum flinched backwards, his arms curling protectively over Lady Lovelace. The carriage lights flickered. Wrench remained staunch. The robot rapped a finger against his skorpidium-carbide skull. "I'm not actually brass," he said.

"On the inside you are." When Wrench had reached into him on the way to the Minster, the brass gears and clockwork had felt shiny and bright, glowing with a sheen she'd not encountered before; not until she'd visited the Artificer.

Bot's eyes narrowed. The seconds stretched out for an eternity, then his face broke into a smile. "And you are skorpidium-carbide all the way through, Brasswitch."

Suddenly aware that she'd been holding her breath, Wrench inhaled sharply. Her pulse slowed, and the carriage's lights shone steady again. She glanced at Plum, who had gone deathly white and looked like he might spew. A feeling of guilt rose up in her. She railed against Bot's bullying, yet she wasn't any better. The thaumagician had been deadset against her plan to burn Flemington's rooms and she'd intimidated him into complying. She wanted to tell Bot how brilliant Plum had been in localising the burning, so it hadn't spread to the adjacent properties or the sweet shop below, but she sensed a line had now been drawn under the incident, so she held her tongue.

"Brasswitch, Ops room one is now yours. Take what you've found and recreate it exactly as it was."

Wrench looked at the mess of papers and string laid out on the desk. "I'll try, but I only saw it briefly. It may not be an exact replica."

"Plum will help you. He has a knack for remembering things. Isn't that right, Plummy?"

"Master Tranter says it's a photographic memory. I don't really see pictures. It's more like patterns, Sir."

"I don't need the details – just get it done. I expect a full briefing in the morning."

"A briefing?" said Wrench. "We should drag Flemington in for questioning and find out what he's up to."

"And how's that conversation going to go?" said Bot. "Please don't tell the Grand Cabal but we illegally searched your lodgings before burning them down and kidnapping your cat. However, if you'd like to answer a few questions for us that would be splendid."

"He's up to no good. Look at what we've found."

"Which is precisely the point of the briefing. We need to continue our investigations and find some evidence we can actually use. Cabal Thirteen survives on the goodwill of the Grand Cabal. I'm not jeopardising it on a witch-hunt. Even if the person we're hoping to burn is Flemington."

✿

Wrench pinned the last string in place and stood back. The corkboard covered one wall of the Ops room, which was a triple-locked train compartment not much bigger than her sleeper cabin. "What do you think?" she said.

Coddled by Plum, a loud thrum issued from Lady Lovelace. "It's good. Maybe not aligned precisely as it was in Flemington's rooms but it's all joined up the same."

Plum was right: the Ops room board was bigger than the wardrobe and so where the paperwork and photographs had previously overlapped they'd had the luxury of spreading them out. Corners of documents that hadn't seen daylight for years were now revealed. Rectangles of white paper, in otherwise yellowed documents, stood out proud with their crisp dark blue ink. Wrench stared at the discoloured documents and an idea began to form. She moved closer to the board, squinting at the photographs and papers.

"What are you doing?" asked Plum.

"Flemington's been documenting me for years, ever since the crash of the *Drake*. Based on the fade of the documents I can build up a timeline of his research and determine what his most recent activity was. What he's most interested in."

Plum nodded, seemingly impressed, then reached inside his jacket and pulled out a battered black journal. "Or we could just look in his investigation diary," he said.

Wrench grabbed the book. "Where did you get this?"

"It was beside his bed. I pocketed it before I torched the place."

"And you didn't tell me because?"

"I didn't want to." The corners of Plum's mouth turned down and he shuffled his feet.

Was this another example of the thaumagician trying to obstruct her? Probably not. Despite having only known Plum for a short time, she'd come to think of him as a petulant child. "Are you sulking with me?"

"Bot hasn't forgotten this, you know. It'll be held over us until we retire."

"Not if we get the better of Flemington; find out what he's up to."

Plum motioned towards the journal. "So, what is he up to?"

Wrench turned to the last page in the diary. "Astrology," she said.

23

"Astrology is phooey." Bot's voiced boomed around the Ops room, trapped by the reflective soundproofing on the walls. Octavia placed tentacles in her ears and Plum pulled the hood on his suit over his head.

As an engineer, Wrench had always been sceptical too. Astrologists were charlatans who played on people's superstitions, making ludicrous predictions based on the alignments of the planets. However, after the things she'd witnessed over the past few days she wasn't ruling anything out. Maybe they did have some arcane knowledge passed down through the generations, and one man's madness was another man's genius. She glanced at the bleary-eyed Plum. He wasn't a morning person, although to be fair he wasn't really an afternoon person either. An air of grumpiness hung around him like a cloud over a cricket match. He scowled, seeming to blame Wrench for the fact that he'd been dragged out of bed at the ungodly hour of eight in the morning.

The thaumagician was living proof that the world was more complex than she'd always believed. After all, she'd thought witchcraft and magic were nothing but folktales. And she'd been wrong about that.

"My horoscope appears to be part of his obsession," said Wrench. "I was born on August the fourth when Bailey's comet was closest to the earth. The comet has a fourteen-year cycle so it's close again this year. Although, why that has any significance I have no idea."

Wrench had stayed up late into the previous night scouring Flemington's notes but either by design or accident they were somewhat cryptic and subject to a good degree of interpretation. They also suffered from the bias of Flemington's own skewed world view, as exampled by the last entry in his diary.

The aberration Chattox claims to be affected by the comet; was WCH affected too and what will happen when the comet returns? Leech has been sniffing about. I'm sure he knows something. Damn Thirteen and its freaks will be the death of us all. Perhaps the astrologers at the Celestines can confirm my fears and give me the evidence to act.

Octavia flicked through the investigation log. "The last entry is two days before Flemington arrested

Wrench. Perhaps he found what he was looking for at the Celestines."

"The Celestines are a cult of lunatics," said Bot.

"I believe they refer to themselves as a religion," corrected Octavia.

"Cult, religion, they're just words. You can't trust people who claim to predict the future from the astrological positioning of the stars and planets."

"The future," echoed Wrench. The Epochryphal Brotherhood had been trying to view the future and Flemington had paid them a visit too. It wasn't documented in his investigation log, but the monk Bot rescued from the manor house had mentioned a badly burned regulator making enquiries. What was Flemington up to? And what was his obsession with Wrench and the future? "Are there remarkables among the Celestines?" she asked.

"Aberrations? We don't think so," said Bot. "Octavia, you've visited them before. What do you think?"

"I didn't sense anything more than the background level of aberration you find on any street in York," said Octavia. "Although, they did claim that their horoscopes could predict the birth of aberrations."

Bot's gears ground, making a noise like a snort. "I'd like to see that in the papers. Gemini; Mars is in its first ascendancy and the alignment with Jupiter means you are going to meet a tall dark stranger – who can breathe fire."

"We don't understand why some people are born aberrations; who's to say the planets don't play some part?"

said Octavia. "No one understood the effects of the moon on the tides until Newton's gravitational theories."

"All right. All right. My mind will remain open to all possibilities," said Bot, rapping his knuckles against his head. "Tomorrow we'll visit the Celestines. Today, I've been summoned to the Grand Cabal and I'm hoping it's nothing to do with your incursion at Flemington's."

"Nobody saw us. We were careful," said Wrench.

"Oh, you were the epitome of discretion, torching his place and making snowstorms in the street."

Wrench's head snapped around to look at Plum. He shrugged sheepishly.

"Don't blame him. He's fast becoming our best thaumagician. I doubt even Master Tranter could do what Plum did with that fire." Bot pointed at Wrench. "You, on the other hand, need to get a hold of your magic. So today, and indeed every day, you will practise."

✿

Anger coiled inside of Wrench like a nest of vipers. Plum had betrayed her. Octavia had been right to pass on Pippa's concerns about the thaumagician; this was another example of him trying to thwart her.

Plum skulked behind a sackcloth target on the weapons range. He clutched his arms defensively across his chest and stared at the ground.

"I can't believe you dobbed me in," said Wrench, prodding Plum in the shoulder. She hardly touched him, yet the force of the blow knocked him off-balance and he tumbled to the floor. Plum stared up at her with a look of wounded hurt in his eyes and her anger transformed to shame. She reached out a hand to help him back up. "I'm sorry."

Plum stood shakily. "That's twice in two days you've knocked me to the ground."

"To be fair, the first time I saved you from a crossbow bolt."

"And the second?"

"Saved me from doing something worse. I didn't mean to hurt you. I didn't realise I'd pushed you that hard."

"You didn't. Like I told you, the magic weakens me. Newton says for every action there's an equal and opposite reaction. Well, for every spell there's an equal and opposite price to pay. You can't create energy; it must come from somewhere, and the place it comes from is me. I'll be alright in a couple of days but controlling that blaze has left me spent."

Wrench remembered the light-headed euphoria she'd experienced when she accidentally made it snow, and her fatigue climbing the stairs afterwards. She'd done no more than a few seconds of magic and it had wearied her. Plum had controlled the blaze for well over an hour while the fire brigade brought the inferno under control.

No wonder he was exhausted. "I had no idea. I guess I don't have an idea about a lot of things," she said, pulling up a chair from against the wall. "Take the weight off your pins while I practise."

"Thanks, I will." Plum slumped onto the chair. "Try to recreate the feeling you had in Humbug and Mints and then focus on drawing moisture out of the air."

From her pocket Wrench pulled out the bag of sweets. She popped a pineapple lozenge in her mouth and rolled it around, savouring the bitter flavour on her tongue. She visualised the water in the air, tiny particles, joining together, forming raindrops, but to no avail. "It's not working," she said disappointedly. "The snow must have been a fluke."

"It will happen," said Plum. "Close your eyes. Imagine you're back in the sweet shop now."

Wrench forced her eyes shut and tried to remember.

"Think back to the smell of the shop, the sound of Humbug's voice, the taste of the sweet, what you felt the very moment it started to snow."

Wrench recalled how she'd screwed up her face when the sour sherbet seeped into her mouth. She bit down on the lozenge, cracking it, and her tongue recoiled against the bitterness of the powder fizzing free.

"Oiy!" shouted Plum.

Wrench's eyes sprang open. A mini-storm blustered in the air. Water fell in torrents from a dark cloud, soaking the thaumagician. Wrench swallowed the remains of the lozenge and ran her tongue over her teeth. The rain cloud dissipated, along with the bitter taste in her mouth.

A weakness overcame her, like when she'd climbed the stairs to Flemington's lodgings. Her legs trembling, she pulled up another chair and dropped onto it. She felt exhausted and elated at the same time. She'd done her second piece of magic, and this time it was no accident. Admittedly she hadn't intended for it to rain on Plum, but at least she was finally making progress. A smile crept onto her face.

"It's not funny," said Plum, shaking a sodden sleeve.

"I wasn't smiling at you," said Wrench. "And it is a little bit funny."

"Not for me. I can't even warm myself up. I'm all out of magic."

"You could teach me how to do fire," suggested Wrench.

Plum shook his head. "Not a chance. My skin's waterproof; it's not flameproof. I'm not teaching you anything dangerous until you have better control."

Taking another lozenge from the bag, Wrench said, "I don't actually need fire, I've got a better idea." She bit down on the sweet, cracking its hard sugar shell and waited for the sherbet to hit her tongue. The feeling of magic fresh in her mind, she felt the surge of energy building even before the tart taste enveloped her mouth. Chemistry was like a machine, a minuscule complex one but even so the elements worked together to produce a result. She focused on Plum's clothes, imagining the water particles. She'd somehow drawn them out of the air to make a rain cloud, so she could draw them out of the material. She pictured a giant hydrophilic magnet pulling the particles away from Plum. Lines of force emanated from the imaginary magnet but instead of attracting ferrous atoms they exhibited a pull only on the combined elements of hydrogen and oxygen: H_2O

Plum's jacket fluttered, seemingly drawn towards the theoretical water magnet, and then a watery jacket-shaped ghost broke free of his clothes, drifting away from the thaumagician. Plum ran his fingers over his velvet sleeves and a mixture of delight and amazement brightened his face.

A buzzing filled Wrench's ears. She ignored it, concentrating on her spell. The sound grew louder, joined by an unpleasant chittering, like a thousand rubbing spider legs. Her body ached as if it was stretching, being pulled in every direction, being pulled in directions that didn't exist. A swirling violet haze marred her vision, but not enough to miss the change in Plum's expression to one of horror.

24

Wrench couldn't breathe. Slithering silver tentacles coiled around her torso, tightening, crushing. A scream died in her throat. She had no air, metallic suckers constricting her neck. Plum surged from his seat and drove his shoulder into her. The water jacket disintegrated and splashed to the floor. Wrench's chair toppled backwards, and she clattered to the scuffed wood planking. The fall knocked the remaining wind from her lungs and she choked, still unable to breathe, her mouth opening and closing like a freshly landed fish.

Cowering on all fours, his skeletal body convulsing, Plum puked. The acrid scent of vomit acted like smelling salts and Wrench gasped a breath of vile, tainted air. She spluttered and took another breath. The tentacles were gone, the only sound her ragged breathing and Plum's moaning.

"I hurt my arm. Again." Plum wiped his sleeve across his face.

Wrench's body wouldn't function. Her arms trembled, drained of all strength and her legs twitched uncontrollably. With supreme effort, she twisted her neck to look at Plum. "Is that normal?"

The thaumagician's face was corpse grey and covered in a thin sheen of perspiration. "About as far from normal as it gets."

"What happened? It was …" Wrench swallowed, trying not to think of the nightmare chittering and constricting tentacles. "… purgatory."

"Not purgatory," said Plum, "maybe somewhere similar."

"What do you mean?"

"I think you created a rupture."

A rupture? Breaking the barrier between worlds. How could that be? There were weak points from the original catastrophe, gates now sealed, or at least netted as Bot had put it, but you couldn't create new ones.

"That's not possible."

Plum pressed his fingertips against her cheek, as if he wanted to keep contact with her, keep her in this world, the real world. "Technically, it is possible. Although, normally it takes a huge amount of effort, planning, occult knowledge, sacrifices, ancient artefacts, and an entire evil hermetic order. You shouldn't be able to punch through to the dark dimensions by accident."

"No. It can't have been. We're both exhausted from magic. We probably just imagined it."

"It was real all right. I couldn't see it," Plum shuddered, "but I sensed it. Something from elsewhere trying to pull you through."

Wrench's hands went to her throat. "I felt tentacles grabbing me."

"Yep. That'll be it. If it's any consolation, I don't think the door was fully open."

"How do you know?"

"Because York hasn't been destroyed in a mindless orgy of gibbering violence."

Some strength finally returned to Wrench's arms and she forced herself into a sitting position. She'd welcomed the fact that at Thirteen she could be herself, no longer having to keep her powers a secret. However, if Plum was right, if she had caused a rupture, that was something else. Something she didn't want anyone to know. "Don't tell Bot, please."

"I wasn't going to." Plum groaned and eased himself next to her.

"You dobbed me in about the magic at Humbug and Mints."

Plum wrung his hands together. "Yeah, well, Bot needed to know so he could decide how to deal with it."

Wrench supposed that was true. If they were in

another tight squeeze, like when they'd faced Carwyn at the church and she started firing off random magic, it could be catastrophic. Then again, surely creating a rupture was far more dangerous, so why wasn't Plum going to tell him?

"And he doesn't need to know about this?" she asked.

"If he finds out, he'll kill you."

Wrench inhaled sharply. "Kill me? I thought he wanted to give remarkables like us a chance?"

"You're too dangerous to let live. He may like you, but he has to think of the possible consequences."

"And what about you?"

A tired smile curved Plum's lips. "I like you too. And I'm trying very hard not to think about the possible consequences."

"You won't tell."

"They'd have to torture it out of me," said Plum.

❁

Drained by the magic, Wrench spent the remainder of the day in bed. Her head thumped like a steam hammer and cramps racked her muscles. Livid purple bruises spotted her arms, torso and neck, a solid reminder that unlike on top of the tower, the metal tentacles had been far from imaginary. There was no "net" over the rupture she'd created, and something had reached through.

Perhaps Flemington had been right to try and electrocute her in the cell. Like Plum had said, she was too dangerous to let live. The regulator believed that as a child she was powerful enough to crash the *Drake*, killing her parents and the train's crew. The suspicion that Flemington was correct had wheedled its way into Wrench's mind. She'd accidentally killed seven people that day, but that was trifling compared to the tens of thousands that might die if she accidentally opened a rupture.

She should really confess to Bot, come clean whatever the consequences. Only, for the first time since the crash of the *Drake*, she felt like she belonged.

A knock at the door drew her from her thoughts.

"I've brought you some dinner," called Octavia.

"It's open," replied Wrench.

Octavia let herself in and deposited a silver tray of scrumptious-smelling food on the table. Wrench had been too lethargic all day to eat. Gazing now at the tender pink beef, golden roast potatoes and fresh mint peas, she realised how hungry she was. Her mouth watered, and a distant memory of sour sweets tingled her tongue. She clenched her teeth together and pushed all thoughts of magic from her mind. The rich aroma of the steaming gravy reached her nose. She grabbed the knife and fork and hacked free a succulent chunk of beef.

"Plum told me what you've been through and I thought you'd need some sustenance," said Octavia.

Gravy dripped from the skewered beef, the fork

paused halfway to Wrench's mouth. Had Plum dobbed her in again? He'd promised not to tell but maybe that was just a ruse to get away from her, scared of what she might do. Her gaze travelled to the plate. Was this her last supper? The condemned prisoner's final meal before she was retired?

"Magic practice always used to exhaust Plum," continued Octavia, "Although, your constitution is somewhat more robust than his, I would venture to say."

Wrench's shoulders sagged with relief and she bit the beef from the fork. Octavia didn't know.

"What don't I know?" said Octavia.

Damn! She'd forgotten about Octavia's extrasensory perception. Just how limited was it? Wrench tried to force away all thoughts of the weapons range, determined not to think about the rupture and the tentacles. The more she tried to ignore it, the more it came to mind. It was like the old trick when you told someone not to think of a pink elephant and then that was all they could think about.

"Oh! That's what I don't know." Octavia's hand went to her mouth. "And I'm not talking about the pink elephants."

Wrench let her fork clatter to the plate. "Please don't tell him."

Octavia smiled. "One thing you become very good at when you have an aberration like mine is keeping secrets." She reached out a hand and pulled Wrench's collar away from her neck. Purple welts coloured the skin where the tentacle had grabbed her. "You're going to need a better way of covering that up. I'll make you a cravat to match your dungarees. Does it hurt?"

"It feels like splash burns from welding," said Wrench. "Only much worse."

"Nasty. I've got some cream that will help with those. I'm a lot better these days, but when I was younger, and angrier, I could pack a hell of a sting," she said, wiggling her tentacles. "Bot was immune, so he tended to bear the brunt of my teenage tantrums."

"You knew Bot as a teenager?"

"I don't think Bot's ever been a teenager."

"No. I meant–"

Octavia stroked Wrench's brow with a tentacle. "I'm kidding with you. Yes, Bot recruited me to Thirteen when I was your age. To be honest it was a miracle I'd survived that long. It's hard to hide an aberration like mine. Even in a circus."

"You were in a circus?"

"It was the only way my mother could think to keep me safe. Carnies have always been treated as outsiders and freaks, they accepted me without question."

"And you were part of their freak show?"

Octavia raised her eyebrows. "No. I was a fortune teller. With an ability like mine I knew what people most wanted and fed it back to them in the form of a prophecy."

Wrench mentally kicked herself for making such a prejudiced presumption.

"It's all right," said Octavia. "Everyone always assumes I was the amazing octopus woman."

"It's not all right, is it though? I'm as bad as the people I'm fighting against."

"When you can read people's minds you soon realise that everyone is prejudiced about something." Octavia rested a tentacle on Wrench's hand. "The important thing is to rationalise those negative thoughts and not let them influence your behaviour. You, my dear, have done better than that. You're trying to change things."

"I've not changed anything. I can't even change myself."

"But you will. I've known Bot since I was a child and I have never seen him treat anyone like he treats you. He knows you're so very special."

It was difficult to imagine Octavia as a child. The woman before her was so elegant and confident. How old was Octavia now? Thirty-five? Forty? Wrench wasn't very good at judging age, but it must have been some twenty years ago. That meant Bot had been saving remarkables since before she was born. How could that be? The technology to build a mechanoid like Bot simply didn't exist back then. Heck, she wasn't even sure it existed now. The mechs used by the regulators to bolster their ranks were masterpieces of engineering but even they weren't a patch on Bot.

"I'm thirty-seven if you must know," said Octavia. "Bot is considerably older."

"That's impossible."

"You're impossible. I'm impossible. Yet here we are living in an age of enlightenment where science tries to explain everything but serves more to shine a light on how little we understand. Bot is an enigma for sure, but many thousands of aber–, remarkables owe their lives to him."

"Plum says Bot will kill me if he finds out what I can do."

"Life has not been easy for Plum. He's suffered more than most and tends to have a somewhat bleak outlook."

"You think Bot would understand? You think he'd let me be?" She didn't want to leave Thirteen, to be alone again. Despite the danger, and the antagonism from the QRF, she was desperate to stay.

"I've seen Bot do terrible things. Things I wouldn't do or couldn't do. Some people think he's heartless, but they don't know him. He's tasked with protecting humankind and that responsibility comes with a cost."

"You haven't answered my question."

"I haven't. Perhaps it's a question only you and Bot can answer."

"Or perhaps tomorrow the Celestines will be able to see my future," said Wrench.

"Perhaps they will. Stranger things have happened." Octavia groomed her eyebrows with a tentacle. "In fact, they happen daily when you work for Thirteen."

25

The Astrologium was set atop a large hill at the edge of the York University campus. Some claimed the Celestines had chosen the location in the hope of gaining some reflected credibility from the university, astrology having fallen from being a science to a superstition over the last century. However, on days like today where a heavy smog from the mills and factories blanketed the city, Wrench could see another reason for the choice of position.

Rising above the clouds, like the isle of Avalon, poked a grassy hilltop and thrusting skywards from its centre was the Astrologium. A multitude of articulated telescopes protruded from the spheroidal, steel-plated structure, giving it the appearance of a giant sea-mine. But they were mere toys compared to "the Cyclops", a massive brass cylinder that extended fifty feet above the roof. At its end, a verdigris dome protected the "eye" of the Cyclops, a diamond polished lens imported from Italy. The Celestines claimed the telescope was the most powerful in the country, a fact hotly disputed by the Royal Observatory in Greenwich.

Wrench had previously only seen the Astrologium from afar when the apprentices had visited the university. Up close it was a truly magnificent piece of engineering. She hoped that once their formal business was completed Bot might allow her time to inspect it more closely.

"Who are we here to see?" she asked.

"Magi Taurus," said Bot.

They broke free of the last few wisps of smog and into hazy sunshine, the warm rays pleasant on Wrench's face after the dirty damp fog. "That's bull, right?"

"You said it."

"I was referring to the star sign. Taurus is represented by the bull."

Bot pointed to a toppled statue of a lady that lay in pieces adjacent to the riveted steel front door. "St Celestine the third. Burned at the stake for suggesting the earth went around the sun. She was a true scientist. I wonder what she'd think of this lot here?" Bot knocked on the Astrologium door. The dull clank of his knuckles echoed inside.

A raw-boned man, whose only resemblance to a bull was the way he snorted as he heaved open the heavy door, greeted them. "Welcome to the Celestines. We're delighted to once again welcome the regulators to our humble order."

He ran fingers like winter twigs over his slicked-back widow's peak. His gaunt cheeks tightened, coercing lips thin as string beans into a smile. The hardness in his eyes suggested he was anything but pleased to see them. Then again, very few people were pleased to see the regulators. They were like the "pure collectors" who scoured the streets for dog poo and sold it to the tanneries for use in leather working. It was generally acknowledged that they were needed, but that didn't necessarily mean you wanted to meet one.

"I'm Bot. This is Brasswitch and we'd be obliged if you could answer a few questions for us."

"Of course," said Magi Taurus, making no move to welcome them in.

"And we'd like to see the orrery," added Wrench. Above her, in the centre of the spheroidal hall that made up the Astrologium, Wrench sensed a machine of marvellous ingenuity.

Magi Taurus looked somewhat taken aback. "Will you be requiring us to run similar programs as your colleague?"

Bot leant closer. "No, we don't need–"

"No, we don't need similar programs; we need exactly the same programs," said Wrench. She suspected Bot didn't know what the Orrery was or what it might tell them. She only had a vague idea herself, having seen a much smaller version at the science museum in York. They couldn't be sure of Flemington's purpose in visiting the Celestines, but finding out exactly what they'd researched for him may provide some answers.

Magi Taurus looked Bot up and down. "You're too big for the stairs. We'll have to use the service lift."

He took them around the side of the building to where a steel caged elevator shaft ran up the back of the spheroidal tower. Magi Taurus hauled the elevator cage door open and beckoned them inside.

Bot stepped into the flimsy cage, which shook unnervingly. The bearings creaked in complaint and Wrench couldn't help but push her mind into the workings of the contraption to reassure herself. The gears were somewhat worn, as was the hoist cable, but there was no obvious danger.

Taurus pulled a lever and the lift groaned upwards, the elevator shaft vibrating ominously. The cage jolted to a halt and they exited onto an enclosed gantry that led to a set of heavy steel doors that matched the curve of the Astrologium structure. The doors slid open in a cloud of steam and Wrench stepped into a masterpiece of engineering.

An iron walkway ran around the edge of the spherical cavern. On the black steel walls points of light glistened, mapping the constellations. At the centre of the immense structure was the orrery in all its magnificence.

A glowing glass orb representing the sun appeared to float in the middle of the cavern. Surrounding it, supported on clockwork-driven spars, were the planets, each scaled proportionally and minutely detailed. Around the planets, driven by more intermeshing clockwork, were their moons.

"You've made a model of our solar system?" said Bot with a distinct lack of wonder.

"It's more than a model; it's a computational analogue." Magi Taurus pointed to a shining red ball that hung suspended near the earth. "The comet is a new addition. It took our astroneers several months to integrate the clockwork correctly once the mathstrologers had detailed the calculations."

"And what does it compute?" said Bot.

"The future, the probability of events, the planetary effects on our existence. It depends on what you ask, and indeed how you ask it."

"What did Captain Flemington ask?" said Wrench.

"I'll have to get his programs to be exact. I seem to remember he was interested in two particular dates. One in the past and one in the future."

Wrench suspected she already knew the dates. Her date of birth and her fourteenth birthday, less than a week away.

Magi Taurus led them around the gantry. Wrench stuck close to the rail, staring in awe at the giant planets and moons arrayed beneath her. Though she wasn't consciously probing the clockwork that controlled them, the sheer splendour of the engineering contrived to leak into her brain, like golden threads waiting to be pulled. The threads congregated at the console where Taurus now stood. He depressed the chunky metal keys on the typewriter, spelling out Flemington, and slid the carriage across, sending the instruction. A metal cradle disappeared into a long brass tube, drawn away into another room by a cog and ratchet mechanism.

"It will take a few moments while it searches for any results," said Taurus.

"What else can you tell us about Captain Flemington's visit?" asked Bot.

"Well, I remember being somewhat surprised. I thought at first he perhaps suspected us of witchcraft. We believe our methods are scientifically robust but there have been many critics in recent years."

"Captain Flemington didn't show any scepticism?" asked Wrench.

"None at all. He was delighted with the results. Well, delighted, and somewhat worried."

The cradle returned from the tube with two stiff white cards slotted into it. Each card was perforated with an elaborate array of holes.

"Here we are. Captain Flemington's cards," said Taurus.

"These are his results?" asked Bot.

"Oh no. This is his program. We must run it through the orrery to get the results."

Taurus fed the cards into a narrow slot on the console. Clockwork whirred, and two brass flags popped out from a heavy iron rod at the side of the machine.

The golden threads in Wrench's mind coiled around the iron rod. This was it, the control that would initiate something both wonderful and terrifying. She wasn't sure she believed in astrology any more than Bot, but whether she believed it or not she was certain the results were going to pertain to her. In Flemington's eyes at least.

"Can I pull the control lever?" she asked. It was only right that she should.

"It's called the taskbar," said Taurus, curtly. "And no one but the Celestines are supposed to operate the orrery."

Bot growled and rested a heavy hand on Taurus's shoulder, causing the magi's knees to bend.

Taurus whimpered and gestured to the console. "I think we can make an exception for the regulators."

Wrench heaved on the bar, dragging it downwards. Gears turned, releasing the massive mainspring, and the orrery came to life.

Along the gantry the lift clattered back into place and the doors rattled open.

"It appears we have visitors." Magi Taurus snorted. "No matter how many times they've seen it before, the other magi still can't resist watching the wonderful mystery of the heavens made real."

The three figures that emerged from the lift were not magi. Some would argue they weren't even human.

26

The heavy booted footsteps of the hulking giant at the centre of the aberrations shook the metal gantry. The right-most of the three, a woman with what appeared to be long chains instead of hair, stepped onto the steel sides of the Astrologium. With no apparent effort, she walked up the metal walls.

Wrench pushed her mind towards the woman and for a moment the lines of magnetic force she was controlling that allowed her to scale the metal came into focus. Then the same oily feeling she'd experienced at the church poured into her conscious, clouding her vision.

The third of the aberrations leapt onto the rail that ran around the gantry. He gripped the thin metal strip with talon-like claws that protruded from the bottom of his pinstriped trousers. What at first glance had appeared to be a multicoloured cloak morphed into feathered wings. With a screech, Parrot-Man launched himself from the rail and soared over the orrery.

Bot held out his regulator star. "Stop right there," he commanded.

The hulk ignored him and raised his right arm, the end of which was shaped like a giant steel hammerhead.

Bot slung the star. Hammer-Hulk batted it away with ease and it clattered over the gantry's side. "I hate it when that happens," said Bot and stormed to meet his adversary.

Hammer-Hulk swung his arm. Bot blocked it, staggering backwards under the blow.

"You pack a punch, I'll give you that," said Bot, drawing back his arm. "But can you take one?" His fist shot forward and struck Hammer-Hulk in his metal chest plate with a thunderous clank. The man-monster flinched but he didn't give ground. Instead he slammed his other hand, which was protected by an iron gauntlet, into Bot's side.

Chain-Head sprang from the wall and landed on the gantry in front of Wrench. "You killed a friend of ours," she snarled, baring rusted iron teeth.

Wrench cursed that she hadn't worn her bracers of Zeus. There hadn't seemed a need; it was supposed to be a simple interview. She tried to think of lemons, but her mouth was dry, and she knew magic was out of the question. It was probably a blessing. At least this foe was human, unlike the things she might drag from the other dimension.

Several strands of Chain-Head's hair spun in slow, menacing circles. Wrench backed away. One of the chains flew at the console, smashing into the taskbar, stopping the orrery. The chain withdrew, and another lashed out, thudding into Wrench's leg. Pain shot through her thigh. She stumbled, her leg deadened. A gash in her dungarees gaped open where the sharpened chain had ripped through them. Only the armoured kevlaris lining had prevented the razor-like links shredding her flesh.

Chain-Head hissed and lashed out with another chain. Metal slammed into Wrench's leg again. The heavy links encircled her thigh and dragged her over. She crashed to the gantry, her face smashing into the metalwork grille. Hot needles of pain spiked her cheek. There was no time to worry about her injuries; she had to defend herself or she was done for.

Chain-Head bared her teeth and the iron shaped into needle-like points. Three chains drew backwards, plaiting themselves into a rigid bar, the end of which formed a fist of razor linked metal. "We're not supposed to kill you, but the master never said we couldn't mess you up a bit."

The fist flew at her. Wrench rolled sideways, and it smacked into the gantry. She glanced at Bot, who was still trading blows with Hammer-Hulk.

"He ain't going to help you, darling," said

Chain-Head, pulling back the metal fist. The links around Wrench's leg uncoiled and snaked up her body to grip her neck. The sharp edges pinched her skin but the kevlaris cravat Octavia had given her prevented worse damage.

Wrench glared at Chain-Head. "I don't need his help." Her jaw tightened. She remembered the first time she'd been picked on at the coachworks, strong hands pinning her down while they'd smeared axle grease over her face. She'd been powerless then but not now. She had no bracers and no magic, but she wasn't defenceless. She'd controlled the electromagnetic fields on the crackle-tram's motors and she could do the same here, with or without the oily interference.

She forced her mind through the sludgy resistance, and just like when they'd emerged from the smog to see the Astrologium, the haze cleared, and the lines of magnetic force came sharply into view. Driven more by anger than fear, she concentrated on the chain securing her neck. With a crack like breaking ice the end link split apart, the two halves clattering to the floor.

Chain-Head stared, unbelieving, at the broken pieces. Wrench seized the advantage. Shattered metal showered the gantry, the chain splitting link by link all the way to its root. Chain-Head's hand went to her scalp and she screamed, silvery blood leaking between her fingers.

Wrench clambered to her feet, directing the chains that formed the metal fist to uncurl. Chain-Head took a step backwards then ran. Wrench reshaped the lines of magnetic force, yanking at the fleeing remarkable's iron-soled boots. Chain-Head sprawled onto the gantry, her hair rattling against the metalwork.

A whoosh of air buffeted Wrench's back then taloned feet slammed into the top of her head. She stumbled, her glasses knocked free of her face. Her kevlaris bowler hat lessened the blow but still she sank to her knees, dazed. Ahead she saw the blurry form of Chain-Head fleeing, then an eruption of smoke blossomed around Bot.

Wrench scrambled for her glasses. A starburst crack ruined one of the lenses. She put them on regardless; she was blind without them.

Bot stomped from the sooty clouds, his eyes angry. A large dent graced his shoulder and a wisp of steam leaked from the joint. "That bloody great parrot dropped smoke bombs on me and then scarpered." He reached out a hand to Wrench, the sound of gears grinding beneath his armour. "Are you all right?" he said.

Was she all right? In the heat of the moment she had no idea if she'd been injured. Blood clung to her face from where she'd smashed into the grilled floor, the bruise on her leg left by the chain throbbed, and she'd cricked her neck when Parrot-Man had hit her. "Better than you by the looks of things," she said.

Bot shrugged, the mechanics of his injured shoulder grating. "I've had worse."

"Do you want me to see if I can fix that?"

"Only if you want your skull crushed, Brasswitch. Where's Taurus?"

Wrench looked around. She'd forgotten all about the magi. From behind a ribbed steel door beneath the console she heard a faint snivel. She tugged the door open. Taurus cowered inside the cabinet, his arms shielding his head.

"Don't hurt me. I didn't tell the regulators anything," he cried.

27

Bot hauled Taurus from the cabinet. "Maybe it's just my suspicious regulator mind but that sounded very much like an admission of guilt."

Still on his knees, Taurus grabbed Wrench's arm. "I'm sorry. I didn't mean to lie. They said they'd kill me. Don't let him send me to the tower. Please!"

When Flemington had come for Wrench on the crackle-tram, she'd been terrified, and nobody had raised a finger to help. Her first instinct was to console Taurus but the blood on her face reminded her that the magi had hidden, leaving her to face Chain-Head alone. She pulled her arm free. "It's not the tower you need to worry about. It's the dungeons beneath."

Steam vented from Bot's back. He leant over the

magi. "You've got one chance. I want the whole truth, Taurus. And no bull."

"I told them you were coming. I had no choice." Taurus wrung his hands together. "They threatened to destroy the orrery unless I informed them if the regulators visited again."

"Who are they?" said Bot.

"I don't know. Truly I don't. The birdman visited about a month ago. He wanted me to run some programs."

"And you ran them?" said Wrench.

"Good gracious, no. I didn't want anything to do with an aberration, so I explained that the system was down while we installed some upgrades."

"Upgrades?" said Bot.

"We'd recently put in the new comet hardware, but the calibration wasn't correct. Magi Aries had been watching Mars; he's been quite obsessive ever since the discovery of the two moons, and from his calculations we were able to tweak the Mars firmware to 2.01 and that did the trick."

"I'm sorry I asked," said Bot. "Get back to the part about the visit."

"The birdman got angry, flapping his wings and squawking about how he'd expected us to be more understanding than all the others. In the end Magi Gemini had to escort him from the premises. A few days later he came back with the other aberrations you saw today. The one with the hammer smashed the statue outside and threatened to destroy the orrery if we didn't run the programs."

"And then you ran the programs?"

"Not immediately. We were still doing the upgrades, and threats or no threats the machine wouldn't work until they were finished. The aberrations insisted on staying around and as it happens their skills proved useful in completing the changes. The things that lady can do with metal are quite amazing."

Wrench's fingers went to her neck. "That's one way of putting it."

"Once we'd done a few test runs and the orrery was working properly I agreed to run their program. It wasn't like I had any choice."

"What was the result?"

"I don't know – they wouldn't let me see. All I know is they wanted to determine the odic force possessed by an individual when the comet was at its closest."

"Odic forces are a myth. Pseudoscience," said Bot.

"As indeed is astrology according to many in the scientific community, yet here you are quizzing me for the results of our orrery."

"Results you claim not to know," said Wrench.

Taurus's eyes shifted sideways, glancing at the console.

"Remember, I want the whole truth," said Bot. "Either now or at the tower, it's your choice."

"I don't know the result – but I do know the program."

For all its magnificence, the orrery was still just a computational machine. Give it the same start parameters and the results calculated would be identical. "Run the program," commanded Wrench.

Taurus positioned himself in front of the console. He removed the previous card, which had ejected when Chain-Head aborted the program, and placed it back in the cradle. His fingers trembling, he tapped out the details on the typewriter keys. C, H, A, T, T, O, X.

"Chattox? That's what you called the program?" said Bot.

Wrench recoiled at the name. She felt an irrational jealousy that her predecessor should have been run through the orrery too.

Taurus dispatched the cradle into the tube. "That's whose odic potential they wanted calculated."

Wrench's gaze swept over the intricacy of the orrery. Flemington had been interested in her connection to the comet, and the aberrations wanted to know about its effect on Chattox's power. They were both supposedly Brasswitches and that couldn't be coincidence.

The cradle returned, and Taurus removed the punched card and fed it into the machine. A flag on the taskbar flipped up and he heaved the lever downwards. Steam hissed from the pipes below the orrery and then a bell rang frantically.

Taurus rushed to the gantry rail and leant over, staring down at the mechanics below. "Oh no," he said.

Wrench joined him. She squinted through the one good lens on her glasses. Large black beetles crawled all over the intricate clockwork, their chitin-covered carcasses being crushed between the turning gears and cogs, jamming them solid.

"They've introduced bugs into the system. This is going to take days to fix," said Taurus.

28

Once again, Wrench waited in the sickbay. This time, however, it was Octavia giving her the moral support. With a gentle brush of her tentacles Octavia examined the cuts on Wrench's face. "How are you doing?"

"Much better than if I hadn't been wearing the outfit you made for me. Thanks."

"It didn't protect you enough."

"Nothing ever can." Wrench gestured towards Bot, who sat on an adjacent bed while Plum and a medic-mechanic tinkered with his armour. "He's made of skorpidium-carbide and he still got injured."

The clang of a hammer on metal rang around the sickbay.

"Ow!" complained Bot sulkily.

"Don't be such a baby," said Wrench. She'd not uttered a sound at the stinging pain she'd endured when they'd cleaned her cuts with liberal quantities of iodine. Neither had she bemoaned the large bruise on her thigh that bore the hue of an overripe damson. She wasn't even convinced Bot could experience pain.

"No, it's no good," said the medic-mechanic. "I can't get it off. You'll have to see the Artificer about this one."

Bot picked at the battered metal with his thick fingers. "We need to see him anyway. Brasswitch has to get her glasses fixed."

"Not fixed, replaced," said Wrench. "I'm thinking goggles. That way they won't fall off in a fight."

"Young ladies should stay out of fights," admonished Octavia.

"Away with you. I'm as good as any boy," said Wrench, looking at Plum. "Besides, it was a lady that attacked me."

Octavia extended a tentacle and prodded Bot in the chest. "You should have looked after her better."

The mechanoid gestured to the dent in his shoulder. "I was otherwise engaged at the time. We hadn't been expecting trouble. We'd only gone to ask a few questions."

"And what did you learn?" asked Octavia.

"Nothing," said Bot, sounding like a sulky child.

"No. We did learn things. We just don't know what they mean," said Wrench. "They're interested in the comet's effects on Brasswitches. They don't want me dead.

And Bot punches about as hard as Plum." Wrench nodded at Plum. "No offence."

Plum shrugged his skeletal frame. "None taken."

"What about me?" said Bot.

"It was meant to be offensive to you." Wrench ran a fingernail over the crack in the broken lens in her glasses.

"Right. I see how it is." Gears ground beneath Bot's injured shoulder. "Brasswitch and I are off to visit the Artificer. Next time I meet that Hammer-Hulk he's going to rue the day he put a dent in my–"

"Ego," said Octavia.

"Pride," said Wrench.

"Armour," corrected Bot.

Todkin cleared an intricate brass instrument from a stool in his workshop and gestured to Wrench. "Looks like you need a sit down. Has he been getting you into trouble?"

"He is trouble," said Wrench. Even seated she was taller than Todkin. He climbed up a set of steps and examined her broken glasses.

"Hmm. Easy enough to fix but as you suggest, maybe some goggles for work." From his tool belt he removed a set of curved callipers and placed the tip against either side of Wrench's head. He repeated the process at various points on her skull, jotting the measurements in a moleskin notebook.

"You have a small head. But, unlike Darwin or Broca, I believe size has no bearing on intelligence." He stepped down from the ladder. "If it did, you would surely be visiting a giant rather than ... well, rather than me."

"So, how long will it take, Clever Cogs?" said Bot.

"You can't hurry genius." His pencil scratching across the notebook, Todkin made some calculations.

With a rattle like a million broken watch parts, Bot dropped a sack that bulged in odd places onto the table. "But you can encourage it to go a bit faster."

Todkin's eyes widened. "Is that ..."

"An incentive for the expeditious creation of Brasswitch's goggles."

"Making the goggles is a simple task." Todkin added a sketch of the new eyewear to the notebook. "However, rather than replace what has already proved to be inadequate, there is an opportunity to include a number of advancements."

"Advancements?" said Wrench.

"Telescopic capabilities, close-up magnification, better vision at night, and oh so much more."

"It needs to be done quickly," said Bot.

"It needs to be done correctly," said Todkin.

"Make a simple replacement for now; you can tinker on an advanced pair later," said Bot.

Todkin held a hand over his heart. "I'm an artisan.

If you wanted simple, you could go to any metal-mickey fabricator."

"I'm a pragmatist. You'll get it done now if you want this." Bot jangled the sack.

Todkin winced. "Please don't do that." He grabbed a set of goggles from a cabinet and, using a complex hinged mechanism, attached an assortment of brass-rimmed lenses to the frame. He climbed the stepladder and placed the goggles on Wrench's head. "Look at Mendeleev's periodic table on the wall and tell me when it becomes clear."

Wrench focused on the centre of the table of known chemical elements. The letters Nb, Niobium, were readable, if somewhat fuzzy, but its atomic weight, written below it in smaller letters, was a blur. Todkin switched lenses in and out of position until suddenly the number 92.9 appeared crisp and sharp.

"That's it," said Wrench. "It's perfect." She'd worn glasses for as long as she could remember but the combination of lenses Todkin had used made the world so much clearer.

The Artificer jotted more notes in his book. "Excellent. I can grind new lenses for your glasses now. The goggles will take a few days."

"I thought we agreed you were going to make a quick pair?" said Bot.

"That is the quick pair." Todkin folded his arms.

A low mechanical grumble resonated from beneath Bot's armour, but he didn't push the issue further.

Todkin flipped his notebook closed and gestured to the dent on Bot's shoulder. "I suppose you want me to fix that too."

"If you wouldn't mind. It's grating somewhat, and it makes me look ugly."

"The armour I can fix. Your ugliness is beyond even my great talents," said Todkin, rummaging in a toolbox.

Steam shot from Bot's neck. "What is it today? Everyone's a critic."

The Artificer selected a set of splitter jaws and plugged them into a steam line dangling from the ceiling. "Come on then – let's have a look at you."

"What, now?"

"No, a week last Tuesday. Obviously now."

"But there's a lady present."

"And?"

Bot folded his arms. "I'm not getting undressed in front of Brasswitch."

"We're removing your outer armour. I hardly think that counts as undressing you."

"It still isn't decent. It's just weird."

"No, you're weird," said Todkin. "Send for an escort to take Wrench back to Thirteen. I'll get her glasses fixed while we wait."

29

A business-like knock rattled the front door of the workshop.

"Excellent timing." Todkin clicked the newly ground lenses into a frame then handed the glasses to Wrench.

She hooked them over her ears and surveyed the workshop. The wonderful creations that lined the walls sparkled bright, crisp and clear. Her previous glasses had allowed her to see but Todkin's masterful craftsmanship brought the world vividly to life.

"Good as new?" asked Todkin.

"Better. They're incredible."

Todkin held out his hand for Wrench to shake. She slipped past it and, stooping, gave the Artificer a heartfelt hug. "Thanks," she said.

"You're m-most welcome," stammered Todkin, his face reddening as Wrench released him.

"And thanks for these." She held up her arms and motioned to the gauntlets of Zeus. "I'm getting much better with them. It took me a while to attune to the mechanism then something clicked and the machinery and I became one. You truly are a genius. They're magnificent, a work of art."

Todkin stroked his beard, the whiskers not hiding the large smile on his face. "They're the work of an artisan."

Bot's gears ground. "Your escort's waiting Brasswitch and the artisan needs to work his mechanical magic on me."

"I'll have your goggles ready expeditiously. It's a pleasure to use my skills for someone who really appreciates them," said Todkin, glaring at Bot.

"I just want my shoulder fixed, *expeditiously*," said Bot, making quote signs in the air with his fingers. "And you're not getting any hugs from me."

Wrench heaved the door open. She smiled, seeing Plum waiting for her. The QRF sergeant stepped into view and the expression dropped from her face.

"Apparently, I've got to babysit you back to Thirteen," said the sergeant, tightening a buckle on his armour. "And if that wasn't bad enough they've sent Mary Magic-pants along too because it seems I might not be up to the dangerous task of walking through the Shambles on my own."

"That is a bit unnecessary," agreed Wrench. "I'm

more than capable of looking after you."

The sergeant grunted and unstrapped his maxim cannon. "Plum, you've got point, Brasswitch in the middle, I'll keep an eye on things from the rear."

Plum sidled next to Wrench. "If anything does go wrong, don't try and use magic. We don't want any elder gods breaking through," he whispered.

"Got it. No magic. No tentacled monstrosities from other worlds."

They trudged out of the snickelway and onto what counted as the main drag through the Shambles. The overhanging buildings with their gnarled oak trusses curbed the light filtering down to the confined street, leaving doorways and alleyways cast in deep shadow. A swirling smog carried with it the smell of sooty chimneys and sewage.

A cat screeched and down a side alley a flash of light was followed by a loud crackle. Wrench stiffened. For a fleeting moment she thought she'd sensed the oily feeling surrounding her. She pushed her mind outwards, searching. All she discovered were the mechanics of everyday life. Nothing untoward. Or to be precise, nothing more untoward than the illegal weapons and alchemical distilleries you'd expect to find in a criminally inclined neighbourhood like the Shambles.

"Stay frosty. Something's not right," said the sergeant.

"I thought it was just a scaredy-cat," said Plum, his voice an octave higher than normal.

"You're the scaredy-cat," said Wrench.

"Knock it off. We have a situation," said the sergeant.

Wrench scanned the alley. "I don't sense anything."

"My senses aren't gained from being an aberration; they're learned in the field, born from combat and surviving missions."

Wrench's heart thumped faster. The sergeant was right. Something was different. A roof slate smashed onto the cobbles further along the alley. Overhead, the buildings leant together, the eaves of the houses nearly touching. A man descended through the gap in the rooftops. Suspended by thick octopus arms that suckered to the brickwork, he writhed downwards.

The crisp metallic click-clack of the sergeant cocking his weapon shocked Wrench from the hypnotic trance created by Octo-Man's descent. Without thinking she spun the Wimshurst discs on her bracers up to speed. Plum raised his hands, his fingers twitching into a magical configuration. More tentacles squirmed from beneath Octo-Man's coat and pinned Plum's arms to his sides.

The sergeant's strong hand gripped Wrench's shoulder and slung her sideways. She slammed painfully into a wall, her cheek pressed cold against the dank brickwork. A flash of electricity bleached the world momentarily white and the burnt tang of ozone filled the air. Wrench gazed in confusion at her arms. Had she accidentally fired the bracers? No. Her body still tingled with the energy stored within her.

The sergeant collapsed to his knees. On the floor beside him his maxim cannon glowed red, its barrel a molten mess.

Further along the alley a blue-skinned woman with thick copper hair advanced, her body crackling with electricity.

"Run," croaked the sergeant.

Wrench turned, but not to run. Her bracers would be useless against the woman, they might even make her stronger, but she could help Plum. Slowing the spinning discs, she dialled back the voltage and straightened her arms. Electricity leapt from her hands, a crackling arc discharging into Octo-Man's chest. He twitched, and his long rubbery tentacles flailed violently. Limp as a discarded ragdoll, Plum slid across the cobbles. With a strangled gasp, Octo-Man keeled over.

Behind her Wrench sensed a dryness in the air as a massive charge built, waiting to be released. She spun around. The sergeant scrambled for his backup pistol, but one arm hung useless and his other hand spasmed, an after-effect of the electric shock.

Lightning-Lady pointed a finger at the sergeant, blue sparks crackling along its length. "Consider yourself deregulated," she said.

Wrench launched herself, sprawling in front of the sergeant. She held her arms above her head, the bracers acting as an earth for the electricity crackling from Lightning-Lady's fingers. Pain forked through Wrench's body. Her muscles tightened, and she gasped; her blood surged hot, hammering her heart. She gritted her teeth. She had to control the energy before it destroyed her. Forcing down the pain she distributed the charge, storing it like she did with the bracers. A throbbing ache taunted every muscle in her body; the power was still too much. She pointed her arms downwards and in a flash the excess electricity earthed into the ground, shattering the cobbles.

Lightning-Lady shrugged. "I can do this all day. Can you?"

She couldn't. Another hit would surely kill her. She'd saved the sergeant once but in the end what good had she done? She was going to die lying in a puddle in the Shambles. Once again, the air became dry, Lightning-Lady's electric charge building. Dry air, wet puddle. Water was the enemy of electricity. If she could control the water, she could save them. Plum had said no magic, but if she didn't do something they would all die. She pulled a pineapple lozenge from her pocket and thrust it into her mouth. Biting down hard, her teeth cracked the sugary shell and sour sherbet spilled across her tongue. Her fingers formed the sign for water and saliva pooled in her mouth. She embraced the wet coldness of the puddle surrounding her, willing the molecules to move.

Above Lightning-Lady the air shimmered like engine oil on a railway sleeper. Wrench concentrated harder, feeling the magic inside her, pushing it out to the puddle. She sensed the water molecules responding, changing state, breaking free of the liquid, evaporating. A dirty black cloud formed in the air. Wrench shuddered, purging the magic from her.

Rain teemed down from the cloud, drenching Lightning-Lady. Electricity crackled over her skin, leaching into the ground. Her face crinkled into a snarl. "Don't think this is over. We're still coming for you." Leaving a trail of sizzling sparks in her wake, she fled into the Shambles.

Wrench reached out a hand to Plum. He looked up at her, his wide violet eyes accusing. "You electrocuted me."

"Actually, I electrocuted him." Wrench motioned towards Octo-Man, but the cobbles where he'd fallen were bare. She scanned the alley. There was no sign of Plum's assailant; he must have made off when Lightning-Lady retreated.

Plum brushed dust from his jacket. "The goon was holding me at the time, so it's the same thing."

"I dialled back the voltage. I guessed you'd be all right."

"You guessed?"

"Would you prefer it if I said I calculated the precise voltage required based on the size of the man, the resistance of his tentacles, and the average inductance of the human body?"

Plum tilted his head. "Did you?"

"Don't be soft." Wrench shrugged. "I eyeballed it."

The sergeant staggered to his feet. One arm hung

limp and his legs trembled. "When you jumped in front of me, how did you know the electricity wouldn't kill you?"

"I didn't. But I knew it would kill you," said Wrench.

"You should have run." The sergeant prodded the remains of his maxim cannon with his boot.

"Would you have run?"

Despite his injuries the sergeant puffed out his chest. "Not a chance."

"Ready for anything," said Wrench.

"Yield to none," completed the sergeant. He offered his functioning hand to Wrench for her to shake. "You're not bad for an aberration."

Wrench scowled, ignoring the offered hand. "And you are still a prejudiced pig. Because I risked my life to save yours, that makes me *not bad*? But any other aberration is by default evil until they've proved themselves worthy in your eyes?"

The sergeant straightened. "Most other aberrations are evil."

"No, they're not. You only deal with the bad eggs, so your views are tainted. Most aberrations live out their days in constant fear of the regulators, trying not to be noticed." Wrench's whole body shook with anger. A chill filled the air and the puddle crackled and froze. From its edges a dusting of frost spread across the cobbles. "It's hardly a wonder that some go off the rails living in perpetual terror of capture, torture and death."

228

Plum put a hand on Wrench's arm. "It was a good speech and I unreservedly agree, but you need to calm down. You got away with doing magic once. Let's not chance it again."

30

It was the day after the Shambles ambush. Wrench's body ached and her muscles intermittently twitched, an after-effect of the electric bolt she'd absorbed. Her head pounded, and the use of magic had left her drained.

Bot was still at the Artificer's and Plum was engaged in his own magical studies. With no one to direct her Wrench was at a loose end. She'd considered visiting the weapons range and practising with the bracers, but the thought of filling herself with electricity was as unappealing as that of practising magic.

Listlessly, she wandered the train. Maybe Darcey might need a hand on the footplate. The engineer was teaching Wrench how the Robinson operated, although Wrench suspected that push come to shove, with a flick of her mind the great locomotive would do her bidding like a dog brought to heel.

She stopped outside Octavia's door. From inside she heard the machine-gun like rattle of the steam sewing machine. The seamstress was the only one of the regulators Wrench felt completely at ease with. Maybe Octavia's abilities played some part, but it felt like more than that – it felt genuine. It was like having a true friend, someone who knew all your secrets, someone you could trust.

Wrench raised her hand to knock.

"It's open," shouted Octavia, pre-empting her.

Wrench ambled inside and slumped onto a chaise longue, exhausted by her short walk along the train. "What are you making?"

The steam sewing machine hissed to a halt. Octavia snipped the thread and pulled a pair of trousers from beneath the needle, holding them up for Wrench to see. "Tada," she said.

The red and black striped trousers were made from strips of sturdy leather and had reinforced bubble-brass plates on the knees, thighs and hips. "It seems that if I'm going to keep you out of the sickbay you're going to need more protection than just kevlaris."

Despite her natural apathy towards appearance Wrench found herself grinning. The garments that Octavia crafted were not merely clothes; they were works of art, fabric engineering. She had somehow tailored the leather stripes to flow around the curved armour plates, lending the trousers a streamlined air that wouldn't seem amiss on a Rutherford Rocket express locomotive.

"Those are magnificent," said Wrench. "Where did you learn to make such wonderful designs?"

"Everyone in a circus has myriad jobs. They may be a clown in the big top, but the rest of the time they're mucking out the animals, fixing tents, and fifty other tasks to keep the circus going. One of my jobs was sewing costumes." Octavia wiggled her tentacles. "With my extra appendages I was able to create outfits others could only dream of. When I joined Thirteen I put my skills to good use. As you've discovered, the job can be pretty hard on clothes."

Wrench smiled sheepishly. "Yes, sorry about that. I'll try not to wreck these ones."

Extending a tentacle, Octavia handed over the trousers. "I'm more concerned about you wrecking yourself, so I'm making you a bodice to match. It'll be a bit heavier than your normal clothes, but the bubble-brass keeps it manageable and with your physique you won't even notice."

"I don't know about that," said Wrench. "I'm used to hard physical labour, but magic is something else – it knocks me for six."

"You'll get used to it in time. Pippa did."

Wrench closed her eyes and rested her head on the chaise longue. Of course Pippa got used to it. Pippa was bally-well perfect.

"Let me fix you a little pick-me-up." China teacups chinked in their saucers and Octavia set about making tea. "I thought you might have visited Sergeant Wilhelm in the sickbay. He could do with the distraction. Regulators' families aren't allowed on the train and I know he misses his children."

Wrench pushed away her guilt. She'd gone past the sickbay earlier but couldn't bring herself to look in on the sergeant. She hadn't known he had a family. Would that have made a difference? No. She had nothing to feel guilty about, it was her that had saved him. Except the sergeant had first pushed her to safety, taking a lightning bolt, sacrificing himself to protect someone he supposedly hated. "I'm sure I'd be the last person he'd want to see," said Wrench, trying to loosen the shameful knot that bound her chest.

"Quite the contrary," answered Octavia. "He's going to make a full recovery and he says that's all down to you. He said you were quite remarkable."

Wrench opened her eyes. "He said I was remarkable?"

"Indeed. I don't think he chose those words lightly."

Octavia placed a tray containing a tea service on a table next to Wrench. She poured a cup of sweet-smelling ruddy tea, into which she dropped a slice of lemon. "I used to make this for Pippa on her worst days. It doesn't do to take it too often, but a little boost now and again doesn't hurt."

"Thanks." Wrench sipped at the tea. "How do you

put up with them? The other regulators, I mean." She couldn't imagine what it must be like. She found it hard enough dealing with the sideways glances and gestures of contempt. For Octavia, it must be a million times worse, actually knowing what they thought.

"I suppose it's just something I've accepted."

"You shouldn't have to. It's wrong. If it was me I'd hate them. I do hate them."

"Hate is pointless." Octavia dipped a biscuit into her tea. "Nothing ever got changed for the better by hate."

"You think you can change them?"

"No." Octavia rested a tentacle on Wrench's hand. "But I think you can."

✿

Wrench slunk into the sickbay. It was odd to be there as a visitor and not a patient. A brass plaque slotted into a holder on the door identified Sergeant Wilhelm's room. It struck Wrench that engraving a plaque with the sergeant's name was a considerable effort to go to. Then again, she'd been to the sickbay several times already in her brief stint in the regulators and perhaps the QRF were frequent patients too.

"Enter," shouted Wilhelm in response to her tentative knock.

Taking a seat by the railed bed, Wrench handed

Wilhelm the remains of the bonfire toffee she'd purchased from Humbug and Mints'. "Sorry, it's all I had left."

"Thanks. Can't chew anyway," said Wilhelm, one side of his mouth drooping.

Wrench placed her hands in her lap and picked at a fingernail. She had nothing to say to the sergeant. The awkward silence lengthened. Despite what Octavia had told her about Wilhelm's words, the space between them still seemed charged with enmity.

"Do they know any more about who attacked us?" asked Wilhelm, breaking the quiet.

"I've heard nowt." Octavia had been summoned to a confidential briefing that Wrench was excluded from, whether it was about the attack she didn't know. "It's got to be connected to Leech and the NIA, surely?"

Shuffling up his pillows, Wilhelm winced. "Or you."

Wrench huffed. "What do you mean me?"

"They attacked us for a reason and it sure as hell wasn't me they were after. They killed Pippa at the Minster; whatever they're up to, maybe they hadn't bargained on Thirteen finding another Brasswitch so soon."

An uneasy feeling about her visit to the Minster and the under-crypt needled Wrench. Like trying to remember a name just out of reach, a thought lurked on the edge of her consciousness. It was important, she was sure of it, but the more she tried to force it into the open, the further it slunk into the dark recesses of her mind. They'd missed something, some vital clue. She tried to picture the scene but unlike Plum her recall was not photographic and she could only picture a vague impression of the under-crypt.

Wrench stood. "Enjoy the toffee."

"You're leaving so soon?" Wilhelm sounded genuinely disappointed.

"There's some place I need to be." It was no good; she was going to have to visit the Minster again.

○

Wrench grabbed her bracers from the wardrobe weapons locker in her room. For the first time since the ambush in the Shambles she felt energised, her lethargy forced away by the prospect of action. She stripped off her patched dungarees and tried on her new trousers for size. They fitted perfectly, as she knew they would, and the armoured plates gave them a snug robustness. She strapped on her bracers and grabbed her bowler hat. No one had implicitly said she couldn't leave the train but given recent events she should probably take Plum or someone from the Quick Reaction Force with her. Neither option appealed. There was no way she was going to approach the QRF for help. Despite having saved the sergeant's life, and the possible thawing of their relationship, she suspected his men would take the view that he shouldn't have been babysitting a remarkable in the first place. And the image of Plum being tortured in the cell was a constant albatross around her neck. She wasn't going to deliberately put him in danger. No, she'd go on her own. She had her armour and her bracers; she'd be fine.

Wrench peeked into the corridor. The coast was clear. She hurried towards the vestibule at the end of the carriage. Ahead, a cabin door swung open and Octavia's voice drifted from inside. Wrench's heart leapt. A tall, red-suited regulator stepped into the corridor and stared down at her. Wrench felt her leg muscles tighten, the ability to walk naturally seeming to desert her. She raised a finger to her bowler hat and nodded. The woman gave the faintest of nods then hurried past on a mission of her own.

Wrench loitered in the vestibule until the woman disappeared from view, then slipped from the carriage. She strode across the platform, her heart pounding, waiting to be called back at any moment. The London express thundered through the station. She sensed the power in its massive pistons and the might of the machine somehow bolstered her confidence. By the time she'd crossed the footbridge she knew she was in the clear. From her pocket, she pulled a brass half-crown and handed it to a carriage driver waiting in the station's forecourt. "The Minster, please," she said, climbing into the back of the cab.

✿

A hundred feet overhead, supported by thick carved pillars, the domed ceiling reflected the harmonious tones of the choir rehearsing. Ahead, row upon row of wooden pews stretched all the way to the distant presbytery. The building was immense. How many locomotives would fit inside it? At least half-a-dozen platforms, for sure. Wrench lurked in a pew towards the rear of the nave observing the comings and goings, getting a feel for the rhythms of the Minster.

A verger polished brasses near the entrance to St George's chapel, complicating her task. She needed a distraction. Nearby, a reverend distributed hymn books for the evening's service from a clockwork trolley. With the smallest of mental nudges Wrench flicked off the brakes. The trolley raced away from the reverend, carving a meandering path down the aisle, spilling hymnbooks as it went. Under cover of the chaos Wrench stole past the verger and into the chapel of St George.

The stone entrance to the under-crypt that Leech had smashed through was now surrounded by a rough lumber frame and door. The lock was inconsequential, and Wrench was soon descending the steps with a candle pilfered from the altar to St George clasped in her hand.

Shadows skittered over the sandstone walls and low arched ceiling. Wrench forced away an almost primeval fear that flickered inside of her. They were clearly just shadows from her candle, not the grasping tentacles of nightmare things from other worlds. Nothing to be afraid of. She spun the discs on her bracers, the reassuring whirr lending her courage. The makeshift door at the top of the stairs had been locked, so no one could be in the under-crypt, only her, alone, in the dark. She hastened to the casket, the discs on her bracers spinning faster.

The phosphor-bronze lid lay open, the hazel wood-lined interior empty bar a layer of ash. Her eyes lifted to the sooty silhouettes on the wall. What had really happened here? They had assumed it was the NIA but what if that wasn't the case? The smudgy shapes looked identical to the one Carwyn had left at the chapel or indeed to the ones Plum had faked at Flemington's lodgings.

A breeze worried her candle and the shadows shifted. This time the shapes were not the product of her imagination: a second light source had entered the under-crypt. Silhouettes of giant tentacles played across the ceiling. Wrench snuffed out her candle and ducked behind the casket. The writhing shapes drew nearer, and her pulse quickened. A tingling ran from the nape of her neck down her spine, the charge from the bracers filling her with electricity. Her breathing slowed, and she brought her arms closer together.

"Don't be alarmed. It's only me," said Octavia.

Wrench peeked from behind the casket. Octavia crept through the under-crypt, a candle in one hand, a four-barrelled Lancaster pistol in the other. Her tentacles probed the air ahead of her, seeking out danger.

"What the chuff are you doing here?" Wrench stood,

her sense of relief marred by annoyance at having been discovered.

"I was worried about you. I picked up on the subconscious doubt of regulator Pendle. She couldn't understand why you were wearing your hat inside."

"How did you know I'd be at the Minster?"

"Once I realised you weren't on the train I did a sweep of the station. The carriage driver told me he'd brought you here."

"Did he?"

"Not in so many words. You do tend to stand out in people's minds. You're no longer the grey girl."

"No, I'm the blue train, or the Brasswitch, or possibly the end of all creation."

Octavia smiled. "Let's stick with the first two. Did you find anything?"

"I've not had a proper chance to look. Something was wrong when I first visited with Bot, only I can't remember what."

"Can I help?"

"Not really." Wrench ran her hand over the embossed sigils on the casket. "You weren't here when we opened it."

"I can be. I can help you remember, share your memories." She tilted the candle and dribbled wax onto a stone plinth then set the candle into the molten pool and waited for it to harden. "Come stand by me."

Wrench hesitated. Should she do this? She was used to

extending her own mind into machines, but they weren't sentient, well mostly not. To have someone probe her thoughts was strange, personal. This was different from when she'd previously let Octavia examine her. Octavia would be reliving her memories, feeling her emotions. She would be experiencing what it was to be Wrench.

"You've done this before, right?"

"It's not my first tea party. Trust me."

Wrench shuffled closer and removed her bowler hat. With a delicate touch Octavia wrapped tentacles around Wrench's head.

"This won't hurt, but you may find it a little disorienting," said Octavia. "Close your eyes and relax. Let me know when you're ready."

Wrench let her eyes flutter closed. It was easier to relax than she'd expected. The tentacles were warm and soft like velvet on her skin. They pulsed ever so gently in a reassuring, comforting way. Wrench sighed, all her troubles melting away. "I'm ready," she said.

31

A procession of images flashed across Wrench's mind. The ambush in the Shambles, the Astrologium, the battle at the church, saying goodbye to Mr Grimthorpe, then she was back in the under-crypt with Bot at her side. The sooty smell burned fresh in her nose and the conversation with Bot replayed.

"No, you're a moron. The casket's empty."

"How do you know?"

"There's something odd about the last lock. It's got a counterbalance that won't allow it to open if there's a weight in the casket."

"Are you sure?"

"See for yourself."

Wrench's eyes sprang open and nausea overtook her.

She gagged and spat bile onto the flagstones. Octavia's tentacles uncoiled. One of them retrieved a handkerchief from the folds of her dress and offered it to Wrench.

Her head spinning, Wrench leant against a stone pillar for support and wiped her mouth. The casket couldn't be opened if something was inside. They'd been so on edge at the time that they'd missed the obvious. Leech couldn't have released an NIA. There was no NIA, just its remains turned to ash.

Octavia rubbed Wrench's back. "Deep breaths. The sickness will pass in a minute."

"Carwyn killed them. Same as at the church." The church where Flemington had been acting strangely, determined to slay Carwyn. He didn't want the remarkable to talk. "I think Flemington put Carwyn up to it, then tried to silence him."

Octavia's tentacles undulated. "Why would he do that?"

"I don't know." Wrench gazed at the casket. Maybe Flemington hadn't wanted it disturbed. Only a Brasswitch could open the locks. Flemington had arrested her and if it wasn't for Bot she'd have been electrocuted at pretty much the same time the only other Brasswitch, Pippa, was being turned into a sooty smudge. That couldn't be coincidence.

Raised voices drifted from the chapel above. Octavia's head snapped up. "We may have some explaining to do."

Bot clanked down the steps, his red eyes scanning the under-crypt.

"Come quickly. We've got to stop Flemington," he said.

Wrench took a step towards him. "What–"

"He's sticking his nose in where it's not wanted. No time to waste," said the mechanoid.

"What happened to you, is what I was going to say."

Bot's eyes narrowed. He turned and stomped back up the steps.

"Your shoulder. It's silver," said Wrench, hurrying after him.

"Todkin didn't have time to electroplate it."

They stepped into the light of the chapel and Bot's shoulder armour sparkled like a million diamonds.

"Oh! That's beautiful," said Octavia.

"It's not a fashion statement. It's a new alloy Todkin's invented: Carblingium."

"Is it designed to dazzle the enemy?" said Wrench, failing to keep the amusement from her voice.

"Brasswitch, I'd wind your neck in. There's a conversation to be had about you running off on your own, but that will have to wait until later."

"I wasn't on my own. I was with Octavia."

Bot stormed from St George's chapel. "That makes it even worse. I could have lost two of my most valuable assets in one go."

Octavia took Wrench's hand. "He said assets, but what he really meant was friends."

Outside the Minster waited two regulator walkomobiles, smoke billowing from their chimney stacks.

Bot headed for the front carriage. "Octavia, go back to Thirteen. I don't want you mixed up in this. Brasswitch, you're with me. Plum's in the carriage; he'll bring you up to speed."

"Take care," said Octavia to Wrench. "I can't see the future. Not in any real sense, but something bad is coming. That much I can tell."

Wrench climbed into the carriage, Octavia's warning loud in her ears. The door had barely shut when the walkomobile lurched into a sprint, sending her sprawling onto the seat.

"Chuff it!" A spasm of pain jolted through Wrench's ribs. She pushed herself upright and hugged her arms around her torso, trying to deaden the stinging sensation. Her body felt like a punching bag. Over the past few days she'd been electrocuted, whipped with chains and savaged by tentacles from another dimension.

"You still suffering?" asked Plum. He sat unnaturally straight, his back pressed into the padded leather seat, his arms held stiff, bracing himself against the carriage's movements.

Wrench sucked in a breath through clenched teeth. "Feels like I've been through a steampress."

"You shouldn't be here. You need to rest. I tried to persuade Bot, but he said he needed you."

"I don't want to miss out if we're going after Flemington."

"We're not exactly going after Flemington; it's more damage limitation."

Much of the recent talk at Thirteen had been about how the captain had not taken the burning of his rooms well. Rumour had it he'd cried for a day over the loss of Lady Lovelace before launching into his *enquiries* with a new-found vigour, claiming an aberration connected to Carwyn must be responsible. The net result of his zeal had left one aberration dead and three more possible suspects awaiting Flemington's robust questioning.

The carriage rocked again. Plum reached out to steady Wrench. She shrugged away from his help, unfolded her arms and gripped the edge of the seat. "So where are we heading?" she asked, ignoring the hurt look in Plum's deep purple eyes.

"The Spread Eagle Tavern. Flemington thinks he's got a lead on a remarkable."

"So, why's this different from any of the others he's hunted down?"

"The remarkable in question is one of Bot's informants, which at best is going to leave Thirteen with some difficult questions to answer."

"Remarkables snitch to the regulators," said Wrench with disdain.

Plum tilted his head. "Because that's so much worse than working for them?"

"It's not like we had a choice, and besides, we're trying to help."

"I guess Tommy Four Thumbs thinks he's helping too. As Carwyn demonstrated, some remarkables are bad, and with the abilities they possess their potential to be remarkably bad is considerable."

Had Carwyn been bad before the villagers shunned him? Or had they made him bad, the constant drip of hatred poisoning him? Wrench knew what it was like not to fit in, to want to belong and not be allowed. She'd been lucky though; Mr Grimthorpe had sheltered her from the worst of it. Carwyn had no such powerful protector.

"Did Bot brief you on the plan?" she asked.

"Not as such. He said something about using his innate skills of tact and diplomacy to defuse the situation."

"He has all the tact of a half-brick in the face."

Plum's finger twitched through a succession of shapes. "Which considering it's Flemington isn't necessarily a bad approach."

Wrench smiled. The fact that the captain had been only seconds away from electrocuting her in the dungeons was enough for her to hate him, but she wondered why Plum and the other regulators loathed him. "How come nobody else likes Flemington?"

"Well, I don't like to talk ill of another regulator," said Plum in a way that meant he was about to do precisely that,

"But apart from being a nasty piece of work with all the charm of the pox, he'll do anything to move up the ranks. He doesn't care who he has to tread on and he sees his overzealous pursuit of remarkables as a means to that end."

Plum was still an enigma to Wrench but she was sure he was hiding something. "What's Bot's beef with him?"

"When the previous head of Thirteen retired, Flemington thought he was in line for the job. Bot was promoted instead and Flemington's been trying to discredit him ever since."

Wrench grimaced. Flemington in charge of Thirteen would be like a fox in charge of the chickens. No wonder Bot had been chosen. Remarkables were what made Thirteen the potent force it was, and she couldn't imagine Flemington working hand in hand, or indeed hand in tentacle, with them. If the attitudes of the QRF were anything to go by, even with Bot at the helm the deep-seated prejudice in the regulators was hard to overcome. How much worse would it be with a bigot like Flemington in charge?

"And what about you, Plum?"

"What about me?"

"There's something going on between you and Flemington. I just can't work it out."

The corners of Plum's mouth turned down and he stared at the floor. "When I was nine my powers started to become a problem. It was like I'd be so charged with magic it had to find a way out. I was with my ma, fetching the day's bread and a horse bolted down the street, dragging the milk cart behind it. I couldn't see because my eyes were bandaged but the sound terrified me. My eyes burned through the cloth and sent a pulse of raw thaumaturgy right at the horse. Poor beast turned to ash mid-gallop. The regulators were called and Flemington arrested me."

"But Bot rescued you, like he did me?"

"Yes. Bot saved me." Plum looked out of the window and shuddered. "Only Flemington interrogated me for two weeks first."

32

Wrench stepped from the carriage. Squat red-brick terraces closed the streets in on both sides, their net-curtained windows grey and uninviting. The tavern was the one bright spot in the street; cast-iron gas lamps hung from brackets on the walls, giving it a homely feel. A floral display below the bottle-glass front windows added to the welcoming ambience.

"This looks quaint. Is it definitely the right place?" asked Wrench.

A body hurtled through the front window, shattering it with a resounding crash.

Plum's fingers twitched into a form Wrench didn't recognise. "Yeah. I'd say so."

"Looks like the party's started early." Bot clanked

towards the door. "Let's see if we're on the guest list."

"He calls it a party, I call it another opportunity to die horribly," muttered Plum.

"Shouldn't someone help the man on the pavement?" asked Wrench.

"Reckon he can help himself."

The man got to his feet and brushed glass from his thick woollen jacket. His large hands had the appearance of granite, as did his face. He cricked his neck, the sound clacking like pebbles on a beach, then he loped back into the pub.

The Spread Eagle's interior was a scene of chaos. Overturned tables and barstools littered the room. Three mechanoid enforcers stood inert by the broken window, their heads hanging limp. On the floor, a regulator battled with the man who'd run back into the pub, while at the bar a four-armed fiend strangled Flemington.

Wrench reached out to the mechanoids. They weren't damaged or broken; however, something was keeping them inert. Where normally their gears, valves and pistons would have felt crisp and clear they were hazy. Her mind sensed the familiar oily feeling. This time it was stronger, not just a barrier to her abilities but interfering with the mechanoids, stopping them from working.

Bot's giant fingers grasped the stone-skinned remarkable struggling with the regulator. "You can walk out of the door or go through the window again." He heaved the man up, so his feet dangled clear of the pub's wooden floorboards. Bot's head moved to within an inch of the man's granite-like face. "But make no bones about it; if I put you through the window you won't be getting back up again."

The man rasped something that sounded vaguely like *door* and pointed to the exit. Bot lowered him to the ground.

Plum and Wrench helped the bloodied regulator onto a stool while Bot marched over to the bar.

"That's enough now, Tommy," said Bot.

Keeping three of his hands clasped firmly around Flemington's throat Tommy pointed at Bot. "We had a deal."

"And I have kept that deal."

Tommy gestured to the trashed pub. "What do you call this?"

"An unfortunate misunderstanding."

"You were supposed to protect me, leave the pub alone."

"And I did. Unfortunately, Captain Flemington plays very much to his own tune. And it's one of those incredibly annoying tunes, like a busker with a penny whistle."

"Well, I'm silencing that tune," said Tommy, returning his hand to Flemington's throat.

"I understand your frustration, Tommy, I really do. Ne'er a day goes by when I don't want to strangle the captain myself, but I can't let you–"

Bot's whole body shuddered, the metal plates of his armour clanking. "Brasswitch!" he bellowed, his body twitching.

Wrench took a step back. The oily feeling that surrounded the mechanoid enforcers rippled through the pub. "It's not me," she said.

Bot growled. "There's another Brasswitch." His voice was stilted, every word an effort. His arm trembling, he gripped Tommy's head. His fingers splayed over the man's skull and he began to squeeze.

All four of Tommy's hands dropped from Flemington's throat and the captain sank to his knees, gasping for breath.

A look of panic on his face, Tommy said, "Not guilty, governor. Someone just killed them mechs and I was grateful for the help but it's nothing I know about."

Straining to turn his head towards Plum and Wrench, Bot stuttered, "F-find the B-Brasswitch."

Wrench hurried behind the bar, following the direction of the oily feeling.

"Where are we going?" asked Plum nervously.

"Can't you feel it?"

"Feel what?"

"The magic," said Wrench, pushing through a door into the pub's kitchen.

Plum shook his head. "I've got nothing. If there's magic, it's not of my kind."

A half-plucked chicken lay atop a battered table.

Next to the fowl rested a pile of mud-covered carrots and potatoes. Hanging from the ceiling on hooks and chains, a host of dull silver pots and pans swung gently as if disturbed by a breeze. Two heavy skillets clattered together, and Wrench looked up. The air was still, but she saw, or maybe sensed, a shadowy current flowing past the pans, along the ceiling, then disappearing into a low wooden door set beneath the stairs.

"We need to head to the cellar," she said and hauled the door open.

"Oh, great," said Plum. "Because nothing bad ever happened in a dark spooky cellar." He flicked a light switch and a feeble Edison bulb glowed orange in the gloom.

The oily feeling shifted, then with a loud plink the cellar returned to darkness. Wrench reached out with her mind, following the wires from the switch to the bulb. Where there should have been a beautiful tungsten coil there was now only a molten mess. The bulb hadn't blown by accident.

Plum made a sign with his hand and a bubble of light appeared floating above it.

"How did you do that?" said Wrench.

Plum gave her a puzzled look. "Magic."

"Obviously magic. I mean how did you do that, precisely?"

"Kind of hard to explain. Kind of difficult to do. And after your last attempts, kind of not something I want to elaborate on."

Wrench peered into the gloom. A set of rickety steps led down, disappearing into the murk. "You first," she said.

"Why do I have to go first?" complained Plum.

"Because you have the light."

Plum looked at the glowing bubble. "Damn!" He descended into the cellar, the steps creaking alarmingly. Wrench followed him down, the wood groaning beneath her feet. The smell of stale beer and damp hung in the air. Against one wall sat a row of wooden casks. Tarnished copper pipes ran from brass valves in the tops of the barrels to the ceiling where they disappeared into the bar above. Beyond the barrels an archway led to a further room. Plum stiffened. A rat the size of a small dog scurried across the floor and disappeared into a broken pipe.

Living in the city, rodents were an unpleasant fact of life. The council's rat pipers would periodically clear a district, but it was only ever a matter of days before they returned. She stepped closer to Plum, who had stalled at the bottom of the stairs. "It's only a rat – let's get this done."

Plum shuffled towards the archway, the hand bearing the light outstretched ahead of him.

The door at the top of the stairs slammed shut and the oily feeling suddenly vanished. The light in Plum's hand flickered.

"Now I feel something," said Plum. "Strong magic." The light flared dazzlingly bright, and Plum screamed.

Wrench squeezed her eyes shut, blinded by the glare. She held her hands over her face. They blocked the light but did nothing to stop the stench of burning flesh. The light died and a thud like a sack of coal slung from a merchant's cart reverberated through the darkness. Purple splotches filled Wrench's vision. Blindly she reached out for Plum, but he was gone.

"Plum! Plum, where are you?" she shouted, her voice high-pitched and reedy.

She dropped to her knees and crawled forwards, feeling for the thaumagician. Her hands scuffed across the rough damp flags, finding nothing. Beyond the archway steam hissed, followed by the clunk and clatter of turning gears. She reached out with her mind to the unknown machine. The oily feeling returned, stronger than ever, pushing back at her, forming an ever-shifting barrier, deflecting her thoughts from the device.

She needed to find Plum and she couldn't do that in the dark. She had no lantern but if she could generate a spark with her bracers it would give her enough light to see. Her mind went to the Wimshurst discs, but they refused to accelerate, plodding around in slow circles, the oily presence retarding their progress.

Behind her a loud crash emanated from the direction of the stairs. Bot burst through the door demolishing a large section of the wall in the process. He piled down the steps, which splintered under his weight, collapsing as he descended.

"Brasswitch," yelled Bot.

"Over here," said Wrench. "I can't find Plum."

Light flooded the cellar through the large Bot-shaped hole. On the flagstones, surrounded by blood, rested Plum's fez. The thaumagician himself had vanished.

A spot-lamp telescoped from Bot's shoulder and played across the cellar. He clenched his fist ready for battle and strode through the archway. Wrench pushed herself to her feet and followed. The room beyond was empty except for a stack of beer casks against one wall and a steam-powered cellar hoist that was stuck in the up position, the lifting platform having pushed open the trapdoors in the street above.

Bot pulled the brass lever on the wall to lower the lift. Steam hissed from the pistons and pumps strained to turn, but the platform didn't budge. "Brasswitch, lower the platform."

Wrench moved her mind into the machinery. The mechanism was straightforward and would have been simple enough to operate had the main gearwheel not been a molten fused lump.

"It's wrecked," said Wrench. "We're stuck."

"Not yet we're not." Bot seized two beer casks and carried them to the next room, depositing them on the floor. He grasped what remained of the stairs and heaved backwards. Gears ground, then with a splintering crack the wood came away from the walls. Bot discarded it and fetched more casks, stacking them to make an impromptu set of stairs.

"Go," said Bot.

Wrench scrambled up the barrels to the kitchen and ran outside. The cellar hoist poked into the now deserted street. She cast her mind about, searching for the oily feeling, searching for Plum. She sensed nothing. Her friend was gone.

33

Wrench sipped a ginger beer at a worn wooden table in the trashed bar of The Spread Eagle. Between drinks she held the squat brown bottle's cool glass against her temple, hoping to quell the needle-like headache piercing her brain. Beside her sat Tommy Four Thumbs and opposite, his face like thunder, fumed Flemington. Nobody spoke. Bot had told them to wait, and so they did. To Wrench's surprise Flemington had offered little resistance to the command. After another botched operation, which was at best only quasi-official, Wrench suspected he was on thin ice. A regulator had gone missing, possibly kidnapped by remarkables, and he needed to do whatever he could to salvage the situation.

Tommy drummed his fingers on the table with all

four of his hands. Flemington glared at him, making no effort to hide his disdain.

The flavoursome fizz of the ginger beer tingled Wrench's tongue and a ripple of magic flowed to her fingers. The ginger beer solidified, turning into a semi-frozen slush. Great, now it worked when she didn't need it. What had happened to the magic in the cellar? Plum hadn't sensed anything until the oily feeling disappeared. Perhaps it not only blocked her abilities but magic too. So why had Plum's light spell worked?

Bot stalked into the room and sank onto a stool, his joints hissing. "Still no sign."

"We should be out there helping to search," said Flemington. "Not in here confined to the naughty chair."

Wrench baulked at the idea of agreeing with her nemesis but for once he had a point. They were wasted here, doing nothing while who knew what horrors Plum was enduring.

"This wasn't chance; it was planned," said Bot. "Someone targeted Thirteen and I need to know why."

"You need to get Plum back. That's the priority," said Wrench. She couldn't shake the vision of Plum being tortured. While he'd been safe at Thirteen she'd been able to dismiss the dream as fantasy; now that he had been taken the image played over and over, vivid in its cruelty.

"We will get him back. However, we have to understand the big picture."

"What makes you think Thirteen was the target?" said Flemington.

"The Brasswitch that did this is powerful. She disabled the mechs, blocked our Brasswitch and did the magical equivalent of sucker-punching Plum. Yet she didn't take you out," said Bot, looking at Flemington.

"Maybe I was just too much of a threat?"

"Yeah, and maybe mechanical monkeys will fly out of my oil plug," said Bot. "No, she wanted the fight balanced so we'd be wrong-footed when we arrived. Then she attacked me knowing I'd send Plum and our Brasswitch to counter her."

"That's a risky plan. Too many moving parts," said Flemington.

"Not if she was prepared to wait. She could see how events unfolded and just disappear if the opportunity to take Plum didn't arise."

Wrench rubbed her temple where the pain was collecting. "The strange presence I told you about before, I felt it here too, only much stronger. Perhaps the Brasswitch originally planned to take Plum at the church."

"Plum didn't go inside," said Flemington. "You left him outside threatening me."

"I left him outside because he had no magic," said Bot.

Flemington's face darkened at the news he'd been duped.

261

Bot cocked his head. "So, she's expecting me and Plum but gets me and Brasswitch and decides to back out, leaving Carwyn on his own."

"She couldn't have known you'd be at the church. It wasn't a Thirteen job." Flemington stroked his beard.

"Carwyn was never going to come quietly. She engineered it so things went wrong and Thirteen would be called," said Bot.

"It still doesn't make sense." Flemington's brow furrowed. "She couldn't have known I'd come to The Spread Eagle."

Wrench stared over her bottle at the regulator. "Why were you here?"

Flemington sneered. "I don't answer questions from aberration filth."

The temperature dropped, and the bottle of ginger beer shattered, its contents now frozen solid.

"Seventy-five per cent of the brain is water," said Wrench. "Plum is my friend, you are not. If you don't answer my question I will ice you." It was a bluff. Magic couldn't be directly used against a person, as the body's aura interfered with the energy. However, Flemington wouldn't know that and she'd delivered the threat with such malice that he capitulated.

"I got sent a message that Daffydd, Carwyn's brother, was the one who torched my quarters. The message contained this." Flemington pulled a regulator red cat collar from his pocket. He fingered the small silver name tag and his bottom lip trembled. "The message said they had Lady Lovelace."

Wrench glanced sideways at Bot. How could that be? Lady Lovelace was ensconced in Plum's cabin back at Thirteen.

"Daffydd's a stone-skin not a flame-mouth," said Tommy. "He don't even like fire."

Flemington scowled. "Well, much as I trust the word of a freak–"

Tommy shoved the table backwards with one pair of hands, lunging for Flemington's throat with the other.

Grasping Tommy's shoulder, Bot forced him back into his chair. "Sit down. You're in enough trouble already. Captain Flemington is going to put his prejudices aside for the remainder of the discussion because whatever else he may believe, he knows Plum is a regulator and we look after our own. Isn't that right?"

Flemington glared at Tommy but nodded.

Wrench flicked a shard of broken bottle from her trousers. "The Brasswitch's magic was stronger than Plum's, so why does she need him?"

"Maybe she's after information on Thirteen?" said Bot.

"Seems to me she's pretty clued up on that front already," said Flemington. "She knew you'd be at the church and she lured you here."

"She didn't lure me here. I came because Tommy sent word he was having issues with you," said Bot, pointing at Flemington.

"No, I didn't." Tommy shook his head. "It was a surprise to me when you turned up."

Wrench twisted her fingers together, wringing her hands. "When we were attacked in the Shambles the Lightning-Lady said, *Don't think this is over. We're still coming for you.* I thought she was talking to me but what if she wasn't? What if they were after Plum all along?"

"Which brings us back to the question, why does she need him?" said Bot.

The image of Plum being branded in the cell replayed in Wrench's mind and a thought began to form. Maybe she knew why Plum had been taken. Why it had to be a thaumagician. She bit down on her tongue, stopping herself from blurting it out. Someone in the regulators was conspiring with the other Brasswitch. Flemington had been at both the church and the pub and she had no reason to trust him. His obsession with her was unnatural and still unexplained and the fact that another Brasswitch had taken Plum was too coincidental.

Bot stood. "We've been played good and proper and I don't like that. Someone has my thaumagician, and I like that even less. I'm going to find them, and then I'm going to make them very unhappy."

Wrench slumped onto her bed, pain and fatigue vying for supremacy over her body. Instead of being allowed to help search for Plum, Bot had sent her back to Thirteen while he headed to Clifford's Tower with Flemington. They were busy organising personnel to conduct house to house enquiries and make up search parties. It sounded good and made it seem like they were doing something useful, but in her heart Wrench knew it was wasted effort.

She'd tried to get Bot to one side, so she could talk to him without Flemington in earshot but the mechanoid was in full command mode and had dismissed her without listening. If she was going to convince him she needed hard evidence to prove her point, and that evidence was at the orrery. She didn't care that Bot had categorically forbidden her to leave Thirteen; Plum needed her help and that was justification enough for breaking the rules.

Her eyelids closed for two seconds. Soft on her back, the mattress tempted her to give in to its charms and sleep for a week, but there was work to do. Forcing her tired eyes open, she dragged herself from the bed. The orrery beckoned, but first she needed to talk to the elusive Master Tranter about Plum.

Wrench hid her bowler hat under her jacket and pulled open the door to her room. A thickset regulator blocked her exit. "Pardon me, ma'am, but Bot left instructions that you were to remain in your room until his return," said the regulator.

"And when might that be?"

"He didn't say, ma'am."

Her anger surged, flickering the lights. "So, I'm to be held prisoner?"

"No, ma'am. You just have to wait in your room."

She slammed the door shut and stomped around the small cabin. Bot didn't trust her and that infuriated her; the fact that he was right not to do so just added to her ire. Well, she'd show him. There had to be another way to slip from the train. The carriage windows didn't open, and the door was no longer an option. Her gaze drifted to the circular heating vent high up on the wall above her desk. It would be a tight fit, maybe impossibly so, although perhaps that wouldn't matter.

From the bottom of her wardrobe she grabbed her tool belt and removed a screwdriver. She lifted the chair onto the desk and clambered on top of it. Compared to the heavy bolts she was used to dealing with at the coachworks, the four screws securing the vent were a cinch to remove. With the flat of the screwdriver she eased the grille free and then replaced one screw, giving it a half-turn so the vent hung suspended. She climbed back down and positioned the screwdriver and screws so they were clearly visible on the desk, then snuck to the hinge side of the door.

Imagining the lines of a magnetic field, she adjusted them so the remaining screw rotated until gravity took effect. The grille dropped from the ceiling, bounced from the chair, then clattered to the wooden floor.

The door burst open, obscuring Wrench. The regulator guard rushed to the desk and scrambled onto the chair. Craning his neck, he peered into the vent.

Wrench slipped out of the door, easing it closed behind her. She rekindled her anger at being kept prisoner and forced her rage into the door's mechanism. The lock melted, fused solid. It wouldn't last for long but she didn't need it to; it just had to hold long enough for her to visit Master Tranter.

The "magic department" took the whole second storey of one of the carriages. The stairs that provided access were barred by a substantial iron gate inscribed with complex sigils. Wrench probed the lock, expecting to encounter formidable magical protection. The tumblers turned unimpeded and the gate clicked open. She hurried up the stairs, not knowing what awaited. Plum had obstructed her previous efforts to take a peek, citing Master Tranter's delicate health as a catchall prohibition, and Octavia had sidestepped any of her questions on the subject.

The stairs led into a room that looked like a cross between a library and a laboratory. One wall was lined with books, their leather-bound spines exuding age. Opposite, jars of chemicals and specimens preserved in formaldehyde filled the shelves. A bench ran along the centre of the carriage. Alchemical concoctions bubbled through the complicated arrays of glassware sat atop the bench.

"Hello?" called Wrench. If Master Tranter was as jumpy as Plum she didn't want to scare him and end up on the wrong end of a blast of magic. There was no reply, only the faint sound of gas percolating through liquid. She walked further into the carriage and called again. "Hello?"

"Plum, is that you?" said a husky voice from behind Wrench. She spun around, her heart pounding. Master Tranter was nowhere to be seen.

"No. It's me, Wrench. Plum's missing."

A snort issued from beneath a black silk cloth covering what Wrench presumed was a large domed birdcage. Although, what sort of bird could communicate so readily was a mystery to her.

"That explains why it's been so quiet. I've been rather enjoying the peace," rasped the voice from beneath the cloth.

"I need to speak to Master Tranter. Where can I find him, please?"

The silk fluttered as if caught in a sudden breeze and then slid free. Beneath was not a birdcage but a large fluid-filled bell jar. A disembodied head floated in the lurid blue liquid, cables and tubes trailing from the brass collar encapsulating its neck.

Wrench gasped and took a step backwards.

The head grinned. "I see that reports of my imminent recovery have been greatly overstated," said Master Tranter, his voice magically projecting beyond the glass bell jar.

"You're just a head," said Wrench.

"My, my. You're far more astute than Plum led me to believe. You've diagnosed my problem immediately. Well done."

Wrench's heart rate returned to normal, the shock of Master Tranter's predicament waning. Two weeks ago, talking to an aquatic severed head would undoubtedly have perturbed Wrench. Today, it didn't even feature in her top ten list of weird things she'd encountered. "I can see who Plum gets his interpersonal skills from," she said, and flicked a finger against the glass.

Master Tranter winced. "Please don't do that," he said, and blew a bubble from his nose. "Now tell me about Plum."

"He's been kidnapped, and I have a theory about why, but I need to know something about Plum and his magic. He's different, isn't he?"

"Yes. The boy is an anomaly, and not merely because he's frighteningly good. What specifically do you want to know?"

35

Wrench clambered onto the roof of the train through a hatch in the magic department's vestibule. She glanced about York station. Thirteen's siding was positioned deliberately well away from the other tracks and no one loitered nearby. She lowered the hatch back into position then padded along the carriage's roof. A confusion of pipes and dials decorated the wall at the carriage's end, making for an easy descent. She clambered down and dropped onto the train track. Crouching below the height of the platform, she stepped from sleeper to sleeper.

To some, being so close to the carriage's giant wheels, axles and springs may have been frightening, but to Wrench they loaned a sense of comfort. The years she'd spent as an apprentice engineer meant she felt more at home beneath the carriage than inside it. She reached the massive hydraulic buffer springs at the end of the track and clambered onto the platform. With a final glance behind, she headed from the station.

Not wanting Octavia to track her again, Wrench walked several streets away before flagging down a cab. The short ride to the Astrologium gave her enough time to clarify her thoughts and devise a plan. Unlike her previous visit, a light breeze sent the city's smog tumbling away from the hill, the grey wisps parting like rapids round a rock. The orrery's spheroidal tower dominated the hilltop, magnificent in the bright sunlight. Wrench took a deep breath and whispered to herself, "Be the blue train."

An underling showed Wrench into Magi Taurus's office. The gaunt, anaemic magi hunched over his desk, scribbling in a journal. He glanced up, then returned his attention to the journal's pages. "On your own today, little miss?" he said, dipping his pen in the inkwell.

Wrench bristled. "It's Brasswitch to you." She pointed her finger at a decorative orrery suspended from the ceiling. Cogs, springs, planets and moons showered downwards, scattering across the inlaid leather desktop.

Taurus looked up in astonishment. Mars bounced from his widow-peaked forehead and rolled across the desk.

"It would be a tragedy were the same thing to happen on a larger scale," said Wrench, gesturing towards the Astrologium.

His hand trembling, Taurus put down his pen. "Please accept my apologies for my rudeness. How can I help you, Brasswitch?"

"Have you fixed the bugs introduced by Parrot-Man?"

"We believe so. We're running some test programs now."

"Cancel those. I need you to run the Chattox program, my program, and one more which may take a bit of extra work."

Taurus spread his hands on the desk. "But that could take all day!"

"What's one day?" said Wrench, flicking Jupiter from the desk. "Compared to a lifetime in Clifford's Tower?"

Taurus slumped into his chair. "Tell me about this special program, Brasswitch."

❖

Wrench leant over the gantry rail watching the planets and moons spin into position. Adjacent to her a pen attached to an articulating arm moved back and forth like the shuttle on a loom, drawing thick black letters and numbers as it went.

After one complete revolution, the solar system slowed to a halt and the bright glow of the artificial sun faded. Taurus ripped off the sheet of paper that spooled from the machine and handed it to Wrench. "These are your results. They're remarkably similar to those we ran for Chattox."

"Except my odic potential is higher," said Wrench.

"Much higher," agreed Taurus.

"Run the final program for when the comet is closest." Wrench stared into space, or at least into a scientifically accurate model of space, while Taurus made some adjustments to the machine. Bot had told her that at certain times the net over the Rupture was weaker, but maybe that wasn't the case. When she'd performed magic with Plum in the shooting range she'd attracted something through. She hadn't weakened the barrier; she'd acted like a magnet. When the moon and sun aligned, the combined pull of gravity created spring tides. According to the Celestines, the planets and the comet amplified the odic forces, making Chattox and Wrench more powerful. Maybe the other Brasswitch was going to use the spike in power to draw something through. Master Tranter had confirmed what she'd suspected, Plum was different from other magic users. Thaumagicians normally converted energy from their bodies' cells into magic, but Plum could store pure magic, which was why his eyes changed colour. The Brasswitch was going to charge him up like a battery and then release all that energy at once, when the comet was closest, creating a beacon to lure the old gods through.

The planets danced across the simulated cosmos and paper spewed from the machine. Wrench scanned the figures, but she already knew what it would say. The greatest effects of the comet would be on August the fourth, St Dereleth's day, her birthday.

The lift doors further along the gantry clanged open. Wrench's heart kicked in her chest. The last time she'd been at the orrery Chain-Head and her cohorts had attacked them. Bot strode from the lift. Wrench's pulse raced and her chest tightened; the mechanoid was angry. With his shoulders hunched forward and his eyes burning red, he stormed along the gantry. How had he found her? She hadn't left any clues for Octavia to follow and she'd not hailed the cab anywhere near the station. Bot stamped to a halt alongside her. "We'll talk about this later, Brasswitch," he said.

Bot's hand shot out and grabbed Taurus's shirtfront. Without effort, he dragged the magi closer. "When we were here last, you said you warned the aberrations."

"I did and I'm sorry. I won't do it again." Taurus clutched onto Bot's thick metal wrist, his legs trembling.

"How?" said Bot.

The pitch of Taurus's voice rose, like he'd been sucking helium. "How what?"

"How did you contact them?"

"G-mail. Brimble Pontefract the Third, if memory serves me correctly."

Bot let go of Taurus's shirt. "Do you have any more?"

"Only one. Miss Penelope Plumplington."

A small leather seat ejected from Bot's back and

foot-pegs extended from his waist. Attached to the seat were Wrench's new goggles. The mechanoid kneeled next to Wrench. "Goggle up and saddle up. We've got some running to do."

36

Penelope Plumplington was anything but plump. Her sleek muscled haunches powered her along York's streets like an express train at full throttle. Bot's feet pounded on the flagstones, steam spurting from his joints as he struggled to match the dog's pace. Greyhound mail was a recent addition to the city's communications. With a higher load capacity than the traditional carrier pigeons they were fast finding favour in the local business community.

Wrench stood on the foot-pegs clinging to Bot's shoulders. She'd spent the first quarter-mile of their pursuit bouncing in the saddle like a pea on a drum skin, before deciding that the seat was obviously intended for more sedate journeys. The wind whipped past her and she was glad of the new goggles Todkin had crafted.

Along with preventing her eyes from watering they had a telescopic function, allowing her to keep sight of the greyhound's distant form.

At first, as they'd headed downhill from the Astrologium Bot had managed to keep pace with the beast. Now on the flat, with the length of Walmgate extending into the distance, they were losing ground. Squalid brick terraces ran both sides of the street, homes to the influx of Irish that had come to the city. With four or more families sharing houses designed for one, the pungent aroma of unwashed bodies and night waste wafted on the wind.

They passed The Spread Eagle pub. Nausea churned Wrench's stomach, the site of Plum's disappearance bringing the vision of her friend being tortured into her mind. Bot pumped his arms harder, accelerating, the reminder of the missing thaumagician perhaps giving him extra impetus.

The gentle curve of the Foss Bridge carried them over the river. Now more of a canal than a river, the smoke from steam barges transporting coal and pig-iron into the city drifted up to meet them. To their left lurked the Shambles but the greyhound surged along the more respectable Colliergate. A hodgepodge of Tudor, Georgian and more modern shopfronts flashed past, the tall buildings casting them in shadow. Some hundred yards ahead Penelope Plumplington veered into Goodramgate and they lost sight of her. Bot growled and ran harder still, his feet smashing into the cobbles.

He skidded around the corner, sparks trailing behind him. The narrow street snaked past the Minster, made narrower still by merchant stalls stacked with vegetables, fresh fish, and all manner of household necessities. Street vendors pushed their barrows through the crowded thoroughfare, shouting their wares. Overhead towered twisted Tudor houses, their second storeys jutting into the street at strange angles and decorated with colourful hoardings advertising everything from Bile Beans to Royle's self-pouring teapots.

"I can't see her," yelled Bot, powering onwards.

Wrench stood further upright and pushed her mind into her goggles. Additional lenses slid into place and the eyepieces telescoped outwards, magnifying her view. They rounded a bend and the street straightened. In the distance, she saw a flash of white and a commotion as a tray of baker's buns went clattering across the street.

"I've got her. She's heading towards Lord Mayor's Walk," yelled Wrench.

"Hang on tight."

"Because I was thinking of letting go," she shouted over the crash of Bot's feet on the cobbles. With a mental flick the magnifying lenses withdrew, and the street's surrounds came into focus. Shoppers and stallholders cluttered the pavements and ahead a Bartholomew's Butchery wagon blocked the road. Bot accelerated towards the looming obstruction, seeming indifferent to the fact that there was no way past.

Wrench held on tighter.

Bot's legs bent and in an explosion of steam he leapt onto the roof of the wagon. The lacquered wood canopy creaked under his weight, then with a loud boing, he sprang over the startled horses. He slammed into the cobbles, his feet skidding across the hardened flint. His arms flailed like a windmill in a gale then he regained his balance and resumed his charge after the greyhound.

"Are you all right?" shouted Bot.

"Just a bit surprised. I didn't know you could do that."

"Me neither," said Bot.

They followed the dog into Lord Mayor's Walk, which turned out to be more of a Lord Mayor's sprint. Again, Wrench used her magnifying lenses to keep sight of their prey, and also to take in the view of the Minster, which peeked above the grass bank and thick city wall to her left. Perhaps it was just an effect of the goggles but the violet hue over the shattered tower seemed brighter than she remembered.

"I think we're gaining," said Bot.

Penelope Plumplington bounded along Clarence Street past rows of squat terraced houses with neat, well-maintained front gardens. Wrench knew little about greyhounds but from an engineer's perspective they appeared to be built for speed rather than distance and Penelope Plumplington seemed to be tiring.

"I know where we're heading," said Bot.

"Where?"

"You said in your vision you saw Plum in a cell."

"I never told you that."

"Octavia told me."

"I never said anything to her." Wrench frowned. Her anxiety about the vision would have broadcast loud and clear to Octavia. Even without trying to read Wrench's mind she probably couldn't have missed it.

"Only two places have cells. One is prisons."

"And the other?" said Wrench.

The greyhound turned into Asylum Lane.

"The madhouse," said Bot.

✿

York Lunatic Asylum was where those deemed to be of an unfit mind were imprisoned, although what deemed a person as unfit was subject to a wide degree of interpretation. Certainly, many committed to the institution were in need of help, but for others their incarceration was a convenient way for a husband to be rid of a wife, or for a family to deal with a troublesome relative.

Bot slunk into a copse of stunted trees near the front of the massive red-brick institution. Three storeys high, it menaced the landscape around it. Rows of iron-barred windows radiated an aura of foreboding, their dark countenance sucking all warmth from the August sun.

"It's time to get off." Bot dropped to one knee.

"Oh no. You're not leaving me behind." Wrench tightened her grip.

"I'm not, Brasswitch. We're staying put here."

"What?" Wrench banged her boots against Bot's armour, like a rider spurring on a horse. "Plum's in the asylum. We need to go and get him."

"And you think striding up to the front door and kicking it in is the best way?"

Wrench shrugged. "That seems to be your normal approach."

"Not when there's one of our own inside. And not when we have no idea what we're up against."

"We know what we're up against: Chain-Head, Parrot-Man and Hammer-Hulk. We scared them off at the Astrologium; we can do it again."

"You're forgetting Lightning-Lady, Octo-Man, and the other Brasswitch. And they're just the ones we know about. Carwyn was probably involved too; we've no idea how many others might be in there."

"We can't leave Plum." Wrench thumped Bot on his sparkly shoulder.

"This is unusual, even for department Thirteen. Aberrations don't normally work well together. You may get one or two acting as a team, but it never lasts. What we're seeing here is unprecedented."

There was something uncertain about the mechanoid. No longer devil may care, act first brag about it later. Wrench had never seen him like this. "You're scared," she said.

"Damn right I'm scared. And if you knew a fraction of what I do you'd be scared too. We need to do this properly. We need to get the QRF and come up with a plan. We can't afford to mess this up."

Wrench's magnifying lenses slid into place on her goggles and she stared down the tree-lined lane that acted as the main approach to the asylum. "That's not going to happen."

Bot stiffened. "Are you threatening me, Brasswitch?"

"No. It's not going to happen because Captain Flemington is racing up the drive with an army of regulators."

"Oh, crap!" said Bot.

37

The Clifford's Tower regulators demolished the front door to the asylum and piled inside before Wrench and Bot had a chance to intercept them. Flemington was nowhere to be seen, having charged into the heart of the building surrounded by a phalanx of seasoned operators. Bot grabbed one of the trailing regulators by the arm and yanked him to a stop. "What's going on?"

"I'm not allowed to say, Sir," answered the regulator, his voice trembling. "Captain Flemington's orders."

Bot's grip tightened and the regulator squealed. "If you value your job as a regulator, and indeed your arm, you'll answer me."

"Yes, Sir," said the regulator, his voice strained. "By robust interrogation Captain Flemington discovered the asylum was being used to shelter aberrations connected with the flame-mouth."

"Carwyn?"

"Yes, Sir."

Bot let go of the regulator. "Damn it. This is worse than I thought."

Screams of the insane echoed from the filthy whitewashed walls. All around, Flemington's regulators smashed in doors and manhandled the inmates with little regard for their wellbeing. Somewhere to the east an explosion shook the building and screams of a different nature rent the air.

"Come on," said Bot. "It sounds like they're playing our tune."

Dust and a haze of smoke wafted up the basement stairs. Slumped against one wall a regulator moaned incoherently. A medic with a large white cross on the back of his red jacket wrapped a bandage around the fallen regulator's mangled leg.

"Don't go down there, Sir. There's too many of them," warned the medic.

"I'm here to even the odds," said Bot and descended the stairs.

The medic reached out to Wrench. "You at least should stay, Miss."

Wrench brushed his hand away. "Chuff that. I'm here for my friend," she said and hurried after Bot.

Fallen plaster and splintered wood littered the floor

at the base of the stairs. A flagstoned hallway stretched ahead of them, its end obscured by steam and a cordite haze. Steel-clad cell doors lined the corridor. Some were open, some were closed, and some hung from their hinges, broken and bent. From the doorways regulators fired blindly into the smoke-filled gloom.

"In here. Take cover Sir," shouted one of the regulators.

Bot ripped a dangling door from its hinges and held it in front of him. "I'm taking cover with me."

An oily feeling washed over Wrench. "She's here, the other Brasswitch," she shouted above the pandemonium.

"Can you keep her from affecting me?"

"I'll try." Wrench pushed her mind out, imagining her own aura surrounding Bot, protecting him.

Bot's leg armour slid open and he grasped the hand cannon. "Let's go get our thaumagician back."

Wrench shadowed Bot, staying behind the cover of the misappropriated door. Missiles hurtled through the smoke, rattling off the impromptu shield. A volley of sharp bangs deafened Wrench and one corner of the door deformed, the steel plate bulging inwards. An explosion sent a cloud of stone splintering from the floor. Pinging from Bot's armour, the fragments ricocheted into Wrench. The bubble-brass plates on her trousers crumpled, absorbing the impact.

"I need backup," bellowed Bot.

Regulators pepper-potted from doorway to doorway, clearing the cells as they advanced. Another thunderous salvo ripped into the shield and the weakened metal gave way, a starburst of holes puncturing the door. Bot hurled the shield into the smoke and was rewarded with several pained screams.

Wishing that Octavia had finished the reinforced jacket to match her trousers, Wrench crouched low behind Bot's thick armoured legs. The flagstone floor was disturbingly familiar. In her vision, she thought she'd seen a dungeon, but she'd been wrong. It wasn't a dungeon; it was the asylum.

Electricity arced through the smoke. Drawn to the metal mass of Bot's armour, it crackled over the skorpidium-carbide plates. He shuddered, and his arms twitched. "I thought you were protecting me?" he bawled.

"From the Brasswitch. I can't do everything."

"It's called multitasking," said Bot. "Watch and learn." He raised his left arm to the horizontal, pointing it along the corridor. The curved armour plate sprang upwards, revealing a rack of three rockets. A flint wheel spun, showering sparks over the trailing fuses, and they ignited in a puff of flame.

Wrench forced her fingers in her ears. With a whoosh, the rockets zoomed into the smoke, exploding in orange balls of flame. Bot levelled his hand cannon and it boomed repetitively, filling the air with steam.

Something crashed within the smoggy haze followed by a scream, more angry than injured. Bot stalked on, his cannon falling silent as the resistance dwindled. The corridor's end loomed into view. On the floor, next to a flight of steps, lay a man covered in blood. He clutched a bullet wound in his shoulder with a crab-like claw.

"Medic," shouted Bot.

Wrench lifted her eyes from the injured remarkable to the door in the end wall. It was ostensibly no different from any of the other cell doors: steel-coated wood with a grilled hatch. However, the specific pattern of bullet holes pockmarking the metal was seared into Wrench's mind. It was the door from her vision. With trembling hands, she pushed it open.

38

The door swung inwards with an ominous creak. A sense of déjà vu gripped Wrench and she froze, unable to breathe, unable to slow her frantic pulse. It was exactly as she remembered from her vision. She clenched her teeth, the scene playing out like she wasn't there, like she was watching through someone else's eyes, waiting for the inevitable.

Her shoulders slumped. The cell was empty. She gasped, sucking in a huge breath, the smoky air tasting wonderful. The vision was wrong. A disconcerting thought niggled her and she pressed her hands against her cheeks, pinching the skin. The pain was sharp and reassuring; this was real and not another dream.

"Are you all right?" asked Bot.

"Plum's not dead."

"But he's not here either. Flemington's gone and blown our only lead."

Wrench stepped into the cell. "Not necessarily." Scratched onto the floor was a drawing. It was the most rudimentary of outlines, but it showed the Minster with its ruined tower and above it, a comet with a flaming tail. "Plum left us a clue."

Bot stooped over the image. "What does it mean?"

"Tomorrow night the comet is at its closest. According to the programs I ran on the orrery, that's when remarkables are most 'magical'. I think the Brasswitch is going to use Plum's magic like a flare to summon the old gods."

"Is that even possible?"

"You said the casket was designed to contain a Non-Indigenous Aberration and slowly leach their power into the atmosphere, like a lightning rod in reverse. What if it could be made to release all that power into the Rupture at once?"

"Plum's not an NIA," said Bot.

"No. Master Tranter says he's like a magical capacitor, a magical battery. The Brasswitch is going to charge him with magic then short-circuit him."

"You met Tranter?" queried Bot.

"We had a head to head, you might say."

Bot grimaced. "And he agrees with you?"

"He agrees it would be possible."

"That's simple then. We throw a cordon around the Minster. I'll guard the casket until the comet's gone then we all go home for tea and scones."

"We'd be going home without Plum." Wrench ground her boot against the cell floor. "We have to set a trap."

"We don't have the resources. This is too big for Thirteen to handle on its own. I'll need the help of the Clifford's Tower Cabal and that means getting Flemington on board."

Wrench eyed the devastation in the corridor. "I don't trust him. The Brasswitch has been one step ahead of us all the way. We need to know whose side he's really on."

"Flemington's a regulator captain, in charge of a cabal. No matter how much we dislike him we can't accuse him without evidence."

"We have evidence."

"No. We have information from a legally dubious search of his lodgings, which we then torched. That's not a path I want to go down. Besides, if he is involved he's hardly going to confess just because we confront him."

"We don't need him to. Get him to a meeting with Octavia and she can tell if he's being truthful."

"He's not going to like that."

"He doesn't have to like it. The fate of the city, possibly the country, is on the line. It's not as if we're strapping him into an electric chair." Wrench rubbed her chin. "Although …"

"We're not going to electrocute Flemington," said Bot.

Wrench spun up her bracers, so they crackled with sparks. "Just a little encouragement wouldn't hurt, would it?"

Bot shook his head. "I never thought I'd be standing up for the man, but Captain Flemington is a regulator and we need to respect that."

"Even if he's a traitor?"

"If he's a traitor he's not going to agree to the meeting."

"You need to do whatever it takes to get him there," said Wrench. Plum's life could depend on it. He was the closest thing she'd had to a friend since the accident and she wasn't going to abandon him. "We have to know what Flemington's up to."

○

The QRF escorted Wrench back to Thirteen while Bot remained dealing with the devastation at the asylum. On her return, she went straight to Ops room one. If Bot was successful, and Flemington agreed to be questioned, they were only going to get one chance to find out the truth. And not just the truth about where his loyalties lay. It might be her only chance to interrogate him about his obsession with her and the deaths of her parents.

She pored over the board of stuff taken from Flemington's apartment, looking for something she'd missed, the proverbial 'steaming gun' as the great detective Shirley Holmes might say. However, after several hours reading and re-reading the cryptic notes, journal entries and newspaper articles, her eyelids drooped, and she was still no further forward. She removed her glasses and pressed the heels of her hands into her eyes, making them squelch.

Dabbing at her tired eyes with an oily handkerchief, she gazed up at the board. Without her glasses, it was a blurred mess, and because of that something stood out. One of the newspaper clippings was different from all the others. Rather than being neatly trimmed with scissors all the way around, it had one ragged edge where part of it had been ripped away.

She pushed her glasses back onto her nose and moved closer to the board. The story detailed the crash of the *Drake* and was similar to that of numerous other clippings but what made this one special was the photo. It showed Wrench and her parents stood on the platform before the *Drake* departed. Half of the photo was missing; the right-hand edge of the picture had been torn away.

Wrench burst from the Ops room and sprinted to her cabin. She barged the door open, ignoring the smashed lock where the regulator she'd previously trapped had escaped. On her bookcase rested the very same photo, but this one was complete. She lifted the frame and stared at the picture. She'd looked at the photograph a thousand times before but had only ever paid attention to the figures in the foreground, herself and her parents. Behind them, over their shoulders, someone was getting into one of the carriages. Wrench removed her glasses and strapped on the goggles Todkin had crafted. She activated the magnifying lenses and zoomed in on the figure. The image was blurred but there was no doubting who it showed. This was the steaming gun she'd been looking for, of that she was certain. She slumped into a chair and removed her goggles. What she'd discovered was most definitely wrong, but what did it mean? Only one person could answer that, and hopefully, if Bot was successful, they would be questioning him tomorrow.

39

Bot had insisted that Wrench left the bracers of Zeus in her cabin but the atmosphere in the briefing carriage still crackled with tension. The captain gripped the edge of the table, his knuckles white. He stared at Wrench, making no attempt to hide his abhorrence. Between them rested a closed box file. Octavia sashayed into the carriage and Flemington sprang to his feet, knocking over his chair. "What's she doing here?"

"She's here to monitor the conversation," said Bot.

"You mean she's going to pry into my brain." Flemington wagged a finger. "The Grand Cabal banned that."

"Have you got something to hide?" said Wrench.

"Everyone's got something to hide. You need special authority otherwise it's a breach of my rights. Show me your authority."

"I don't have any," said Bot.

Flemington sneered. "Then we're done here."

"Which is why after we have safely rescued Plum, I will leave Thirteen." Bot tossed an envelope onto the table. "My resignation letter. Signed and dated."

"No!" said Wrench. "You can't. Thirteen needs you." She'd finally found somewhere that she fitted in, a place where she belonged. If Flemington was in charge the remarkables would suffer. Thirteen would be destroyed.

Bot placed a hand on Wrench's shoulder. "We have to do this. For Plum."

A crooked smile twisted Flemington's lips. "Your word on this and I get to keep the letter."

"My word," agreed Bot. "But you have to be honest with us."

Flemington retrieved the chair and sat at the table. "You've got ten minutes."

"Why did you visit the Epochryphal Brotherhood?" said Bot.

"I didn't."

"They said a regulator with a burned face visited them."

"Well, it wasn't me."

Bot turned to Octavia. "He's telling the truth," she said.

"Did you lure us to the church with Carwyn, hoping to kidnap Plum?"

"No!" Flemington pulled a face of surprise. "I didn't even want you there interfering."

"Why did you go to the Astrologium?"

For the first time the confident veneer dropped from Flemington's facade.

"It was just routine enquiries."

Octavia shook her head.

"You've got to be truthful or the deal's broken."

"I was investigating Leech. He was clearing too many dangerous aberrations." Flemington sat back in the chair. "The Astrologium featured in a number of his enquiries; he'd visited several times with Chattox and I couldn't see why. I wanted to know what they were up to."

"He's being truthful but he's holding something back," said Octavia.

Flemington flicked a hand in the direction of Wrench. "I got them to run a program on her."

Wrench leant forward across the table. "Why?"

"Because you're a dangerous aberration. Leech cleared you, but I know you're a killer, just like Carwyn and the others."

"Leech never investigated her," said Bot.

But he had. Wrench shuddered at the memory of being strapped in the electric chair being submitted to the full weight of Flemington's anger as he ranted at her about the crash of the *Drake*. The crash Leech had investigated.

That was where this all started. Wrench opened the box file resting on the table and withdrew a framed photo. A photo she had stared at for eight years, memorising every feature of her parents' faces, making sure her memory of them would never die.

"This is a photograph of the *Drake* before it crashed. Why are you and a young lady getting into the rear carriage?" said Wrench.

The colour drained from Flemington's face and he folded his arms. "I'm not. That's ridiculous. That blur in the background could be anything."

Wrench didn't need Octavia to tell her he was lying. She slapped her hands on the table. "Why were you on the train when my parents died?" she shouted.

"Because I was going to propose. The lady was to be my fiancée, only you killed her, burned her alive. How do you think I got this?" Flemington pointed to his scarred face.

"No passengers were supposed to be on the train. It was a test run."

"I pulled some strings. Abused my position as a regulator. I wanted to make it a day to remember. And it was. You saw to that."

"I didn't crash the train. I didn't kill my parents."

"If you're so sure, let's ask her to delve into your mind," said Flemington, pointing at Octavia.

"This isn't about Brasswitch. It's about you," growled Bot. "Is that why you've been stalking her?"

"I knew Leech had bungled the investigation into the *Drake*'s crash. I didn't know that this Brasswitch was responsible at the time but when she turned up in the investigation at the coachworks I connected the dots. She's killed before, and if you don't deal with her now, she'll be the death of us all."

"That's not how we work at Thirteen," said Bot.

Flemington snarled. "Not now. Once you're gone and the job is mine, things will change. Oh yes. Things will change."

"That's only going to happen if we find Plum," said Bot.

"So, stop this charade and tell me what you need."

"One last question," said Bot. "Are you totally loyal to the regulators?"

"Yes, I am."

Octavia nodded.

40

It had taken the rest of the day to coordinate the resources needed for the plan to work. Flemington was to marshal as many regulators as he could and hold them at the tower in reserve, so as not to tip their hand. His cover story was that they were going to raid the asylum again. To reinforce this, he was to *accidentally* let slip that they had information the aberrations had returned but they needed to wait for confirmation from their source. In their previous encounters, the Brasswitch had always managed to have the jump on them, so surprise was essential to turn the tables.

Meanwhile, Bot, Wrench and the QRF were to sneak into the Minster and take up positions from which to spring an ambush. Bot had been silent on the matter of how they were to access the Minster unnoticed and Wrench didn't push him, aware that perhaps he couldn't rule out that the leak was coming from the QRF.

○

The canvas-covered delivery wagon rumbled over the granite cobbles of Stonegate. Wrench peered through a gap in the canopy. The thick glass windows of the warped Tudor buildings sparkled with a scarlet hue cast by the comet. Further along the street, towards the Minster, revellers celebrated the passing of the meteor, which in a few hours would be at its very closest. They had the look about them of university students: starched white shirts, long black tailcoats and frivolous hats. Not so many days ago Wrench would have been just like them, blissfully ignorant of the horrors that Thirteen and the regulators protected the country from. Bot pulled on the reins and the horses slowed to let a scrum of drunken revellers stagger into the White Hart tavern. The wagon turned into the yard at the back of Torvill and Trent gunsmiths and Wrench caught a glimpse of the Minster. The magical maelstrom above the shattered tower pulsed, lighting the night sky, and this time there was no doubt that its luminescence had grown.

The wagon trundled to a halt. Wrench jumped down and pushed the yard's gates closed, dropping the bar securing them in place. Now hidden from view, the QRF dismounted and followed Bot into the gunsmiths. The door was held open by a thin, grey-haired man who sported a marvellously curled moustache. He could easily have been mistaken for an accountant were it not for the polished six shooters he wore on each hip and the look of a killer in his eggshell-blue eyes. "I got your message," said the man.

"You knew this day would come, Trent," said Bot.

"I'd rather hoped it wouldn't, not in my lifetime at least."

"Me too," said Bot. "Just don't get all twitchy with the trigger."

"I've never shot anyone who didn't draw on me first."

"Undoubtedly. But there's a bit more at stake here."

Trent led them down a flight of stairs into a stonewalled basement with a target range at one end and a steel-riveted door set into the wall at the other. From his waistcoat pocket, he pulled a small gold key which appeared incongruous with the heavily reinforced door.

He twisted the key in the lock and with a clunk, the door swung open. Lining the walls of the vault was enough weaponry to start a small war. The QRF already brandished firepower of a calibre far exceeding anything Torvill and Trent had to offer, and Wrench wondered why Bot had brought them there.

Trent lifted a revolver from a rack at the end of the vault, opposite the door. He placed the heel of his hand under the empty rack and slid it upwards. Beneath, a large keyhole was recessed into the plasterwork. Trent slid the pistol's excessively long barrel into the hole and twisted.

Wrench sensed the mechanism behind the wall. The weapon's foresight acted like the bit of a key and rotated a cam, sliding the locking bolts aside. Clockwork whirred, and the vault's end wall swung into a tunnel behind. A damp musty smell with a hint of sewers filled Wrench's nose.

A lantern emerged from Bot's shoulder and shone into the tunnel. "You remember on the tower when I said I'd taken a few secret precautions?" said Bot.

Wrench nodded.

"This is one of them. It will take us to the Minster unobserved."

The walls were made from a grimy red brick that formed a low arched tunnel. Bot led the way, shuffling along in an uncomfortable-looking half-stoop. Wrench followed the hunched mechanoid. Trent trudged beside her, in his hand a battered leather case. Behind them marched the QRF. The floor was made from worn stone flags with some sort of pattern on them. It wasn't until they'd been walking for several minutes that Wrench realised the flags were old gravestones and the markings weren't patterns but worn-down inscriptions.

A cool breeze wafted along the passage and the smell of the air changed; no longer that of a sewer, it possessed a caustic, chemical tinge. They entered a stone vaulted chamber that reminded Wrench of the under-crypt, only many times bigger. Tarnished brass tubes that looked like giant shell cases filled the chamber with only a few narrow paths weaving between them. Each tube was the size of a locomotive's boiler tank. Thick copper cables ran overhead between the domed cylinders, forming an interconnected web. From the closest tank rubber-covered wires ran to a clip hammered into the stone wall near the passage entrance.

Trent put down his case and flicked the catches open. From inside he withdrew a wooden box with a T-shaped plunger atop it. Wrench didn't have to sense inside the box to know what it was for. She'd seen similar devices used to detonate explosives when blasting away rock for railway tunnels. The plunger would spin a dynamo, generating an electric charge that would trigger the blasting caps on the cylinders.

With nervous precision Trent removed the rubber wires from the clip on the wall and twisted the exposed copper ends onto the plunger's terminals.

Bot rested a chunky hand on Trent's forearm. "Only as a last resort."

"I've survived two wars and seven duels. Believe me when I say I have no desire to die today," said Trent. "But if there's no other choice, you won't find me lacking."

"You're a good man," said Bot.

"No, I'm not. Just a foolish one." Trent upended the case, using it as a seat.

Bot beckoned the QRF closer. "It probably goes without saying, but it would be a jolly fine idea not to bang into the shells as we pass through."

They wended their way between the maze of cylinders. The faint smell of ammonia stung Wrench's nose. She didn't know how much explosive was packed under the Minster; however, she was certain it would not only destroy the cathedral but a considerable amount of the surrounding city. It felt odd to be walking so close to something so dangerous, something that in the blink of an eye would wipe her from existence. She examined her warped reflection in the dulled brass surface of a cylinder. Did she have the power to stop the catastrophe? Was the face that stared back at her truly a Brasswitch, or was the only real brass the metal beneath her reflection? She guessed very soon she was going to find out.

Bot drew to a halt at the base of a flight of stairs. "These lead to a secret door into St George's chapel. Once we're inside, consider yourself in enemy territory."

Wrench stepped onto the stairs in front of Bot. "Actually, you're not coming," she said.

Gears whirred, and Bot flexed his shoulders. "What?"

"It's supposed to be a surprise. The Brasswitch is going to sense you the moment you go up there."

"I'm not sending you without the QRF," said Bot.

"Yes, you are," said Wrench. "She'll sense their weapons, so I'm going by myself."

"Don't be ridiculous. What can you do?"

Wrench unstrapped her bracers. "I'm a Brasswitch at the peak of my power. I can do whatever I want."

41

Wrench carried a candle. Even the simple mechanism on a lamp for raising and lowering the wick might lead to her discovery. The wall at the top of the stairs incorporated a secret door that was a miracle of ancient engineering. She eased it ajar and the candle flickered in the breeze; its glimmer illuminated the dusty back of a thick velvet curtain.

Wrench snuffed out the candle and listened for any sign of activity. Hearing nothing, she pushed her way through the heavy material to emerge at the rear of St George's chapel. She ducked behind the altar and took stock. Out in the south transept Chain-Head and Parrot-Man stood guard with another remarkable Wrench didn't recognise. He had a tail like a monkey curling from the rear of his breeches. Below his tasselled red fez was a face more simian than human. In his hands, the monkey-man appeared to be carrying a pair of giant brass cymbals.

The glow of hundreds of candles shone from the ragged entrance to the under-crypt. Wrench waited until the remarkables in the transept had their backs turned, then darted through the hole smashed in the wall and down the stairs. Stealing from pillar to pillar, she made her way to the railed area surrounding the phosphor-bronze casket. The silhouettes of Chattox and Leech still blackened the wall, but the sooty tang was gone, replaced now by the aroma of burning sage and sandalwood.

Bowed and broken, Plum knelt before the casket. Stripped to the waist, his body was a bag of bones, his shoulderblades and ribs clearly visible. His back was to Wrench, the milk-white skin scarred with the brands of his torture, strange twisting sigils burned deep into the flesh.

Wrench cast her gaze about. The under-crypt appeared otherwise empty. "Plum. It's me," she whispered, hurrying towards him.

"Wrench," he croaked, his voice as broken as his body. "I knew you'd come."

"I couldn't leave you," said Wrench.

"No," said Plum, his voice stronger, commanding. "I knew you'd come." He stood. His body was somehow no longer withered, but powerful in its emaciation. Magic crackled over his skin. He turned to face her, his eyes glowing the deepest purple.

Wrench took a step backwards, almost physically repulsed by the magic. "Plum. What's happening?"

"I've had enough, Wrench. The looks, the hateful comments, the revulsion. You said it yourself: we're remarkable. We shouldn't be hiding in the shadows, fearing our neighbours, living in terror of the knock on the door when the regulators come to take us. Tonight I will summon the old gods, flood the world with power and aberrations will become the norm. No longer rare freaks but the majority. The rulers."

Nausea gripped Wrench, her head giddy. This couldn't be. She'd come to save Plum, but not from himself. "This isn't right. It's not what we do. You'll destroy the world."

"That's what they want you to believe. Lies spread by the fear-mongering cabal. The world wasn't destroyed when the Monks of Mayheim summoned the old ones before."

"Because people fought against it. Sir Dereleth sacrificed himself to save us."

"Not to save us. To save them. You're an aberration too. Join us. It's time for the remarkables to rise."

Wrench had always wanted to belong. To be part of the group rather than the outcast. Even at the regulators she was an outsider. They needed her and perhaps some even respected her, but did they actually want her? With Plum and the other remarkables there would be no half-glances and hurtful comments whispered behind hands.

But how long would that last? And how many innocent people would she be condemning to death?

"This isn't the way, Plum. If the old gods don't destroy the world, the war between remarkables and everyone else will. What we have now is wrong, but this isn't the way to change it."

"It's the only way to change it. We've been persecuted ever since the Rupture. They don't care about us."

"Some of them do. I can't let you do this."

"You can't stop me."

Pain encircled Wrench's arms. Thick tentacles wrapped around her, crushing her muscles and stinging where the suckers met her exposed skin. "No electricity this time," said Octo-Man. He dragged her towards the casket where waited a regulator with a scabbed burn scar on his face. She flexed her arms, struggling to break free of the thick rubbery coils. Octo-Man squeezed tighter, forcing the air from her chest. Without her bracers, she felt powerless. She probed with her mind but there was nothing mechanical about Octo-Man and she found no purchase. She pushed further, searching for the Minster's bells or the steampipe organ. Anything to summon help. From nowhere, the oily feeling surrounded her, stronger than ever.

"Save your energy," said Plum. "When I killed Pippa, I inherited some of her powers. An unexpected bonus that's enabled me to interfere with your abilities."

Wrench stopped struggling, shocked by Plum's

confession. Her body felt cold and the nausea returned. She swallowed down acidic bile. "You killed them?"

"Just Pippa. I wanted them to help; I thought they'd be sympathetic." Plum gestured to the man with the burn scar. "Leech had been clearing aberrations for years and saw the merits of my plan. However, Pippa baulked at the idea. I had no choice; I couldn't let her go free."

"Don't delude yourself to brush off the guilt. There's always a choice."

"And Pippa chose death. That's on her, not me." Plum's gaunt features contorted into a deranged grin. "You too have a choice. Perform magic to try and stop me and risk summoning the old gods or stay in the casket and wither to dust as your power is sucked from you."

Wrench knew her magic wasn't strong enough to defeat Plum and if she tried she'd be giving him exactly what he wanted. Unappealing as the casket was, it might buy her some time to think of a way out of this or for Bot and the QRF to investigate. And if all else failed, there was always Trent.

Octo-Man lifted Wrench off the ground and, unresisting, she let herself be lowered into the hazel wood-lined interior of the casket. She flinched, settling into the grey dust covering the bottom of the coffin.

"Any last words?" said Plum. "And do try and make them interesting. I find it hard to describe how sickening I found your whingeing. Boohoo, magic's too difficult.

Boohoo, why can't you teach me what you do? Boohoo, my parents are dead. For a supposed Brasswitch you really are quite pathetic."

Anger seethed inside of Wrench. "This isn't going to end well for you," she threatened.

"Perhaps that was on the cards the moment I was born; however, I think not. Isn't that right, Leech?"

For the first time the man with the burned face spoke, his voice a sycophantic whine. "Yes, Master. The Epochryphal Brotherhood showed me a glorious future of aberrations ruling the world."

Wrench pointed at Plum. "You're not part of that future. That's not what I saw."

"Didn't anyone ever teach you, it's rude to point?"

The air around Wrench thickened, pushing her back into the casket. Her fingers splayed outwards, an invisible force pressing her hands flat against the hazel wood lining. Two of the spikes topping the railings surrounding the casket bent and broke free. They drifted above Wrench, turning slowly on their axis.

Plum leant over the coffin. "I know your feeble attempts at magic never got beyond water, but I wouldn't want you to rain on my parade." The spikes shot forward, impaling Wrench's hands, nailing them to the casket's wooden interior.

Wrench clamped her jaw shut, refusing to scream at the searing pain.

A look of disappointment on his face, Plum said,

"If it's any consolation, you only have to endure the torture for a little under an hour, not like the two weeks Flemington had me in the tower. Bot may have rescued me, eventually, but the damage was already done."

The casket lid closed and darkness shrouded Wrench.

42

Wrench lay immobile, the wounds in her hands angered by the slightest movement. She panted in short shallow breaths. How much air did she have? It probably didn't matter; whatever Plum was planning it was going to happen soon.

She used the agony to force away the claustrophobia that gnawed at her mind; she had greater concerns. Bot had intimated that the energy was drained from the occupant over hundreds of years; however, Plum needed her magic released in a pulse of power. He must have either altered the casket, or he intended to perform a dark magic ritual. He'd talked before about sacrifices being required to summon the old gods and perhaps that was what she was. Under Plum's direction, her odic potential would be drained in an instant, a beacon of magic drawing the old gods like moths to a flame.

Ignoring the warm trickle of blood that leaked from her hands, she probed the workings of the casket's locks with her mind. They appeared no different to when she'd opened them before. She could probably even unlock them again, but with her hands skewered in place, she wasn't going anywhere.

The locks were the same, but was the casket altered in any other way? She pushed her mind further, fearful she might arouse Plum's suspicions. Beneath the stone plinth on which the casket lay, something had been added, some form of magical circuit. The layout of the components had a certain familiarity. The transformers at the Epochryphal Brotherhood were of a similar design. Perhaps Leech's visit to the monks had not only been to gain hints of the future but also to acquire the technology. When activated, the transformer would suck the magic from Wrench and pump it skywards. She let her mind follow a lead-shrouded copper cable from the transformer, out of the under-crypt, up the Minster wall and – that was strange; the cable branched. The old section continued upwards to an antenna that would dissipate the power, much as she'd expected, but a second, newer section of cable passed through a diode, ensuring the magic could only travel away from the casket. Had Plum added this too? No. Although not part of the original design it was too weathered to be a recent addition. She let her consciousness travel along the cable, which ran across the roof all the way to the ruined tower, to the odic capacitor.

When she'd opened the casket with Bot they'd expected to find a monster; instead they'd found only dust. The additional cable had accelerated the draining of the NIA's energy.

Wrench held her mind at bay, scared of what had happened the last time she'd looked into the odic capacitor. Scared of seeing her father, or at least something pretending to be her father.

Again, she felt a memory lurking. There was something familiar about the device, yet how could that be? Until Bot had taken her to the tower that day she'd not even known it existed.

Tentatively she eased her mind into the machine. Being so distant, insulated from the Rupture, she hoped to be able to explore its workings without the threat of other worldly hallucinations. Yet immediately the smell of pipe smoke filled the casket, a blend made especially for her father by Pip Finnegan's Tobacconist on Stonegate. The elusive memory became clearer. A blazing fire, her father sat at his desk, pipe in mouth, annotating an engineering plan. She lay on a soft rug playing with her favourite toy, a golden puzzle sphere made of concentric discs that would contract and expand with the movement of their ingeniously hinged segments. Except now she saw that it wasn't a toy; it was a scale model, a prototype of the odic capacitor.

Tears welled in her eyes. Her father had built the capacitor, using his genius to keep them all safe and now Plum was intent on spoiling his legacy. She'd be damned if she'd let that happen. She pushed further into the device, determined to understand its workings. The toy she'd played with as a child had expanding rings – why had her father done that? He'd been fastidious about the robustness of design so he'd made the rings expandable for a reason. She probed deeper, gaining insight into the brilliance of her father's creation. In a feedback system, perfect as any she'd ever seen, the rings' distance from the core automatically adjusted to balance the capacitor's efficiency, dealing with surges from the Rupture.

What would happen if she pushed all the rings to their maximum? Could she drain enough power from the Rupture to thwart Plum's plans? She reached out with her mind and expanded the rings to their limits. Nothing changed, their effect on the Rupture unmeasurable. She waited, holding the rings taut but it made no odds; the Rupture was just too powerful. Defeated, she let go and the rings snapped back into place.

The inside of the casket flashed violet for a millisecond and her skin tingled. What the heck? She repeated her actions, pushing the rings to their maximum and then letting go. They contracted in an instant and again the casket blinked purple.

It wasn't a perfect analogy but in many ways thaumaturgy was comparable to electricity: the power dissipated by the capacitor was like direct current. However, when the rings suddenly contracted it created an alternating wave, half of which could travel through the protective diode, into the casket, into her. Instead of sucking out her magic, the casket could amplify it.

Wrench reached out to the capacitor and began expanding and contracting the discs in quick succession. Thaumaturgy magnified by the comet flowed from the Rupture, through the capacitor and down the shrouded cable.

A tingle ran through her body and the air in the casket stirred. The pitch black was forced aside by a violet glow that seemed to emanate from a million tiny specks. The tingling of her skin escalated to a shocking pain, which made the gashes in her hands seem like a minor irritation. Teeth clenched, her muscles held taut in torment, she kept the discs expanding and contracting, fast as her mind would allow. Her body absorbed the magic, a capacitor of its own, and through the anguish, she felt her power growing, like when the Wimshurst discs charged her with electricity.

The odic forces were many magnitudes more intense than mere electrical potential and every single cell fizzed with energy. There was no need to think of lemons, or use silly hand signals; the magic was hers to direct. She was the magic. The metal spikes tremored, then pulled free of the wood, free of her hands. Violet light shot from her eyes and the casket lid exploded, shattering into pieces.

Wrench levitated from the coffin, her body rotating upright. Plum stood transfixed, frozen like a rabbit in the beam of a hunter's lamp.

She floated to the ground, dust spilling from her clothes and Plum's trance broke. "Kill her," he shouted.

From behind, tentacles wrapped around Wrench's arms and throat. She remembered the feeling of helplessness when Octo-Man had dumped her in the casket and her anger flared. She sent a pulse of power through her skin. With an anguished scream and the smell of sizzled suckers, the tentacles withdrew.

Plum's fingers formed the sigil for fire and a jet of flame shot from his hands.

Wrench held out her wounded palms and the fire splashed harmlessly against an invisible barrier.

His shoulders sagging, Plum's arms dropped. He looked beaten, but his eyes were still the deepest purple. Wrench wasn't taking any chances. She focused, directing her magic at his hands and a chill mist swirled around them, like breath on a frosty day. She drew more moisture from the air, freezing it solid, so ice enveloped Plum's fingers, securing them in place.

"Give up. I don't want to hurt you, Plum. I've won."

"Not so." A lunatic's smile contorted the thaumagician's face. "You've started what I couldn't."

A tentacle curled around Wrench's waist. "I've had enough of you and your groping suckers," she said and sent a shock of magic to her skin. The grip on her waist tightened and Wrench gasped. It wasn't Octo-Man securing her but a translucent metallic cable. Her magic pulsed and the cable-like tentacle became darker, more solid, its grip on her more painful.

A demented chittering filled the under-crypt and a voice like a million echoes chanting in a language she didn't understand droned behind her.

Wrench twisted to look at the source of the noise and wished she hadn't. The thing that clasped her was colossal, with writhing segmented tentacles and a giant yellow eye made from a thousand smaller eyes. It was clearly too big to fit in the under-crypt and yet it did. Or perhaps not in the under-crypt, beyond the under-crypt, as if an extra dimension had been created especially for the purpose. The arm that seized her was all too corporeal, but the remainder of the beast appeared ethereal, almost transparent in places.

"Plum, help me, please," she shouted, hoping the sight of the writhing horror would shock him to his senses.

The thaumagician dashed his hands against the floor, smashing the ice surrounding them. His fingers trembled from the cold, but he managed to form them into a sigil and a beam of violet light shot at the giant eye.

The beast roared, the sound a thunderous gargle of pain, and its grip momentarily loosened. Her muscles straining, Wrench pushed the coiled tentacle from her waist. "Run!" she shouted and staggered towards the under-crypt stairs. Plum remained static, his gaunt body quivering. His brow furrowed, and a look of determination contorted his face. The beam from his fingers brightened and the beast grew more solid. Wrench faltered. He wasn't helping her to escape; she no longer mattered to him. He was intent on adding his magical power to the beast, dragging it into their world.

She had to stop him. Only, she couldn't use more magic; that would draw the creature nearer. Snuffing out a candle, she grasped the heavy iron candelabrum, the pain in her damaged flesh excruciating. She didn't want to kill Plum. Despite what he'd done to Pippa it didn't make it right. All she had to do was to stop him, stop the magic. She raced towards Plum and swung the candelabrum.

The sound of the metal striking bone churned Wrench's stomach and she let the candelabrum clatter to the floor. The thaumagician crumpled, blood seeping from a gash on his skull. The magic died, and the beast keened an angry scream.

Wrench backed away. The monster lashed out. Its tentacles wrapped around the sturdy under-crypt pillars and it pulled itself towards her, its translucent body becoming more solid as it heaved itself into their dimension. Wrench fled up the steps and ran straight into Bot. Gunfire and screams filled the chapel. The QRF battled Plum's army of aberrations, their BBGs laying down a barrage of bedlam.

"Looks like we arrived in the nick of time," said Bot and loosed a volley of shots into the fray with his hand cannon.

"You're too late. They've broken through."

Bot ceased his firing. "Who has?"

Wrench's answer was lost beneath the sickening squelch of the beast squeezing up the under-crypt steps. It emerged in a seemingly never-ending blob of eyes and tentacles, slurping into the chapel.

43

Wrench clasped her damaged hands over her ears as best she could, trying to block out the boom of the QRF's weaponry. The remarkables had fled when the creature appeared from the under-crypt and so now the QRF emptied their magazines at the beast. Despite the calibre of their weapons and the ferocity of their fire the net result was disappointingly insignificant. Even the massive shells from Bot's hand cannon were absorbed into the monster's silver skin, melting like lead dropped into a crucible.

The weapon's impact was so negligible that the beast was either unaware or uninterested in Bot and the QRF. It squelched through the Minster, resolute in purpose, although the nature of that purpose remained unclear.

Bot's pistol clicked empty. He signalled to the QRF and made a cutting motion across his throat.

The firing ceased, and Wrench pulled her hands from her head.

Bot returned his weapon to the holster in his leg. "We can't use magic, and shooting it seems ineffectual. Any thoughts before we hand over to Trent?"

"What makes you think Trent's solution will work?" said Wrench.

"Nothing's indestructible. It's like when you get a cut; it'll scab and heal. However, if we do enough damage all at once its ticket will be punched for sure."

"I do have an idea," said Wrench. "You're not going to like it."

"It can't be worse than using Trent."

"We go to the broken tower. I channel magic from the odic capacitor and then blast the beast to smithereens."

"You're right, I don't like it. It's got no chance of working and will probably kill us all," said Bot. "But under the circumstances, worth a try. How do we get the monster to the roof?"

Wrench shrugged. "That's where it's going, anyway. It's heading for the biggest source of magic around."

Blithely smashing pews and anything else in its path, the beast dragged itself towards the tower door.

Bot signalled to the QRF sergeant. "Get your men out of here. Either we end this, or Trent does. Either way it's not going to be pretty." He sank to one knee and the saddle emerged from his back. "Jump on. We better beat it to the door."

Wrench clambered onto Bot's back, grateful that she didn't have to climb the steps up the tower again. If she was going to die, she didn't want to die tired.

The Rupture pulsed brightly, casting a mauve hue across the top of the tower, reminding Wrench of Plum's eyes. Her mouth turned down, a moment's sorrow piercing her. He'd done wrong, but he'd been driven to it by hatred and prejudice.

"So, how's this going to work?" asked Bot.

"I'll draw as much power as I can from the odic capacitor and when I'm fully charged I'll blast the beast," said Wrench with more confidence than she felt, trying to be the blue train. She'd absorbed the magic in the casket and was gambling their lives on the hope that she could repeat the process here.

The crash of a door being smashed rose from below.

"Better jump to it. Doesn't sound like you've got long."

Wrench approached the globe and the heavy cables trailing from the capacitor snaked to life. In an imitation of the vision she'd had the first time she'd visited the tower, they slithered up her body, coiling around her legs and arms. Immediately she felt the jolt of magic.

Another crash from the tower, this time much nearer.

"That was the last door," said Bot. "How're you doing?"

"It's working. I need more time."

Bot clenched his fists and long blades shot from his knuckles. "I'll hold it for as long as I can."

Argent tentacles squirmed through the archway, probing the air, sniffing the magic. Bot slashed left and right. The severed tentacles dropped to the floor, pooling into mercurial liquid blobs before evaporating in shadowy swirls of mist.

Wrench's body spasmed and her parents stood before her. Her mother smiled softly, a smile that Wrench missed terribly. It was the smile that said everything would be fine, the smile that said she'd done well, the smile that said she was loved more than anything in the world. Her father reached out a hand and stroked Wrench's face, his eyes full of pride.

Wrench's heart twisted, the pain of their loss no less than the day she'd woken in the hospital to be told of their deaths.

Her mother squeezed her hand gently, furrows forming on her brow. "This isn't the way, sweetheart."

"You must stop this now, Wren," said her father, his face becoming stern.

Wrench jolted. He had never called her Wren. As far back as she could remember he'd always called her–

"WRENCH!" Bot's desperate cry cut through the fog of her dream.

The bulbous beast oozed through the tower's archway, crushing Bot beneath it. The horrific reality honed back into focus. Squeezing her fingers was not her mother's hand but a metallic tentacle. And what she felt on her face was not the gentle caress of her father but hooked suckers attaching to her skin.

With an exhalation of breath Wrench let the magic free, purging the power from every cell of her body, sending it coursing forth in a crackling wave.

The beast reared, for a moment becoming more solid, as if it existed in many more dimensions than the world was designed for. Then with a tumultuous squelch, it exploded in a shower of metallic slime.

The capacitor's cables fell away from Wrench's body and she dropped to the floor, drained, powerless to move. Her gaze fixed on Bot, who lay motionless by the archway, his armour dented and crushed. "We did it, Bot," she mumbled, but there was no response from the prostrate mechanoid.

Wrench fought the weariness that consumed her. She wanted to close her eyes and sleep forever, but she owed Bot a debt. She forced her little finger to move. Pins and needles pained it, spreading through her hand into her arm. Using the agony to drive her on, she dragged herself across the flags. Pain throbbed through her hands like they were in molten metal. She groaned, too tired to scream but kept on clawing her way towards Bot. She collapsed next to him and twined her fingers into his, her hand dwarfed by the massive metal digits.

"You called me Wrench," she said. "At least I think you did. Things got a little bit weird for a moment."

Bot didn't respond, his lifeless metal hulk cold and still. Wrench let her mind drift down to her hand and into Bot. "But what you really need now is a Brasswitch."

Despite the lethargy that consumed her, she pushed into Bot, searching for a spark of life. He was a machine, she was a Brasswitch, and she would fix him. She pushed further, deep within his chest, and there it was, a faint red glow like an ember in a fire. She took what little strength she had left and fed it into Bot, breathing her life into the spark. She felt it grow warmer and brighter. Her vision dulled, and her breathing slowed. "Live," she mumbled, and her world darkened.

✿

Wrench's eyes flickered open. Overhead the Rupture churned, but not as brightly as before. How long had she been out? She had no idea. A dull throbbing filled her ears. She turned her head. Beside her, Bot's armoured body trembled, and beyond that hummed the odic capacitor, unharmed, keeping the Rupture closed, keeping them safe.

"You knew my father," said Wrench.

"I did," answered Bot, his voice weak.

"He built the capacitor for you."

"No." Bot squeezed Wrench's hand. "He built the capacitor for you. His sole payment was a promise that I would protect you from the regulators."

Wrench coughed, and pain electrified her ribs. "How's that working out?"

"Pretty good so far." With the unhealthy sound of grinding gears Bot pushed himself up on one elbow. "However, all things considered, let's never do that again."

Every inch of Wrench's body hurt like hell. "Agreed," she rasped.

Above them, Flemington slunk into view, a snide smile on his face. "You won't have to. You've resigned, remember?" He waved a wax-sealed envelope over their heads. "And things will be very different at Thirteen when I'm in charge."

Flemington's eyes glazed over and he toppled forward. Behind him stood Sergeant Wilhelm, his rifle butt raised where he'd struck the captain. The sergeant picked the letter from the floor and, sparking a match with his fingernail, set fire to the paper.

"Sergeant, did you just assault a superior officer?" said Bot.

"Nothing superior about him," answered Wilhelm.

"True. But I gave him my word," said Bot.

Wrench wheezed and spat blood onto the flagstones. "You gave your word that after Plum was safely rescued you'd offer your resignation." She turned her head to the sergeant. "Did you find Plum?"

"No, Ma'am. No sign of him or Leech."

His mangled armour grating, Bot sat upright. "Excellent. Back to Thirteen for tea and scones it is then."

The sergeant reached down and offered Wrench his hand. "I mean no disrespect, ma'am, and I'm sure you're more than capable of standing without my help, I merely offer my assistance should you choose to use it."

Wrench took his hand and pulled herself to her feet. "Thank you, sergeant, but I'm not a ma'am. I'm a Brasswitch."

44

Wrench hobbled into the briefing carriage to find the party in full swing. It was two weeks since the events at the Minster and her body still felt like she'd been thrown under a train. Her hair had turned from mousy brown to a metallic mauve, an after-effect of the magic that no one could explain. She pushed herself through the revelling regulators looking for Octavia.

At the front of the carriage sparkled Bot, his battered armour now completely replaced with carblingium. He raised a glass and flicked it with his finger, making a ting-ting sound. The room quietened.

"Ladies and Gentlemen, we are here today to celebrate the retirement of regulator Chattox. She served

Thirteen without fear or favour and at the time of her retirement she did not falter. Please raise your glasses to regulator Chattox."

"Regulator Chattox," chorused the room.

"There is work to be done, but not now. Today we celebrate, tomorrow we recuperate, then we investigate," said Bot, popping the cork from a bottle of champagne to a round of cheers.

In the aftermath of the Minster Schism, as the incident was being termed, the QRF and Flemington's regulators had rounded up many of the remarkables involved, but Leech and Plum were still in the wind. Questions were being asked by the Grand Cabal and despite the destruction of his resignation letter, Bot's future at Thirteen was in doubt.

Wrench weaved through the drunken crowd to find Octavia huddled in a corner.

"You don't like parties either?" said Wrench.

"Far too much uninhibited emotion sloshing about the room for me. I find it most exhausting."

"Let's go somewhere quiet. I want to ask you something," said Wrench.

Octavia pushed the door to her rooms closed and the sounds of the party vanished. Wrench sensed something unusual about the room that she'd not picked up on before and she wondered if it had been designed to be equally effective at blocking out emotional noise.

Octavia took a seat and motioned to the chaise longue for Wrench.

"I wondered when we'd be having this chat," said Octavia.

"You know what I want?"

"At the Minster, I helped you remember your previous visit. You want to know if I can help you remember the crash of the *Drake*."

"Can you?"

"I can." A tentacle curled into a question mark. "Are you sure you want to know?"

Wrench had given the issue much thought over her two-week convalescence. Was it better to live with the hope that she wasn't responsible than to possibly know for certain that she was? She had gone back and forth on the issue so many times she'd lost count but had finally decided that she needed the truth. It wasn't something she was prepared to leave any longer. The party along the corridor was evidence enough of the dangers they faced and although Octavia was not at the sharp end of Thirteen there was no guarantee that she would always be available another time.

"I'm sure," said Wrench.

"Lay back. This will be traumatic," said Octavia.

Wrench lifted her legs onto the chaise longue and positioned her head on the velvet-cushioned support.

Octavia lowered her tentacles onto Wrench's temples, encircling her forehead.

"Close your eyes and relax," said Octavia.

Wrench was on the footplate of the *Drake* with her parents. The countryside rushed by, the wind tearing at her clothes. Her father laughed happily, clutching her mother's hand as he encouraged the driver to go faster. A burning knot of fear tightened in Wrench's chest. An oily feeling enveloped Wrench and the brakes on the engine locked on. The air filled with the scream of metal on metal. Her mother wrapped her arms around Wrench, shielding her. The carriage's momentum flung the *Drake* from the rails and the steam engine twisted, hurtling towards the embankment. Behind it a coach slewed sideways. A woman smashed headfirst through the coach's window and the oily feeling vanished. The *Drake*'s massive wheels ripped into the embankment and the bramble-covered grass rushed towards Wrench. She buried her face in her mother's shoulder.

Octavia pulled her tentacles away. "You don't need to remember the next bit," she said.

Wrench's heart hammered in her chest, her breathing sharp and shallow.

Octavia stroked Wrench's hair with one tentacle. "It's done now. You can be calm and relax."

"It wasn't me," said Wrench. She gulped down a huge breath and clutched her arms across herself, trying to slow her breathing. "There was another Brasswitch on the train."

"Flemington's fiancée," said Octavia.

"But why did she do it?"

"I'll help you find out, I promise." Octavia took Wrench's hands. "For now, it's enough that you know it wasn't your fault. You can forgive yourself."

And she could. Nothing would bring her parents back; she'd accepted that. Just like she'd accepted she was a Brasswitch. However, she was not the Brasswitch responsible for the crash of the *Drake*, that burden belonged to another, and with Octavia and Bot's help she'd find out who. Of that she was certain.

ACKNOWLEDGEMENTS

The Rise of the Remarkables: Brasswitch and Bot has had many supporters along the way whom I would like to thank.

A big HUZZAH to Linsay Knight and the team at Walker Books Australia for turning my manuscript into this wonderful book. Thanks for your continued support.

Thanks to my agent Josephine Hayes at the Blair Partnership for her advice and for championing *Brasswitch and Bot*.

Thanks to the NZSA for support via their mentorship program and to my mentor Barbara Else who helped me beat my ideas into shape.

Thanks to Adele Broadbent and Jackie Rutherford for feedback on my early drafts and to Brandi Dixon from Charcoal and Brass for feedback on my later drafts.

Thanks again to Storylines and Tessa Duder for all their help on this journey.

Thanks to all the reviewers, booksellers, book reps, librarians, school librarians and customers who have supported me by reviewing, recommending and buying my books.

Thanks to Bex at Little Red Robot for drawing the awesome cover and for the graphics on my website www.garethwardauthor.com.

Thanks to Adam and Lynda for pinball, pandemic and helping me when I lost the plot.

Thanks to our dog Tonks for inspiring me with her love for life.

And special thanks to Alex, Max and Louise; I am so very proud of you all.

ABOUT THE AUTHOR

Gareth Ward (aka. The Great Wardini) is a magician, hypnotist, storyteller and bookseller. He has worked as a Royal Marine Commando, Police Officer, Evil Magician and Zombie. He basically likes jobs where you get to wear really cool hats. Born near Oxford in the UK, he went to University in York and currently lives in Hawke's Bay, New Zealand where he runs two independent bookshops with his wife Louise.

His first novel, *The Traitor and the Thief*, a rip-roaring young adult Steampunk adventure, won the 2016 Storylines Tessa Duder Award, the 2018 Sir Julius Vogel Award for Best Youth Novel, a 2018 Storylines Notable Book Award and was a finalist in two categories at The New Zealand Book Awards for Children and Young Adults. His sequel, *The Clockill and the Thief*, is also jolly good. You can learn more about the fantabulous world of Gareth Ward at www.garethwardauthor.com

"TICK-TOCK, CHIP-CHOP,
CUT OUT YOUR HEART AND REPLACE WITH A CLOCK,
STITCH IT AND SEW IT AND STITCH IT AGAIN,
HEARTLESS, INVINCIBLE WITH COGS FOR A BRAIN."

GRYM BOOK OF NURSERY RHYMES

Sin is DYING, poisoned by his blue blood. His troubles
deepen when the traitor who poisoned him escapes from
the custody of the Covert Operations Group and sets out
for REVENGE. COG tasks Sin, his friend Zonda Chubb
and their frenemy Velvet Von Darque with recapturing
the traitor, WHATEVER THE COST. Taking to the air in
pursuit, they must battle skypirates and the terrifying
CLOCKILL to complete their mission. But with his
condition worsening, can Sin SURVIVE long enough to
save his friends, himself and the day?

ALSO AVAILABLE BY
GARETH WARD

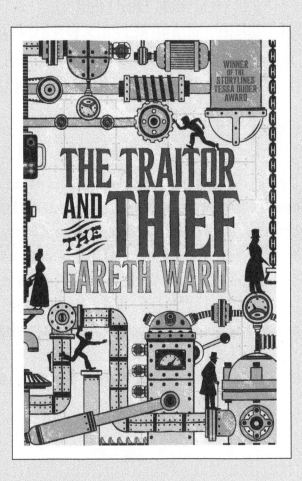

"IF YOU JOIN US, YOU TOO MAY DIE, BUT YOUR SACRIFICE WILL SAVE THE LIVES OF MILLIONS. COG DOES NOT FIGHT FOR THE EMPIRE; IT FIGHTS FOR HUMANITY."

Discovered thieving at Coxford's Corn Market, fourteen-year-old Sin is hunted across the city. Caught by the enigmatic Eldritch Moons, Sin is offered a way out of his life of crime: join the COVERT OPERATIONS GROUP (COG) and train to become a SPY. At Lenheim Palace, Sin learns spy craft while trying not to break the school's CAST-IRON RULES. Befriended by eccentric Zonda Chubb, together they endeavour to unmask a TRAITOR causing HAVOC within the palace. After an assassination attempt on COG's founder, Sin realises that someone close to him could be the TRAITOR. Sin is forced into an ALLIANCE with the school bully, Velvet Von Darque. But can he trust her? And will COG try to bury him with the SECRETS he discovers?